The Magical Journey of
John and Adele

The Magical Journey of John and Adele

Ancius M. Murray

Matador
Unit E2 Airfield Business Park,
Harrison Road, Market Harborough,
Leicestershire. LE16 7UL
Tel: 0116 2792299
Email: books@troubador.co.uk
Web: www.troubador.co.uk/matador
Twitter: @matadorbooks

Cover design by Dominyka Anciūtė

Paperback ISBN 978-1-80514-152-5
Hardback ISBN 978-1-80514-442-7

British Library Cataloguing in Publication Data.
A catalogue record for this book is available from the British Library.

Typeset in 11pt Minion Pro by Troubador Publishing Ltd, Leicester, UK

Matador is an imprint of Troubador Publishing Ltd

Kai aš ir tu kalbuosi tavyje. Kai tu ir aš kalbiesi manyje.

When it is only you and I, it is in you we speak. When it is only I and you, it is in me we speak.

1

In the Dark

The beams of two headlights crossed the darkening sky which hung over the motorway. An old silver hatchback streamed through the hills rising towards the mountains, and through sparse woods. The traffic emerging from the city had been left behind hours before, and occasional passing cars were the sole sign of human civilisation in this remote countryside.

Two passengers in their late forties, a man and a woman, were travelling in the car. Their boredom and the silence between them seemed to be in tune with the monotonous sound of the raindrops that were beginning to fall from the grey sky and onto the windscreen. A brochure on the back seat, depicting a luxurious spa nestled in a sunny mountain valley, seemed in sharp contrast to the dull and dreary atmosphere inside the car.

"John, there should be a filling station in a mile or so," said the woman. "Are you sure we've enough fuel to get to our destination?"

"Don't worry, Adele," the man replied automatically,

obviously lost in thought. Then, looking at her, he said mockingly, "Why don't you just tell me the truth? You want to stop to buy some useless trinket, like a fridge magnet for your endless collection, or one more coffee mug that says, 'I love Paris'. You want to do that, don't you?" He smiled sarcastically.

Adele did not want to venture further into territory that would lead to an unpleasant argument. She turned her head to the window.

Ten miles later, John took an exit heading to the mountain road. "Look, there we are. Only fifty miles before we reach the paradise promised in your precious brochure," he announced in a bored tone.

They continued to drive, observing the still, melancholic landscape. The disappearing light as the sun set made it seem even sadder and more forlorn.

Adele leaned towards John and looked at the dashboard. "Hold on, doesn't this small yellow light mean that we'll run out of fuel soon?" she asked.

"Don't worry," John said once again, firmly this time. But he was unable to hide the anxiety in his voice.

The steep and winding road seemed to be intent on exhausting the worn-out car and its nearly empty petrol tank. A second light, this one red, lit up on the panel.

"Damned car!" yelled John. "This old engine burns petrol like a monster!"

"John, I told you we should have filled the tank at the last station we passed! Why is it always like this? Can't you deal with a simple problem? You fill the tank; you drive the car!" Adele crossed her arms and fixed her angry gaze on the road.

"This so-called 'simple problem' could have been solved if you hadn't dragged your feet over buying a new, more fuel-efficient car, and despite us getting several very good offers, you didn't want to sell this thing!" John cut in, unwilling to admit his negligence in not planning ahead for petrol.

He accelerated, determined to continue the journey to its end. But the end came more quickly than he had planned: it came at the next corner. The car spluttered several times before John managed to pull it into a small area off the road. Then it stopped still. They had run out of fuel.

2

The Couples' Counselling Office

The piece of ground where the car had come to a sudden halt was surrounded by tall trees. It was already dark, but the long black shadows on the gravel indicated that there was a source of light somewhere.

"Is that moonlight?" asked Adele, trying to remain calm and in control of her rising unease. "I didn't notice the moon before. There can't be any other light in this isolated place."

They both got out of the car. While Adele stayed close to it, John walked around and discovered a narrow path leading up a hill. Light shone down from above.

"Adele, there's a house up there. Let's see if they can help us."

The unlucky pair went up the hill for several hundred metres until they reached the house. Warm light shone from its large windows. When they got to the gate, they saw a sign affixed under a lamp at the entrance.

"'Couples' Counselling Office,'" John read aloud, surprised. "What kind of a crazy house is this? Who do they work with?"

He made a wide-reaching gesture, stretching out his arms. "There are no couples around here!"

Does he think we're no longer a couple? The worrying thought crossed Adele's mind.

"Anyway, it doesn't really matter what they do. I don't care!" said John indifferently. "We're here for help. Let's get on with it!" He approached the door and knocked on it with a good, hard rap.

A minute later, a tall, handsome middle-aged man opened it. His features were even and in proportion. A dark yet greying beard gave him an air of authority, but one that lacked arrogance. His wide grey eyes were welcoming and kind. "Good evening. Nice to see you," he said, as if their appearance at his front door were no surprise to him at all; as if he had been expecting them to come.

John and Adele looked at each other. They both noticed the man's Eastern European accent.

"Please come in; you're welcome!" He opened the door wide, and called out cheerily to someone inside, "Marija, the clients are here!"

"Good evening. We're sorry to disturb you at such a late hour. My name's John, and this is my wife Adele. We're not clients," John hastened to explain. "We just need some help because we've run out of petrol."

The man looked deeply into John's eyes. "Are you sure this is the only kind of help you need?" he asked. Then, without waiting for an answer, he introduced himself. "I am Darius, a couples' counsellor. I help couples when they find themselves in trouble. This is Marija, my wife and colleague."

He turned to a slim, fair-haired woman who had joined him by the door. She leaned gracefully against her husband and smiled at the strangers.

Darius added, "Wouldn't you like to come in?"

"I'm sorry to disappoint you, sir! We're not in trouble," John said firmly, but then corrected himself. "That is, we *are* in trouble in the sense that we need a little bit of petrol to get to the nearest filling station. Do you… understand me properly? Can you help us?"

"Don't worry; just come in. I'm sure we can do something for you," said Marija in the same Eastern European accent, looking at Adele in a warm and friendly manner.

Adele had already started to shiver in the chilly evening air.

"Would you like to try my apple cake and have some hot tea?" suggested Marija.

"Yes, please! That's very kind of you." On impulse Adele stepped into the house, and a dubious John followed her.

They entered a spacious living room which, far from resembling an office, seemed to welcome them with its cosiness. The room was furnished in a style of fifty years ago. There was a soft red oriental carpet, a large wooden bookshelf filled to the brim with books, and a fire burning in the grate.

"Please, have a seat." Darius pointed to two comfortable armchairs.

Two seconds later, a Skype ringtone went off in the background. "Just a moment…" Darius crossed the room to where a computer equipped with a high-resolution camera stood on a big table. "Hello, Mary Catherine!" he said enthusiastically to the caller. "We have two clients this evening and we will need your precious help for at least a week, I suppose."

John and Adele nearly fell out of their armchairs.

"Are they out of their minds, these guys?" said John to his wife under his breath.

But his rising protest was interrupted by the soft, melodious voice of a woman with a clear Irish accent. "Hello, Darius; hello, Marija, dear friends! I'm glad to see you; I'm really looking forward to working with you on all of this. Will the clients need general advice or will they have to follow The Road? Have you already decided?"

"The case seems complicated; they probably need the second

option." Marija joined the conversation. "But you can see them yourself, sitting with us just over here."

She turned the computer screen and its camera towards John and Adele. An attractive woman with wavy dark hair and sparkling eyes was visible on the screen.

"Yes, you're right, Marija: they definitely need to follow The Road," Mary Catherine confirmed gently, but in full confidence. Her expression showed that she was giving all her attention to the 'clients' in front of her.

That was enough. John jumped up from his chair, grabbed Adele's hand, and turned to the door. "Are you making fun of us? We're not guinea pigs for anything. Just tell us that you don't want to help us and we'll solve our problem ourselves!"

Darius appeared untroubled by John's reaction. He said calmly, "All right; it's up to you to decide. In any case, you are welcome to stay here for the night. The doors will stay open for you."

John stalked back to their car and got inside. Still confused, Adele went with him. She also got in and closed the door.

It was pitch dark outside. The tiny rays of light from the house on the hill were the only traces of the odd encounter they had just had.

3

A Night of Disillusionment

"John, you dragged me outside without asking and I didn't even get any of Marija's tea. Look, I'm still shivering," Adele said, her disappointment audible in her voice. "I agree they were a bit eccentric, but I felt at ease with them. They were kind and maybe they could have helped us, but you took away that chance. Now our hope of help is gone!"

"Damned car!" John shouted in anger, shaking his fist at the vehicle.

"There's no point in shouting, John!" Adele said, losing her patience. "You have to admit that we ended up in this situation because of your overconfidence and arrogance. *You*, of course, didn't fill up with petrol in time, as any normal person would, and now look what's happened! I tried to tell you but you never consider my opinion; you think you know best all the time. You act as if you're superior. Why don't you listen to me? And now, in your ridiculous, stupid arrogance, you're shouting—"

"*I'm* ridiculous?" John interrupted. "If I listen to you, we'll spend our holiday at every single petrol station along this blasted motorway. A normal wife wouldn't buy stupid, cheap toys at every chance she gets, like a teenager would!"

"It's you who treats me like a child!" exclaimed Adele. "You're always checking what I spend and what I buy, like your dad did with your stepmother."

John clenched his teeth. "Yes, my dad controlled Margaret's spending! You know well that she hoarded things, stacking them in every corner until there was no empty space in our house. But leave my family out of this! Have a look at your mother, who nearly had to sell her house to pay off her foolish debts."

"I can't believe you're saying this." Adele stared at John. "My mother treated you like her own son and was always so generous to you: if you'd relied on your dad's money, you would never have finished your high-flying postgrad studies."

"I finished my doctoral studies because I worked hard – unlike you, who gave up at the first failure," continued John furiously.

"Your opinion doesn't matter to me, Professor!" Adele bit back sarcastically. "I'm not interested in what you have to say. I'm fine with my degree. I'm not using my status to impress young female students, like you do."

John's body strained like a tiger preparing to jump. "That's not fair! Don't accuse me of infidelity! There are no grounds for that. If you can't tell the difference between an innocent chat and betrayal, then I've nothing else to say to you."

They were silent for a while, looking out through the windows at the dark night and the empty road. There were no stars in the sky, and no moon. No passing cars came to help them out with petrol. They felt like prisoners lost in the middle of nowhere. This hopeless situation in which they were now trapped made them even angrier, and gave rise in their minds to all those many irritations and annoyances that occurred in their life together. These tiny aggravations emerged suddenly, exploding to the surface like bubbles from a bottle of carbonated water which had just been opened. Their desire to observe social niceties had evaporated hours before, with the last of the fading light that evening.

"If you want to know why I am attracted to my students, take a look at yourself," John started up again bitterly. "I can't remember the last time there was much action in our bedroom."

"Now you're saying that *I'm* the one to blame for all of our problems in bed? I can't see why you refuse to understand that women need a different approach than men do in order to get excited. I've tried to tell you that so many times – if you don't believe me, read the books!"

"Oh, yeah, I read them! I am fed up with all those silly instructions that turned our sex life into a lab experiment. Is there any excitement, arousal or fun there? Any spontaneity?" John stopped talking for a moment but his facial muscles contorted desperately, betraying his inner struggle with an avalanche of emotions. "You never pay attention to your appearance anymore! The things you wear are dowdy. With your baggy trousers and long skirts, you remind me of my grandmother. Couldn't you sometimes wear clothes that are sexier, or more glamorous? I would be pleased to see you show off your figure once in a while, in high heels or a miniskirt."

"That's cruel of you to say! I can't wear that kind of thing, John, and you know very well why." The tears welled up in Adele's eyes and she hid her face in her hands.

At once she had an image of her teenage self, dressed in a short, tight skirt, fishnet stockings, and high heels. She had been walking down the street with her classmates, going home after a school Halloween party. They chatted happily, raising their voices over one another, recounting the fun they had had at the party. Adele hugged Jing Mei and Clare as they said goodbye; then she turned the corner to go home, which was several hundred metres away.

She had been walking down the street when she suddenly noticed three shadowy male figures behind her. They were clearly following her. Frightened, she started to run, but in her high heels she could not escape the men, who were much faster. One of them caught her by the back of her blouse and held her forcibly, preventing her from moving forward. She fought hard to escape.

"Hey, sex bomb, don't pretend you're a nun. Look at the way you're dressed. Come with us and we'll have fun!" laughed a second assailant, roughly pulling her against him.

Adele had thought that the situation was lost, but suddenly a policeman had appeared and had run to help her. The three men had fled. They had jumped into a car parked nearby and got away.

It had taken less than five minutes for Adele to reach home after that, but the incident had left lasting psychological scars on her. She was fearful of walking alone, even for a short distance, in the dark. She was frightened of having anyone directly behind her at any time, even during the day. The most lasting effect of all was that she could not endure wearing anything that she perceived to be the least bit revealing. Each day as she dressed, she avoided anything that would call attention to her.

Now, overwhelmed by her emotions, Adele got out of the car and slammed the door. She crossed the road and walked down a slight slope to a field, which was faintly illuminated by the light coming from the hilltop house. The moon emerged timidly from the clouds and threw additional light onto the field. Adele looked around, searching for a boulder or rock on which she could sit and calm down. But her solitude did not last long. A few seconds later, the rock she thought she saw ten metres or so ahead started to move. She cried out in fright and jumped back, but then realised that it was only a cow. There were more of them in the field. The cattle moved towards her, curiously inspecting their unusual night-time visitor.

"Where have you gone?" She heard John's anxious voice and his quick steps coming towards her. He emerged from out of the darkness. "Are you all right?" He touched her shoulder, but she did not react. "I'm sorry, Ad. I didn't mean to hurt you."

Adele heard the guilt in his voice. "I understand," she sighed. There were a few moments of silence. "But it's been happening quite regularly for some time now," she continued, exhausted.

"Let's go back to the car," John said.

"John, I'm tired. I've reached my limit. I've had enough…"

They looked into each other's eyes.

"John, the two of us are really in trouble now", Adele said slowly, emphasising every word. "Darius's troubled couple. That's us."

John opened his mouth to object, but the words stuck in his throat. Suddenly, he was acutely conscious of the oppressive atmosphere that had reigned between them for several years now. After their son Patrick had left home to study, the chasm separating them had grown ever wider. It seemed that for each of them the very presence of the other was a source of irritation rather than one of contentment. They took no pleasure in each other's company. The smallest details of everyday life led to sparks between them, followed by the misery of incessant arguments. It had not always been like this. The early years of their relationship had been very happy, and John longed to live as they had in the past… He looked up the path leading to the house.

"Let's try our luck in that curious house," said Adele.

John yielded. "All right. At least we can spend the night there."

Slow and exhausted, they retraced their steps to the house. The light shining from the windows seemed to welcome them back. John knocked once again. They heard soft steps, and this time it was Marija who came to the door. John drew a breath, preparing to explain the situation, but it was she who spoke first.

"Come in, John and Adele. I can see that you're terribly tired. You don't need to explain anything; just come with me. Would you like to leave your shoes over here and put on these slippers? I'll take you to your room."

They followed her up to the first floor, their feet dragging on the stairs with fatigue. Marija continued down the landing and opened the door of the bedroom furthest from the stairs. She took a spare blanket from a wardrobe on the landing, and handed it to Adele.

"Goodnight to you both," she said kindly. "See you in the morning for a cup of tea or coffee," she added soothingly.

The two travellers were worn out. They had neither the strength nor the desire to look around the bedroom. The only object attracting their attention was a large feather bed. They got undressed and fell into it as if they were passengers boarding a lifeboat from a sinking ship. John turned to lie on his side. Adele gazed through the window for several minutes. She looked at the moon which offered its light to her. It was more luminous now than it had been when she was in the field. As if encouraged by this moonlight, she touched John's hair lightly. But he was on a distant shore, carried away by his dreams. Adele wrapped herself in the soft blanket, and she too sank into a deep sleep.

4

Morning Tea

The next morning, Adele and John were awakened by strong sunlight and birdsong coming from beyond the bedroom window. The morning looked bright and lively and the fragments of their memories from last night seemed completely unreal. They showered, dressed, and went downstairs. Coming through the hall, they noticed several certificates and diplomas from well-known universities, framed in gold and hanging on the walls. The room they entered was filled with the pleasant sounds of breakfast being prepared. The big table in the middle was set for five people. John surveyed the room: there were still only four of them present. Darius and Marija cheerfully invited them to sit down. There was a radio near the breakfast table, and Cat Stevens' 'If You Want to Sing Out, Sing Out' was playing. This positive message encouraged Adele and John to approach the table and join their hosts.

"Please, have some breakfast. Here you are!" Darius pointed to a pot of tea, a pot of coffee, croissants in a wooden bowl, seeded bread rolls, ham, cheese, butter, and jam.

John and Adele felt hungry, and started to serve themselves.

"This bright morning seems a world away from the darkness of last night," said John.

"Literally, indeed!" remarked Darius, and everyone around the table laughed.

"Was it so hard last night?" asked Marija.

"Oh… well… perhaps this isn't the time to bother you with all the details, but we had a bit of an argument yesterday," answered John.

"Yes, that's understandable," Darius said. "Once you are in the midst of a disagreement, the argument takes off in many different directions. You argue about lots of things: money, relatives, education, or questions of intimacy. This inflames the situation and everything ends in tears." He sipped his tea. "It's all very exhausting."

Astonished, John and Adele stopped eating and looked at each other.

Adele reacted first. "How could you possibly know what we were talking about?"

"And in the right order!" added John. "Except for my stubbornness at the beginning."

"I didn't want to be impolite concerning the beginning," resumed Darius with a half-smile.

"Have you been spying on us?" Adele asked, slightly irritated.

Marija calmed her. "Not at all! Believe me, what happened between you last night is less personal than you might think."

"Less personal… umm… what does that mean?" Adele asked, apparently reassured, but with rising curiosity. "Our quarrel concerned *very* personal issues."

"What I mean, Adele, is that your unconscious habitual reactions happen in predictable ways. This is common to many partnerships…" Marija drank her coffee slowly, still looking with empathy at the couple, "when they find themselves in trouble."

Those last words made a strong impression on John and Adele, and they looked at each other again.

John coughed, shifted in his chair, and said, "In actual fact, we acknowledged last night that our marriage really *is* in trouble…"

Everyone at the table remained silent for a moment. Adele was immersed in her thoughts, contemplating a small wooden sculpture on a chest of drawers at a little distance from the table. It comprised two slender trees, one dark and one light, encircling each other in a humanlike gesture of affection.

John took a breath to steady himself, and then said, "Did I understand you to say yesterday that you provide counselling to couples? Was that a serious offer on your part?"

"Yes, we do provide counselling," confirmed Darius, without elaborating further.

"All right, then!" John said. "When we get back from our holiday, perhaps we'll contact you for a consultation. What do you think?" He turned to Adele.

As if awakened from a dream, Adele nodded her head.

"That's not possible," Darius said, calmly but firmly. "We start to work with our clients immediately. That is our method." He looked at Marija, who was following the conversation attentively; then he continued, in a gentler voice, "Believe me, if you go now, you'll never come back. You feel optimistic at the moment, because last night's storm has just passed over you. But your relationship difficulties are more complicated than that. It is very important that you address the source of your problems. Today's positive mood can evaporate quickly, and once it does, you will no longer have the desire to see us again." He gazed at his teacup for a moment, and then, looking up, smiled at Adele and John. In a lighter tone, he added, "Besides, you have no fuel."

"Well, I think we'll find a solution to that," John said, barely hiding his annoyance.

"I don't mean fuel for your car. That is, of course, important, but I mean fuel for your partnership; the steam, the source of energy driving you forward into your future," replied Darius. "If you look at a couple – that is, at their partnership as a whole – you will see that that partnership moves through different stages, such as formation, evolution, maturity and so on. It has its own path, it has its ups and downs, it goes through smooth patches as well as crises. In order to go forward continuously, it needs fuel. When people first fall in love, the initial energy is there in the passion they feel for one another. Mother Nature provides it, and the couple themselves don't need to do much to keep their relationship alive. The strong attraction between them provides the fuel. But the time soon comes when this fuel granted by nature has been consumed and the overwhelming passion begins to diminish. If by that time the couple have children, their shared concern for their offspring provides a powerful source of fuel that can last for a long time. If there are no children, building a home and creating a life that will benefit both partners can also be a source of energy. But as the children grow up and begin to live their own lives, or once the desired lifestyle has been achieved, the couple can feel that they have lost the source of their partnership's energy. That is due to the fact that the main life goals expected of a couple by nature and society have been achieved. This is the time for those partners to replenish their relationship's fuel. Often, couples begin to look to the external world for something to keep them together. This could be material things – a new house, a new car, another holiday – or it could be something more personal, like grandchildren. But either way, they remain dependent on many uncertain factors, and as a source of energy in the relationship it is unreliable.

"A lack of energy in a relationship can show in increased conflict, reproaching each other for insignificant things, and frustration. There are also problems in negotiating the details of daily life. The couple can't agree on what to have for dinner, which movie to watch, or how to spend the weekend. In time, the husband begins to criticise his wife's new hairstyle, and the wife doesn't like the way her husband slurps his soup or scrapes his knife on his toast… small things start to grate on them to an extent that is out of proportion to their importance. Of course, there are always disagreements between two people in a relationship, even if the fuel is well stocked and the tank is full. But such disagreements are normally a sign that the couple are in the process of seeking the best way to realise their hopes for the future. We consider these to be constructive conflicts. But when the relationship's fuel tank is allowed to run dry, the conflicts are no longer constructive. The arguments usually relate to the past, and concern old, unhealed wounds, unfulfilled dreams, or missed opportunities, because… there is no shared future. The couple have no common vision of their life together. They feel trapped."

Darius finished speaking and reached for the teapot to fill his empty cup. John looked at him and their eyes met. John had been instinctively prepared to keep his distance from Darius, but inexplicably Darius returned his gaze without embarrassment. There was nothing in his expression that made John uncomfortable. He felt no pressure, no judgement, no air of superiority. He felt safe.

"How can a couple discover their source of energy?" asked Adele, who had been listening attentively to Darius's explanation. "How can we discover it for ourselves?" she added silently.

"Every couple is different, so we can't say yet," replied Marija. "You will work it out in your own way. With our method we try to help activate the couple's inner resources. We give them the tools to develop a more meaningful relationship and to confront their problems with a fresh perspective. In order to gain this fresh perspective on each other, and to discover what keeps you together, you need to go beyond your usual everyday situations.

This is why we are offering to you the programme we call The Road. It will take just over a week."

"But we've already paid for our holiday!" exclaimed John. "Adele loves a spa so much; it will be impossible to cancel it!"

He looked at Adele, certain of her approval. But Adele did not give him any sign of agreement. She was obviously considering Marija's proposal seriously.

"Well, I think we can change our plans for a good reason," she announced suddenly. "And if we cancel our booking today, we can still keep half of the money."

"But, Ad, what are you talking about?" John interjected, extremely annoyed now. "This is irresponsible! It's also a pure waste of money. You're always like this: you pay no attention to how we spend or what we spend it on!"

"Oh, I certainly do! But I can't say that our last holiday at the spa was very pleasant," snapped Adele. "You were either angry or irritated with me the whole time. I felt like we were in a boxing ring together, not on a relaxing holiday."

"Because it was impossible! I couldn't relax: every minute, you changed the plans we'd agreed on," retorted John. "We missed the theatre performance because you weren't ready on time, you couldn't decide on a restaurant for our anniversary, and I had the impression that you were there on a shopping binge, not a vacation!"

"You always control everything, as though we're living in a defined scenario, and I—"

Adele's sentence was left unfinished because Darius interrupted her by raising the palms of his hands. This silenced the couple and they realised that their quarrel had become too personal. It was totally out of tune with the bright morning and its lovely birdsong. They felt ashamed and lowered their eyes, trying to suppress the surging wave of emotion between them which risked ruining everything. Feeling like guilty children, they waited for Darius to give them some direction.

But instead, he looked at them intently and said calmly, "Have you noticed that you were already 'in the past' in your quarrel?"

This question made a marked impression on John and Adele. They stared at Darius.

"It seemed to me that your intention was to discuss your future plans," he continued. "But there was no future in your discussion; not even a present. There was only the past. However, in true fact, that past does not exist any longer. Please excuse my plain speaking – I'm very direct – but this situation reminds me of a comic strip in which the driver of a car looks behind him instead of at the road ahead. In fact, he is driving to Nowhere."

This was an apt description of the situation in which John and Adele had found themselves trapped. They had nothing to add to it. They could not contradict Darius. They remained quiet. There was no logic that they could present to prove that they had the ability to resolve the problem themselves. Minutes passed as the sunny morning, the chirping birds, and the light music slowly re-established harmony in the room.

Adele broke the silence first. "John, we really need to address the problems in our marriage. Let's take this opportunity to do it!"

John took a deep breath. He looked at Adele, trying to read in her eyes how serious she was about attempting this unusual endeavour. Her expression left him in no doubt: Adele was sincere in her desire to undertake this programme. The depth of the emotion in her eyes reminded him of the times when they had felt happy just being together. He could not explain why those moments, which had been so precious to him, had become so rare that they had almost vanished with the passing of time. He was also not entirely sure that this new venture upon which they were deciding would actually help them to regain the affection and closeness they had lost. However, he understood the importance of the present moment. He took Adele's hand

and smiled half-heartedly. "If you want this, we'll do it. In the end, we have nothing much to lose." Then he turned to Darius and Marija and asked them, "What are your instructions? What should we do?"

Adele looked at him gratefully.

Just at that moment, there came a gentle knock at the door.

5

The Road Map

Darius hurried to open the door and invited the visitor inside. It was Mary Catherine, the woman Adele and John had seen on the computer screen the previous night. Wearing blue jeans, a lightweight white blouse, and an elegant, colourful necklace, Mary Catherine was well matched to the bright morning. Her smiling face looked young. Her green eyes sparkled with joy and wonder at life, and she seemed ready for adventure. Greeting everyone at the table, she sat down to join them for breakfast.

"You are just in time," said Marija, filling Mary Catherine's orange ceramic cup with hot lemon verbena tea. "Just a few moments ago, John and Adele decided to follow The Road."

"John, Adele, I am so happy to meet you. I can't wait to get to know you better," said Mary Catherine.

Both sensed the sincerity in her words, and this created an immediate feeling of trust. There was a strong connection to her that the couple felt but could not explain. Relaxed by Mary

Catherine's words and presence, Adele smiled and looked at John in encouragement.

"You'll manage everything perfectly; no worries at all," Mary Catherine reassured them.

Taking in her words and the soothing manner in which they were spoken, the last remnants of the couple's confusion and embarrassment were swept away.

"So, we're ready to start!" John declared resolutely, and Adele nodded in agreement. "What is it that we need to do?" he asked, repeating his earlier question. "I understand that we are to stay here a week?"

"No," replied Darius. "You will actually be following our Road programme. That is, over the coming week you will go to certain places and carry out the tasks we set for you. You will receive the Road Map, and then you will start your journey. Our job is to guide you. We will send you relevant information every day by email or by other means. I hope you have a laptop and a phone with you? Should you need our help in challenging situations, I will be available on a hotline."

Darius caught sight of the anxious expressions on the faces of Adele and John. Involuntarily, they had looked over at Mary Catherine, expecting her to provide further explanation and reassurance.

"Mary Catherine will have a special role in this programme," Darius promised them. "You will come across her during your journey. She is an expert in helping to manage emotions, and she is very empathetic. You will benefit from her presence and support."

"Oh, yes!" Adele exclaimed. "That's clear to us already."

"Of course." Darius smiled. "She has brought you fuel. This time, I mean sufficient petrol for your car to enable you to reach the nearest filling station."

That last clarification made everyone else at the table smile as well.

"But why do we need to go on a journey? Why don't you just give us advice on how to strengthen our relationship right here and now?" asked John. "We have the time." He was clearly still doubtful about the need to travel for a week to solve their problems.

"Advice, books and lectures just give you hints and provide you with general ideas," Darius answered. "To comprehend their meaning fully, you have to experience it through your own personal journey. Your everyday life is like an established pattern based on your past experience, habits and convictions. Even if one day you heard a life-affirming idea from the Dalai Lama himself, it would not be very likely to change your life if you kept on following the same pattern. Your good intention to improve your life in line with this new principle would drift further and further away, until that idea was buried somewhere in your subconscious mind. Good advice is only helpful if you put it into practice as soon as you receive it. It is very important to be brave enough to break away from old patterns of behaviour that do not work for either of you any longer. The Road allows you to enter into situations in which, we believe, each of you will have the opportunity to discover unexplored aspects of your own character and personality as well as those of your partner. By working through the practical challenges and tasks we set for you, we hope that you will acquire new ways to deal with day-to-day difficulties in your relationship. That is our goal."

"Well… I suppose it sounds feasible," John said. But he was clearly not fully convinced.

Marija and Mary Catherine glanced at each other, and each knew that further explanations concerning the content of The Road programme would not be helpful.

"Honestly, it's not as complicated as it may seem," Mary Catherine said reassuringly.

"Really, you can see it as an adventure," added Marija. "You will actually be on holiday, so why not spend your time in a different way?"

Caught by a wave of enthusiasm and inspired by this encouragement, Adele turned to John. "John, we've made the decision. Let's do it!"

"All right, I think we're ready to begin. But I have to ask you about payment for your services. Do you need it in advance?" John addressed this question to all three of them.

"The main part of the work will be done by the two of you, and during your journey you will cover your own expenses," answered Darius. "We will guide you, and the result will depend on your efforts and your awareness while you are on The Road."

John was suspicious. "You mean to say that there's no charge? You don't take any money at all? You're telling me that you're spending your time on us for free?"

"Well, not exactly…" Darius smiled calmly. "By taking couples on The Road, we are actually repaying a debt of gratitude to someone who taught *us* without expecting a monetary reward. We are showing our appreciation. There are things in life which cannot be bought or sold, and they have nothing to do with money."

John and Adele did not say a word after this odd yet persuasive statement. Darius, Marija and Mary Catherine's bright, sincere faces spoke for themselves and radiated trustworthiness. No additional explanations were needed. John was still curious about this mysterious debt their benefactors were seeking to repay, but he understood that this was not the appropriate time to ask about it. For now, the subject was closed.

"So, shall we sort out your petrol?" asked Mary Catherine, and she invited John to follow her outside.

"Adele, would you like to walk a bit and see my garden?" inquired Marija. "The sky is so clear and the weather so warm that it would be a pity to stay indoors."

John, Mary Catherine, Adele and Marija left the house.

Tranquillity reigned once again. Darius sat down at his desk to gather his thoughts. He was in a state of full concentration for preparation of the Road Map.

6

Inspiration in Marija's Garden

Adele followed Marija, and a delightful view appeared in front of them. A large area behind the house was filled with fruit trees, flowering shrubs, and eglantine roses. Chokeberry trees as well as gooseberry and raspberry bushes were planted along the garden wall. The garden was not particularly well organised, but breathed harmony. One narrow path led to a bird bath underneath the raspberry bushes, and another path led to a swing hanging from the branch of an apple tree.

"Oh, look, a swing – how charming!" exclaimed Adele. "You have an exceptional garden. There are plants here that I have never seen before."

"I'm not surprised that many of these plants are unknown to you." Marija smiled. "I brought some from my own garden beside the Baltic Sea." She pointed to them as they passed. "Those over there are thujas, which are in the same family as the cypress tree. It seems that they thrive well and withstand the strong winds here. These are quince, blackcurrant, and sea buckthorn bushes. You can make an excellent jam from their fruit."

The women followed a stone-paved path down to a small pond containing water lilies. Marija suggested sitting down on the low wooden seats beside the pond. Adele could not resist touching the soft, translucent surface, and then she looked into Marija's eyes, which were as soft as the water.

"How do you manage to keep it all so clear?" asked Adele. She was unable to decide whether her question related to life, to the water, or to Marija's eyes. She suddenly recalled the pond at her grandparents' farm, which had required near-constant skimming due to twigs, fallen leaves, and flower stems tumbling into it.

"It's important to look after the pond and not to neglect it. Just as we love water's sound and transparency, water likes our presence too," answered Marija. "I often come here."

"And Darius? Does he come also?" asked Adele. Then suddenly she realised that with this straightforward question she was perhaps straying into a private domain.

"Yes, he does! He likes to come here with me," answered Marija frankly and unambiguously. "Even though he prefers to escape to the mountains or to his library, he understands my love of nature and he was of great help to me in setting out much of what you see around us. I always find that for women – for us – a connection with nature is essential. Its beauty provides calm, but also gives us energy. What do you think?"

"Yes, you're right! I feel revived in the garden too," Adele answered.

They sat quietly, admiring the picturesque view of the violet-green hills in the distance illuminated by the sun. It was already noon. A warm, soft wind caressed Adele's face, triggering bittersweet emotions in her. She felt contented in one sense, but she was also downcast. She thought of her past attempts to bring a little bit of the natural world into her own, as well as John's domestic life. *Why does John avoid having a garden?* she wondered to herself. *Why does he detest the idea so much?* Several years ago, when they were looking for a new house, she had found one with a wonderful piece of land that she had adored. The price was reasonable but John had given ridiculous reasons in rejecting the house, such as the height of the gate, the number of windows, and its proximity to the local church. Recalling this, Adele felt a cloud of sadness envelop her. In the end they had stayed in their old apartment, which had no garden; only a tiny patio at the back that barely allowed for a few pots of flowers and kitchen herbs. John refused to have any kind of plant indoors.

Marija perceived the change in Adele's mood. She looked at her intently and said, "Sometimes we have to be strong and firm in expressing our needs. We must make an effort to fulfil our hopes and dreams. If we give up on them completely, we wilt and fade, little by little, like plants without water."

These simple words reached deep into Adele's heart and she felt a pleasant surge of energy move through her. She would reopen the garden discussion with her husband as soon as possible; of that she was determined. *I'll be responsible for expressing my own needs in this relationship, and I won't compromise one inch,* she thought firmly. Then suddenly she realised that her strong resolve and combative posture were at odds with the tranquillity and serenity of the garden, and she began to laugh out loud. Marija joined her in laughing conspiratorially, as if an important secret were being kept between them. *Well, all right, then: to preserve peace I can step back by half an inch,* Adele conceded. *We'll finish this journey first. I can wait a week and then speak to him.*

As if reflecting their mood, the sun's rays chased each other happily over the surface of the pond. Suddenly, a tiny frog hopped out onto the grass, and seemed to stop for a moment to stare at the two women.

Marija leaned forward to look him in the eye. "Would you like to talk with us too?" she asked. "Or just stare?"

The little frog paused, blinked at her, and then hopped away.

Their laughter rang out through the garden for quite a while until, energised, both women stood up.

"Adele, come over here with me! I'd like to show you some of my favourite flowers," Marija said.

Adele followed in contentment.

7

Refuelling

John and Mary Catherine walked down to the road. Warmed by the sun, the path seemed much more pleasant to descend than it had proved to be the previous night. John's car, now in the company of Mary Catherine's small but robust jeep, no longer looked as abandoned as it had on their arrival.

Mary Catherine opened the back door of her own vehicle and took out a small canister of petrol. "Here you are! This should be enough to reach the nearest filling station," she said.

Her kindness, combined with the pleasant anticipation of moving forward as well as that of launching out on an adventure, made John feel light-hearted. While filling the tank he began to smile, pleased to commence the journey.

Mary Catherine shielded her face with her hand and regarded the sky. "It's beautiful today, so you'll have lovely weather on setting out."

"Oh, yes! Weather conditions are great." But John still had something on his mind. On impulse, he asked, "By the way, could I ask how you met Darius and Marija?"

"Oh, well, that was a day I'll never forget," said Mary Catherine. "It happened in Paris, nearly ten years ago..." She extended her arms into the open air and made a happy little turn, like a child.

"So, tell me!" John handed her the empty canister. Though normally not very interested in the details of other people's lives, he was very curious to learn who these mysterious people really were. He suggested walking down the hill a bit, and prepared to listen to Mary Catherine.

"So it was in Paris," repeated Mary Catherine. "I was invited to give a presentation at a seminar on well-being. It was held in the Hôtel Biron, the Musée Rodin, and brought together a large group of participants. After the seminar there was a short meditation organised by the water pond in the sculpture garden. I was a little bit late for that because I lingered in the garden, admiring the sculptures, so when I arrived I couldn't find a place to sit down without disturbing the others. Since the guided meditation was just starting, I began to feel very uncomfortable and was considering leaving.

"Just then, my attention was drawn to a woman and a man on a stone seat a few metres ahead, facing the water. I could see their reflections in the still water, and then suddenly, birds taking flight rippled the surface. That broke their images into brilliant smithereens, animating the two reflections as if by magic. At that very instant, the woman turned and motioned to me to come and sit beside them. Softly, she called my name. I can't really explain it, but on seeing her gesture and hearing my name I felt as though electricity ran through me. My intuition told me that staying with them for this meditation would be exactly the right thing to do. Once the meditation had ended, I thanked them for their unexpected help, and asked them who they were and how they knew me.

"'Don't you recognise us?' asked the man. 'We're also here for the seminar, and we listened with great interest to your presentation. Sorry if we seemed a bit overfamiliar, but we realised that you really needed to join the meditation, and we felt that it was also important for us.'

"So, as you have guessed, I'm sure, those two people were Marija and Darius. We visited the exhibitions in the museum together, and then spent all evening talking and sharing our views. We learned a lot from each other, and had much in common straight away... But of course, we all needed just a bit of time to discover why circumstances had brought us together that day." Mary Catherine ended her story and smiled.

"That's interesting," interjected John. "I met Adele in a similar way..." He paused before taking up the subject again. "So, you have kept in contact with Darius and Marija ever since?"

"Yes – since then our lives have been intertwined, and to me they are both colleagues and friends," resumed Mary Catherine.

"And you always work together?"

"Yes..." Mary Catherine answered slowly. "We've never really been apart since... even when we were working in different places, or different countries at the same time."

"Darius mentioned that someone taught you... erm... could you tell me more about that?"

"John, that doesn't really matter to *your* situation at the moment. During our lives we meet many wise people who have something important to tell us. But only those whom we trust entirely can become our Teachers and inspire real changes in our lives."

John's curiosity about this unusual team was not satisfied. The more he asked, the more he wanted to know. But he still had no real answers. "So, at the seminar in Paris, what was your presentation about?" he asked, trying again to solve this intriguing puzzle.

"I gave my presentation on plant awareness – that is, plant consciousness," answered Mary Catherine, looking intently at him.

"Plant consciousness?!" cried John. "It sounds like science

fiction. Do they *have* consciousness? Could you call them intelligent?"

"Yes, of course!" answered Mary Catherine, calmly and confidently. "My research shows that plants react differently depending on the behaviour of those who take care of them. I also find that plants have more influence on our mood and our feelings than we imagine."

John was perplexed by this unusual field of research, of which he had no knowledge and to which he could contribute nothing. He could not even make an informed comment on the subject. In one more attempt to throw light on this mystery, he asked Mary Catherine a direct question. "But... working as a team with Darius and Marija... ah... in helping couples to stay together, what has that to do with a knowledge of plants?"

"Quite a lot!" exclaimed Mary Catherine. "You can't imagine how many connections there are. Once you begin to discover how complex plants are and the capacities they have, your perception of yourself also begins to change. Human beings live in the natural world, yet they're so unaware of its characteristics and potential. Do you know that plants can help bring together the mind, the emotions, and the health of the body in one positive life force?"

John could not reply to this question.

Mary Catherine continued, "The essential oils extracted from plants are very powerful. They can treat illness and produce a feeling of well-being. They can also help us to think more clearly and relax more deeply. If we allow these oils into our bodies, into our air, and into our lives, the power of nature comes with them. It's a good way to feel more at ease with the world and with each other. That is really important in any relationship, and very beneficial to couples moving towards a new way of thinking. The aromatherapy that I practise now has wonderful effects on them. In our team, I get to do the happiest part of our work."

"I'm a bit apprehensive about this 'work', as you call it. I really don't know what Adele and I are letting ourselves in for…" John looked pensive.

Mary Catherine stopped and looked deeply into his eyes. Though she said nothing, John sensed that she perceived and fully understood his fears and apprehensions. But he also knew in that instant that he and Adele alone would take responsibility for their decision.

Mary Catherine bent her head towards a still-blooming wild rhododendron bush and inhaled the scent of its mauve blossoms. Looking up, she said suddenly, "My cottage has a nice garden, and it isn't far from here. I hope you'll visit it – I'm sure you'll like it."

"Of course… that is, I mean… some day… sometime in the future," John responded. However, the unexpected invitation made him anxious. His chest felt heavy. He wanted no part of any garden.

They walked in silence for a few more minutes; then Mary Catherine asked John if he had ever picnicked or played a game in the open air, what books he preferred to read, and how he liked to spend his leisure time. Engaged in pleasant conversation, they turned to go back to the house.

8

Setting Out on the Road

As John and Mary Catherine came back into the house, they met Adele and Marija returning from the garden. They all entered the living room, where Darius was already waiting for them. He invited everyone to sit around the table. John and Adele were more relaxed after their walks and had started to enjoy being in this already-familiar place. They were hoping that Marija would suggest bringing out some refreshments, but it was Darius who broke the silence with his firm, clear voice.

"I am glad you feel at ease. Now is the time to set out." He laid out a map and a sealed envelope on the table in front of John and Adele. "For The Road programme you will need a detailed description of the region. The envelope contains your instructions for your first destination. Please open it at the first filling station, which you will find on the map. The green cross marks your present location."

John and Adele pulled the map towards them and began to scrutinise it with great curiosity, like junior scouts on an excursion. It had been a long time since they had last used a real paper map. At home they normally drove around familiar areas, and when travelling they relied on satellite navigation. The map was detailed and marked out cities, towns, villages and side roads, as well as places of interest and national parks.

"So, if I have it right, our journey will be limited to this area?" John asked, obviously relieved.

"Hmm… Yes…" answered Darius lightly, with his ambiguous smile. "Unless, of course, you get lost and find yourselves outside the district." Then he pointed to the envelope. "By the way, you will also find our contact details in here. As I've already mentioned, if you need us urgently, call… at any time."

Hearing that last sentence, John started to feel uneasy. Perplexed, he looked at Darius and thought, *Why the hell would we need an urgent consultation? What's going to happen to us?*

"I wonder whether we'll have to go to such extremes," remarked Adele. "I can't imagine calling you at three o'clock in the morning!" She laughed nervously, but the others remained silent.

Mary Catherine was watching John and Adele attentively. Seeing that they were perturbed by Darius's mysterious instructions, she sought again to reassure them. "Don't worry – we'll be meeting up during your journey. Everything will fall into place," she added, smiling kindly.

"Anything else?" Darius asked, addressing the couple with a decisive, business-like air. He paused briefly to allow for any questions but did not give Adele or John an opportunity to enter into a detailed conversation. "So, now it's time to go!" He looked at them intently in a manner that obliged them to concentrate on his words. "And remember: no matter what happens on The Road, you are there to learn."

He got up from his chair, clearly signalling an end to the preparations for their journey. The bright morning had advanced: it was, in fact, already after midday. John and Adele thanked

Darius, Marija and Mary Catherine, and in a few minutes they had reached their car. The engine started immediately; it had long awaited its fuel. The car sounded better and seemed to drive more smoothly. John turned it around and drove down the hill towards the filling station identified on the map. Immersed in their thoughts, he and Adele were very quiet.

It was John who eventually spoke. "Honestly, I feel as though I'm dreaming, Adele. All this just doesn't seem real."

"John, I feel the same, but it's not a dream," answered Adele, looking down at the map and the envelope in her hands.

John continued to drive without speaking, but his facial expressions showed that he was reflecting deeply on something. "This is, after all, a region with quite a lot in it. It's very scenic, with the mountains, lakes, forests… We'll have the chance to explore it a bit. I've been thinking about taking an extended road trip for some time now," he said, emerging from his reverie.

"Well, that's good to hear! This will be interesting," Adele agreed enthusiastically. "The three of them seem very close to nature, and they really appreciate its benefits."

"No doubt; especially Mary Catherine," laughed John, surprising Adele. "You know, Adele, with your studies in ecology and the environment, you would have a lot in common with Mary Catherine. You could have an interesting discussion with her. You might find her ideas intriguing: she told me that she did research with plants and proved that they have consciousness. I can't believe it…"

"You shouldn't be so sceptical!" Adele replied earnestly. "I listened to a radio documentary recently. Apparently, it's believed by scientists that plants have the capacity to recall experiences within their changing surroundings. They have a sense of kinship, the ability to protect each other, and they can even influence the behaviour of insects and other animals in their own interests. Maybe people should consider that they might be intelligent beings? They may quite possibly possess inner wisdom and be conscious. I'm really intrigued by such an alternative way of thinking about them."

"Mary Catherine told me that she's become an aromatherapist and applies this knowledge to help others with their health and well-being. I wonder what other alternative methods the three of them use in their work with couples?" said John. "I don't want to get involved in anything bizarre. I'm asking myself, *What is going to happen to us?* They said something about tasks. What—"

He wanted to continue, but suddenly saw the filling station at which they were meant to stop. He pulled into it and filled the tank, and they went inside. John paid and then dropped a coin into the funny piggy bank on the counter, thinking of his son as a little boy. Seeing that a corner of the shop offered refreshments, he suggested having a snack and a drink before continuing their journey.

"I'm really curious to know our first destination," Adele said impatiently as they sat at a table near the window. "Can I open the envelope?"

John sipped his Coca-Cola and looked at her approvingly.

9

First Destination

Adele opened the envelope and found one page with the contact details for Darius, Marija and Mary Catherine, and another with their first task. Sitting opposite her, John noted her expression changing suddenly from curiosity to disappointment.

"What is it?" he asked. "Can you read it?"

Adele pushed the sheet of paper across the table. There were only two sentences written on it.

BOOK A HOTEL THAT YOU BOTH LIKE IN THE CITY OF NEWTOWN AND STAY IN THIS CITY FOR TWO NIGHTS. YOU WILL RECEIVE FURTHER INSTRUCTIONS TOMORROW MORNING.

"What? Newtown?" John exclaimed. "That's the last place I would visit in this region. It's just a big industrial city, a port; I was there once and there was nothing good about it." The task seemed to ignite anger in him; greater anger than unpleasant memories of a place merited.

"That's really disappointing," added Adele in frustration. "We didn't leave our own noisy, crowded city to find ourselves back in the same stressful situation."

They both felt unhappy and all at sea with this first assignment. Neither the task they had been given nor the destination itself motivated them much. But they did not like the idea of abandoning this journey. The excitement of entering into the unknown had already begun to appeal to them. A fresh desire for adventure had taken hold as they had driven away from the mysterious house on the hill in which they had stayed the previous night. The house and its intriguing team of three had made a marked impression on Adele and John; an unforeseen encounter that pushed them to explore new horizons. Pleasant anticipation of their adventure to come dissipated John's negative feelings about this assignment. He knew, on reflection, that this task would play to his strengths. He would make all the necessary arrangements and organise every concrete detail of their stay in Newtown. Noticing Adele's dejected posture, he tapped her hand. She lifted her head and met his eyes. They were lit up in a manner she had not seen for a long time.

"We can do this, Ad," John soothed her. "We'll book a hotel, stay there, and then hopefully we can leave this boring city in two days. Let's see what we can find online. Hold on a minute…" He left the table to retrieve his laptop from the car, turned it on, and opened the web browser to begin the search. He typed 'hotel Newtown' and the search engine listed a substantial number of links. He clicked on the site they usually used to book hotels. "Here we are! Almost four hundred hotels in and around Newtown," he announced with new vigour. "What do we need? We need a cheap hotel in order to spend two horrible days in this city!"

This last sentence made Adele frown, but she joined John in the search for accommodation. He set the filter for two-star hotels, and as they scrolled through the descriptions and the photos, she noted their poor quality and high prices. "These are pitiful!" she exclaimed.

John was slightly irritated but extended their search to include three-star hotels. However, the even higher prices discouraged him. The improvement in quality was barely noticeable, and this left him puzzled.

"Maybe it's best not to do a blind search? Let's look for suggestions on the best accommodation in the city," proposed Adele.

"No – I always look at the price first and then the photos to make sure the quality is worth it," John declared confidently. "I won't waste money following the biased opinions of people who liked a hotel just because of the view, the colour of the walls, or the well-rehearsed smiles of the staff at reception."

"Come on, John! Don't be stubborn. Let's at least have a look at the best they have."

Unwillingly, John clicked the link to view the top offers. The screen showed a list of the hotels with the highest guest ratings. He started to scroll down, skipping the most expensive ones, but Adele stopped him.

"Look! This one, The Park Hotel, looks gorgeous." She started to read the description. "'This renovated Victorian-style hotel, situated in the city centre and surrounded by gardens, will make your stay unforgettable. The hotel is renowned for its restaurant and exceptional cuisine and boasts a rich interior including a luxurious acoustic hall. It organises private concerts with performances by celebrated musicians from all over the world...'"

John was also impressed, but the words 'luxurious' and 'style' clearly troubled him. He omitted the hotels of superior quality from his search in favour of looking for the cheaper offers, concluding, "Our budget won't extend to that!"

"Yes, it will!" contradicted Adele, angry and disappointed by his stinginess. "We still have quite a lot of money put aside for who knows what purpose. We didn't buy the new house; we left

Patrick in cramped university digs instead of taking that small apartment for him at a good price to help him to start his own life; we didn't travel last year to Bali, which I've been dreaming about for a long time; *and* we didn't buy annual tickets for the concert hall. You insisted that we economise. Why?"

"Don't exaggerate! I simply don't want to waste money left and right. As for Patrick, believe me, the university accommodation is good for his social life. If we get him an apartment, he won't learn the value of money. And what if when he graduates he takes a job in another city? Maybe some day we'll have a clear idea of what we need and we'll spend our savings in a way that really means something to us. I promise you, Adele."

"But, John, listen to me," exclaimed Adele, touched by John's sincere promise. "Time is going by and we're turning grey waiting for something that might never come until we are too old and worn out to do anything enjoyable with our savings. We can really turn to our advantage the time we have to spend in this city, and use some of our money right here and now!"

John considered Adele's point of view. He admitted to himself that her argument was reasonable, but at the same time he just could not acknowledge defeat. He had been raised in a family in which irresponsible spending was a persistent problem, and so he associated careless spending with a lack of security for the future. Over time John had established his own strict principles for managing the family budget, and he tried to follow them rigidly. "Adele, we've already lost a considerable sum because of the spa cancellation, and besides, we've been arguing too long. It's late afternoon and it'll be dark in two hours. Let's be practical. We'll find a simple, good-value hotel, and then discuss the question of money later."

Adele was far from reassured by John's logic. She felt strongly that his obsession with saving money prevented them from enjoying their life together. For her, it seriously limited the choices they made in their marriage, but she knew that she would be unable to persuade him, and since the evening was advancing, she gave up.

John continued to scroll. "Oh, look, Adele! What an attractive offer: it's The Ambassador Hotel, only two miles from The Park Hotel." He started to read the description, which seemed quite reasonable.

"And what are the guest reviews like?" asked Adele, sighing and tired of this long search.

"This place suits us perfectly, and I don't need to look at anyone else's feedback. Let's book it." John completed the booking, and a few seconds later received the email confirmation.

The road to Newtown wound through craggy hills, little silver lakes, and an evergreen forest. The setting sun threw its orange-gold rays across their windscreen, shining into John and Adele's eyes and warming their faces with its last light. Both were thoughtful, exchanging only a few words en route. John felt that his life had been thrown into a high gear since their arrival at the house on the hill. The quick succession of peculiar events – meeting the team of counsellors, their presentation of The Road programme, his and Adele's decision to participate in it, and their journey to Newtown – had taken place in a single day. His mind was also occupied with fragments of unpleasant memories of when he had last visited Newtown as a student. He was resisting the idea of going back there, but he was also trying to remain positive. He did not want to disturb Adele by telling her the real reason why he disliked the place so intensely.

Adele noted with disappointment that the picturesque landscape was now being replaced with high-rise apartment blocks and industrial construction sites. It was difficult to imagine how they could have any fun in a city like this. As if nature were responding to her mood, it began to rain heavily. As darkness fell, driving became difficult in the dense traffic. John was starting to show signs of fatigue, so Adele tried to keep him alert by talking to him and turning on the radio news.

The motorway ended and fed into the ring road. They took the exit that led to the city centre. Adele and John were pleasantly surprised by the well-kept streets, the public squares with gardens, and the nineteenth-century buildings. But, to their great annoyance, the satellite navigation led them outside this lovely area and towards the harbour and its surrounding district. As in most ports, the streets here were designed to provide the most direct route to the main dock and the port areas in order to facilitate trade. All the buildings looked the same, and their ground floors were given over to shops, bars, and other small businesses such as pharmacies, hairdressers, and travel agencies.

On finally reaching their accommodation, John and Adele saw that The Ambassador Hotel was no exception to this monotony, apart from its name. Written in old-fashioned, blazing blue neon, it had an air of pretentiousness for such a modest neighbourhood. The couple entered the hotel and walked down a narrow corridor to find themselves in a tiny reception area. A young man at the desk interrupted his computer game most unwillingly, mumbling a word that must have been meant as some sort of greeting. He asked them to fill in some forms and then gave them the room keys. As soon as they turned towards the stairs, he resumed his hunt for monsters on his screen.

When John unlocked the room, its appearance left them both speechless. It was extremely small, with faded, colourless wallpaper that looked decades old. A little window looking out onto the noisy street was located just above a double bed which itself took up more than half of the room. The threadbare rug, visible from the foot of the bed to the door, reflected the long history of life lived within this space. It was marked by coffee stains, red wine spots, and cigarette burns. *The photographer who took the photos for that booking site was a real virtuoso,* thought John, comparing the images he had seen when booking to the reality now confronting him.

10

Getting Around the Impasse

In desperation Adele turned around, looking for somewhere to put her suitcase. The wardrobe with its doors falling off the hinges was the only piece of furniture apart from the bed and a fitted shelf by it. A large print of Hans Holbein the Younger's *The Ambassadors*, hanging opposite the bed, seemed like the ultimate bad joke. It was the last straw for Adele.

"Unbelievable! This is what you call an attractive offer?" she exploded. "If you had taken a minute to read the guests' comments, we could have avoided this disaster. But you didn't listen, as usual! You didn't take what I wanted into account. Remember, the task is to stay in a hotel that we *both* like!"

John had no reply to make. Privately he admitted that he had made a mistake, but now it was too late to change anything. "Well, at least there's a bed here, even if it isn't fit for real ambassadors," he quipped.

On seeing Adele's face, he realised that it was the wrong time to start making jokes, so he decided to attempt to remedy the situation. He tried to take her hand, but she withdrew it and stepped back.

"I'm sorry, it's my fault," John said. "Let's go out and find a decent place for dinner. We have enough time to do that."

Adele was still seething with anger at his stubbornness, but felt that there was nothing left to say, and so she kept her emotions to herself. She followed John out of the room, at first refusing to walk beside him.

As they left the hotel, the light sea breeze began to blow away their negative thoughts. It had just rained, and the air was fresh and sweet as they started to walk towards the city centre. After several hours in the car the exercise felt rather pleasant, despite the greyish streets. In half an hour the streets got wider and more interesting. Tall black lamp posts on either side gave off more light. They started to look around for restaurants but it was not easy to spot one, since the commercial area through which they were walking was occupied mainly by offices and department stores that had already closed. John suggested turning into a side street in the hope of finding a café or small restaurant. But when they did this, it appeared that the street they chose had only fast-food places.

It was getting late and they wanted to turn back, when suddenly Adele shouted, "Marija, it's us!" She rushed towards a woman who had crossed the street and disappeared around a corner, and John, surprised, followed her. Reaching the corner, they saw the woman rummaging in her bag, for keys or something similar, at the door of a nearby building. It was clear that, despite a strong resemblance, she was not Marija. "I could have sworn I saw Marija," Adele murmured to herself.

They continued around the corner and the street opened out into a very fashionable pedestrian zone. Looking around, they saw a charming restaurant with the inviting name of Your Destination. They hurried inside and were met by a smiling server.

"Good evening, and welcome. Our kitchen is still open," the server said, and led Adele and John to their table.

This was exactly the place they needed. The peach-coloured walls were decorated with wooden ornaments and shelves filled with antique objets d'art. Exposed timber beams supported the ceiling, and all of this created a warm, relaxing atmosphere. The restaurant was only half full. The calming conversations of the customers, diluted by soft music, made the place even more harmonious and lovely.

John surveyed the decorations on the wall. One shelf in the centre was occupied by four slightly worn vintage marionettes sitting together. They wore pointed burgundy hats with bells, like jesters in the Middle Ages. Their jackets were crimson and black. John looked up at them, and then down at his own black jacket with its red lining. "I feel like one of you," he whispered. "I have had people pulling at my strings all day long." With a sigh, he took off his jacket and hung it on the back of his chair.

Adele had already taken her place at the table. They opened the menus, which were contained within smooth wooden covers. Their eyes jumped from one appealing dish to another, all listed in calligraphic text.

"I'd like to order everything!" exclaimed John. "It looks as though they have a really creative chef."

"We should ask for today's special. Then it'll come quicker," proposed Adele. "I'm famished."

The server brought them some bread and butter. They took his suggestions and ordered some regional specialities. The crusty bread was still warm from the oven and the herb butter melted in their mouths. Shortly after, the server brought their drinks. There was a freshly pulled pint of stout in a cool glass covered with drops of moisture for John, and a glass of sparkling apple cider for Adele. Sipping their drinks, they decided to explore the reading corner of the restaurant. They found some interesting books about the region's history, tourism and art, and there were also leaflets about the city and its upcoming events, as well as the most widely read daily newspapers. Adele took a brochure and started to read it. She learned that a classical music festival would begin from tomorrow.

"Look, John!" She turned to her husband. "There's going to be a Stradivarius quartet concert tomorrow. It's amazing to discover this on our first night in this city. And do you know where it's taking place? In The Park Hotel!" she continued, without waiting for his answer.

The server came with their main courses and invited them to return to their table. Noticing Adele holding the brochure, he remarked, "Madam, if you're interested in The Park Hotel, it's just at the end of this street." But then he added quickly, "It's important to know that rooms are hard to get in summer unless you're really lucky." He carefully arranged the dishes on the table, invited them to enjoy their meal and politely stepped away.

The meals looked great and were delicious. Adele squeezed fresh lemon over the bream she had ordered. It tasted as if it had just been caught. The lamb chops on John's plate were generously covered in a spicy mustard sauce and accompanied by fresh salad greens and potatoes fried in butter with nutmeg. John and Adele almost inhaled their food. Their plates were emptied in a flash; then the server brought in a trolley of sweets and fruit from which diners could select their favourite.

"I'm going for a dessert," announced Adele, leaving the table to look at the sweets and put in her order.

"Good idea! I'll take whatever you choose for us." John sat back and opened up the newspaper that he had just found in the reading corner. One article concerned perceptions of financial security in society. He was surprised by the results of the research discussed therein. It seemed that some of those surveyed who were millionaires several times over still felt financially insecure. In contrast, many with very modest incomes described themselves as affluent. This was because they had just about enough money to do what they found fulfilling in life – a bit of travel, helping their children, or enjoying hobbies and leisure activities that brought contentment. John had to admit that the results of the survey were very convincing, and mirrored Adele's view that they should enjoy their income more, rather than worry constantly about whether or not their savings would be sufficient for their future. He then recalled, with some embarrassment, his own logic in overriding her view during their search for a hotel. *What the hell?!* he thought. *What do I really believe? Theoretically, I agree that money is there to be enjoyed, but why do I go on behaving differently in my daily life?*

He was so lost in thought that he had not noticed Adele returning to the table. His reflections were interrupted by the server, who placed a mouth-watering chocolate mousse before him. They took their time in enjoying the smooth, beautiful chocolate.

"What a great place. It's a real pleasure to be here!" Adele exclaimed, putting the last spoonful of creamy mousse into her mouth. A few moments later, her face clouded and she sighed, "I can't bear the thought of going back to that Ambassador place."

They paid and left the restaurant, then stood outside indecisively, obviously unwilling to make their way back to their hotel.

"If you like, we can walk to the end of the street and visit The Park Hotel. Maybe we'll be lucky enough to get tickets for the concert tomorrow?" suggested John.

Adele was pleasantly surprised by his suggestion, and happily agreed. Indeed, she was ready to go anywhere to put off returning to that detestable room.

They walked along the street until they reached a large park. A brightly lit path through a manicured lawn, lined with neatly presented flowerpots, led to an elegant building. The shiny gold lettering of the sign left them in no doubt that this was the hotel they had been seeking. The symmetric facade seemed to want to embrace the park between its left and right wings. In front of the main entrance there was a circular drive with a fountain in its centre. John and Adele were drawn to the light streaming from the large windows, like moths to a flame. They approached the building, admiring its architecture, and then stood hesitantly at the entrance for a little while.

"Well, since we're here, let's have a look inside and find out more about the concert," John suggested.

They nodded to the doorman, who pushed open the entrance door, saying, "Good evening, madam, sir, and welcome to The Park Hotel."

The foyer was spacious, with high ceilings, columns, and arched doorways; and furnished with chesterfield sofas, soft armchairs upholstered in emerald green, and small mahogany tea tables. Little groups of guests sat comfortably, chatting and enjoying their drinks. John and Adele moved towards the reception. The thick aubergine carpet muffled the sound of their steps. Several receptionists dressed in midnight-blue uniforms were ready to receive guests. Among them was a tall woman with fair skin and ginger hair. She noticed the couple and invited them to come to her desk.

"Good evening. How can I help you?" she asked courteously.

"Good evening. We've just arrived in the city today and we saw a brochure about the concert here tomorrow evening. We'd like to know if it is open to members of the public who are not staying with you?" began John.

"Certainly – we organise concerts for our guests, but other visitors are also welcome. One minute, please; I'll check to see if we have any tickets left." The receptionist began to search for the information on her computer. "Yes, some tickets are still available. Would you like two?"

"How much do they cost?" asked John.

In the meantime, the receptionist studied the information on her screen, and when she found what she was looking for, she turned back to them and said, "By the way, if you're interested, I've just received a booking cancellation for our package which includes a one-night stay in a double room, two tickets for the Stradivarius concert, and dinner." She printed out the details of the package, together with its price, and then put the paper in front of John and Adele. "This is a very good offer, and ordinarily our rooms are booked well in advance," she concluded, and then politely remained silent, allowing the couple to make their decision.

Adele wanted to accept the offer straight away, but she knew it had to be a joint decision. It was not her choice alone. She was reluctant to trigger another argument about money, and so chose instead to say nothing as she waited for a little miracle to happen, all the while looking at John with a hopeful expression.

The ideas discussed in the article John had just read in the restaurant were in full swing in his head. He picked up his smartphone and browsed it briefly; then touched his chin with two fingers and pronounced, "Of course – we can't pass up such an excellent offer, can we?" He looked at his wife.

"No, we definitely can't!" Adele replied quickly, with no hesitation.

"We'll take it." John filled in the booking form and secured it with their credit card.

"Thank you, Mr and Mrs Ross. We'll be expecting you tomorrow at noon. Have a nice evening."

They left the hotel. Adele was delighted but still surprised by John's consent to take the package. Then he waved to a taxi waiting at the front entrance near a large white azalea bush.

"It's very late and we're both getting tired. Let's not waste time walking." John opened the taxi door for Adele. "The Ambassador Hotel, please."

"Sir, are you sure about that? It's a bit of a kip," quipped the driver, having seen them leave the Park Hotel.

"That's correct," John answered, not going into detail.

"You're suspiciously generous tonight," said Adele as they got out of the taxi at The Ambassador Hotel. "I'm really very glad about this decision, but what are we going to do with our booking here?"

"Don't worry! I checked the conditions on my phone," John assured her. "We have up until midnight to cancel for the second night. But we need to hurry!"

They dashed to reception, where the same young man was still busy with his computer game. Apparently, he was not very surprised by their desire to leave the hotel the following day. He quickly completed the necessary paperwork, as though he were very accustomed to cancellations. Once he was certain that the couple needed nothing more, he rushed back to his virtual kingdom, which in the absence of its saviour had been invaded by an army of monsters.

11

Trying Even Harder

After their long day, John and Adele returned to their room and fell into bed. They were no longer bothered by the pocket-sized space they had to sleep in until the morning, nor by its faded old wallpaper or its spartan furniture. They plunged into their dreams and left all their anxieties behind them. The salty sea air blew in through the open window. The waves, churned by a strong wind, crashed against the pier. Now and then there came the ring of a ship's bell, and the occasional sounding of horns. But none of these sounds from the port disturbed the couple's sleep…

John looked at the curtains waving in the breeze and the pattern of neon lights cast onto them. He had a sudden, unnerving sense of a stranger's presence in the room. In the corner by the door he saw the young man from the reception desk staring at him with an ominous smile. A shiver went down John's spine, and he felt cold. Like a wild animal being stalked by a predator, he stayed silent and tried to become invisible as the stranger continued to lurk in the corner. The intruder stood still, watching John and Adele with a diabolical expression. John felt that something awful was about to happen. Then, unexpectedly, the stranger's outline faded and he slowly disappeared. His face, with that horrible smile, was the last part of him to vanish.

Still terrified, John jumped out of the bed, leaving Adele on her own. He then found himself outside in the dark street. Ahead of him, two men were fighting with a third man. John recognised the third man but could not remember his name, nor where they had met. The poor guy was losing the fight, and fell to the ground. The two others started to kick him.

"Stop! Leave him alone!" yelled John. "You're going to kill him!"

Slowly, the assailants turned towards John. He saw their frightening faces and their glaring eyes and froze in fear. Abandoning the man on the ground, he tried to escape, but his feet were rooted to the spot. Now he could only watch as the attackers, who had turned into a pair of monsters, left the other man and approached him rapidly...

John gasped, and sat up in bed. He was in a cold sweat, and breathing heavily. He stretched over towards the open window, and the fresh air made him feel better. Then he turned and looked down at Adele, who was in a deep sleep. Simply by watching her breathing, he calmed down. He lay down again and moved closer to her. Eventually, he fell back to sleep.

Both slept longer than usual, and when they woke up it was already late morning. They felt restored and decided not to waste any more time in this dingy place. Adele's happy chatter about their approaching stay at The Park Hotel chased away John's memories of his nightmare. They went down to the dining room, where two adults and three small children were finishing their breakfast. John and Adele were expecting to serve themselves, but there was no buffet visible. They sat down at a table, waiting for someone to come and take their order.

"Let's give Patrick a quick call," said Adele. "We haven't spoken to him for almost a week." She took out her phone and selected Patrick's number.

He answered after a few rings, but was very apologetic. "I'm really sorry; I'm in a hurry and I can't stay on the phone. Are you and Dad having a good time at the spa?"

"Oh… yes, we're having a wonderful time," Adele said, happy to hear her son's voice. But she hoped he would not have further questions. She knew that she would be unable to give him any real explanation of what she and John were doing on The Road. "Is everything all right there?"

"Of course it is!" Patrick answered, showing his impatience.

"Daddy says to say hello."

"Bye – enjoy yourselves!"

The call ended. Hurt, Adele looked at her mobile in surprise.

"He seems to be fine," concluded John, having overheard the conversation.

"Oh, but that was a bit rude. He was so abrupt! Maybe he's keeping a secret from us?" Adele said in a low tone.

"I think he's met someone," offered John.

"Hmm… I wonder…"

"Now, Adele, leave him in peace!"

After a pause, Adele added, "I must admit, though, that I was relieved that Patrick didn't ask any specific questions about our holiday… and now, John, it seems that we've begun keeping secrets of our own, too…"

Just then, someone came out of the kitchen and told them that they could choose either the croissants and yoghurt or the bread and ham for their breakfast. John tried to negotiate a hot breakfast but was told that they had just served their last plate of it. He gave up and ordered the croissants and yoghurt. Adele took some bread and ham.

When the food arrived, the couple were surprised by the small portions and the tiny, insufficient coffee pot. As John looked around, everything he saw was cheap and mean: the tables, the chairs, the napkins, the plates… He felt that there was no appreciation of the guests, and that the hotel was determined to retain every penny possible. The word 'stingy' came to his mind. Suddenly he imagined himself, old, dishevelled and pale, sitting in a small, drab room with the same cheap print of *The Ambassadors* in front of him. He did not want to end his life like that. "I have to change!" he murmured.

"What?" Adele asked.

"Nothing," said John. "Let's get out of here!"

They checked out, climbed into their car, and set off towards the city centre. It was still too early for them to go to The Park Hotel, so they decided to have a good coffee on their way. They parked the car in Newtown's central square and went to the nearest café, where they ordered oven-fresh Danish pastries and real Italian cappuccinos in white porcelain cups.

"Maybe we can check to see if we have more instructions?" Adele suggested.

John took his laptop from his backpack and browsed through his mailbox. There was an email from the Couples' Counselling Office, sent a few minutes earlier. With growing curiosity, he clicked on it and started to read. Suddenly, he blew out his breath. "Oh, no! These guys really know how to spoil my day! But I think this will make *you* happy, Adele."

Adele took the laptop from him and read the new task out loud.

GO SHOPPING TOGETHER AND BUY SUITABLE CLOTHES AND ACCESSORIES FOR DINNER AT A LUXURIOUS RESTAURANT.

"They definitely want to ruin my morale as well as our

finances!" John declared in a desperate tone. The very idea of going shopping with Adele made him feel sour and out of sorts.

"But, John, this is a great idea! We can each choose what we like, but then give the other feedback on what we feel looks best," exclaimed Adele, convinced by the practicality of the new task. "And the second part of this task is already arranged, because we have an elegant dinner to look forward to as part of our package!"

"You're certainly very excited about this task, especially the shopping part," John replied without enthusiasm.

"That's right, I am! I'd love to go shopping with you," Adele said in full sincerity. "We haven't done that in a long while."

"But I don't see any sense in wasting our time and money in shops," continued John, unwilling to give up his resistance to this assignment.

"Well, keep in mind what Darius told us: that whatever happens, we're here to learn," said Adele firmly, using this as her ultimate weapon of persuasion.

John was lost for words that would serve to contradict her. He tried to recapture the tranquil mood he had been enjoying earlier in the day. It was the new task that had taken it away from him.

"Learning is seventy per cent practice. Make your life delicious with us!" Suddenly John noticed a television commercial on the screen on the wall in front of him. Apparently, it was for a cookery course for beginners, as evidenced by a clip showing a couple in their eighties clumsily but cheerfully kneading dough. It looked funny, and made John smile. His anger dissipated, and he began to feel his equilibrium return. *All right, then. I can use this task as a way to practise developing more patience*, he decided.

Adele could not see the advertisement John was watching, but the smile on his face was a clear sign of his decision to engage in the task. "John, I'll do my best to make sure that our shopping trip is fun for you," she promised, taking his hand and squeezing it reassuringly.

They left the café, and on their way back to their car, Adele noticed a sign indicating a piano bar. She had played the piano as a child, and still never missed the chance to listen to professional pianists. The narrow steps down to the bar led to just below street level, and she walked down them, curious for information. The doors were closed, but a big, colourful poster announced that the bar was open from ten o'clock each night and offered live music and a dance floor.

When they got back to the car, she said, "John, I'd love to come here tonight. What do you think?"

"Let's complete our tasks first! Then we will see," John replied, obviously not enthralled by this new idea. He started the engine.

Eventually they approached the circular drive of The Park Hotel with its sparkling fountain. The place was just as beautiful in daylight. They pulled up at the front entrance and John gave the car keys to the valet. They checked in and went up to the third floor overlooking the park. Their room had a welcoming air and was tastefully appointed in every detail. All this invited them to linger there longer. They wanted to relax and read through the hotel's information brochures, but they were pressed for time. The concert was to start at seven o'clock and they still had to find out where to buy suitable clothes. They went back to reception, where Adele picked up a detailed shopping map and opened it with great excitement. She moved towards the entrance.

John allowed her to go in front of him through the revolving door. Then he entered it after her, took a deep breath, and whispered, "OK, out of the trenches! I'm a soldier ready for battle."

12

Shopping Together

Normally, on the rare occasions when they shopped together, Adele always seemed to drag out the time as she viewed every item on the racks and shelves – cushions, pictures, candles, kitchen gadgets, lipsticks, and books – as a prospective purchase. Furthermore, John was asked a hundred times to give his opinion on the items she had selected, but in the end that opinion was usually disregarded. They often disagreed on Adele's choice of clothes and what she should wear for special occasions. Essentially, for John, shopping with Adele had always been more of a punishment than a pleasure. He had believed that the feeling was mutual. That was why he avoided shopping with her. This time, though, he decided to try to change his attitude.

In order to choose their attire for the evening, they first sought out a popular shopping centre in Newtown, but what they saw there did not seem to be of high quality or very elegant. They then decided to look for smaller shops that might have an assistant to help them choose and try on what they liked. They approached a small but well-stocked and beautifully decorated display window. The shopfront read, 'Men's Apparel, Established 1863'. They stopped in front of it, both admiring a dinner jacket in the style of the 1920s, made of smooth, fine black silk with a white satin lining.

Adele looked at John. Thinking that the silk would complement his blue eyes and his dark hair, and especially his strands of grey that stood out under the light, she took his arm. "Let's go in!" Then she pulled him through the door.

A man of about eighty approached and said courteously, "Good afternoon. How can I help you?"

"We have a special dinner to go to this evening," explained Adele, "and my husband is in need of a jacket. We saw the one in your window."

"The black silk… yes, that is a special one. It is made from Kashmiri silk."

The proprietor of this shop knew everything there was to know about men's clothing. It was not an area of his life to which John had ever paid much attention. But when he saw the look in Adele's eyes as he stood in front of the mirror in a snow-white dress shirt, a red cravat, and the black evening jacket, something changed. He knew then that it had been an excellent idea for them to shop together in order to dress well for their evening to come. John availed of the gentleman's extensive knowledge by purchasing a couple of well-tailored shirts and a wonderful navy cashmere sweater that made Adele's eyes shine again with pride when he tried it on for her. They thanked the proprietor heartily and left, eager to stop at a perfumery or a pharmacy to find a natural, traditional cologne for John to use before putting on his new jacket that evening. They soon found one: a German blend made from bay leaves, coriander, alcohol, and a touch of musk. The elegant label on the bottle detailed the history of this cologne, which had first been sold in 1726 to the nobility of Aachen.

But as the afternoon drew to a close, John was conscious that the shops would remain open only for another hour or so, and that Adele had not been anywhere at all to look for her clothes for their dinner tonight. He felt a stab of guilt. She was still chatting about their luck in coming across such well-made clothing at such reasonable prices when he anxiously took hold of her shoulder.

"Adele, dear, we need to look for something for you. Time's getting short."

Adele caught her breath on hearing the word 'dear' from John. She had rarely heard it in the past few years, and it was like a salve to her heart, but this was not the moment to reflect on it. She nodded at him quickly, but her face took on a worried expression.

"What's the matter?" he asked quietly. "Don't you want to look for your clothes? Would you like me just to wait for you? Would you rather go in by yourself?"

Adele looked thoughtfully at her husband's face. "I'm not good at choosing these things; I mean, clothes for occasions," she said slowly. "Ever since… you know… ever since…"

"We're not even going to think about that," replied John quickly. "You're going to find something really nice, and we'll complete our task and have a great evening."

Adele looked doubtful. "I'm not sure how… But I'll try not to disappoint you."

Finding something suitable, however, was much easier said than done. John had had no idea that women's clothes, even those meant only for special occasions, could come in so many different styles, colours, fabrics, lengths, cuts, finishes and prices. It was astonishing to him how, given so many options, women could even begin to make a choice, and Adele was certainly no closer to making a decision than she had been when, an hour before, they had entered the first women's clothing shop. Moreover, she moved from one section to another, wasting precious time looking at inappropriate garments that, in John's opinion, had nothing to do with the goal of their assignment.

"John, look at this nice green pullover! Do you think it matches my eyes? And this linen country-style blouse – doesn't it look fun? I was searching for a similar one for our spa visit," chattered Adele, whose search was being ever more drawn to totally unsuitable items.

Her absent-mindedness started to irritate John. "Adele, *please* try to concentrate on the task! Look for something to wear this evening," he chided her gently. His head was starting to spin from looking at all the clothes hanging around him. "Do you mind if I step outside for a minute?"

He left the shop and bought a glass of sparkling water from a kiosk in the street. A quarter of an hour later, he came back and found Adele moving towards the fitting room, carrying several dresses in her arms. Catching sight of all the outfits she had chosen, John doubted that she had really listened when he had asked her to concentrate on the task in hand. She tried on all of the dresses she had selected and had to admit that none of them suited her. They went out of that shop and entered another… then another… leaving each place more despondent than the last. The evening was approaching, and some shops were already closing. They were both afraid that Adele would be left with nothing to wear for their evening together, and John felt again the pang of guilt. He had everything he needed and more, but Adele had nothing. She was enjoying the shopping trip less and less.

Finally, she sighed and said, "Let's go back to the hotel. This is hopeless."

"Look, Adele." John pointed to the pharmacy in which they had found his cologne. "What about going in there and asking for a perfume for yourself? I can wait for you here, and you can at least have that for this evening."

"Oh, well…" Adele hesitated. "I suppose I could go in, if only for a moment… If I can't find anything, it won't really matter…"

"It *does* matter!" said John.

He took her to the door of the pharmacy. The lights were on and the door still open. Adele went in reluctantly, and John turned around and glanced at the street. It was then that he saw it. The dress. In a bow window, standing out on a tiny little corner. He had not noticed it before. This part of the city had been built in the eighteenth century, and carried all the charm of that architecture. It was a ladies' dress shop, and the dress was the only one in its window. He did not know enough about fabrics to identify what it was made of, but he had never seen anything like it. It was indescribable. The dress was light, but not at all transparent. It appeared to float; to be suspended in the air. He was drawn to it as though he had fallen under a spell. He could not explain why. The dress seemed to have some kind of power over him; it exerted a magnetism, but a positive, life-affirming one, not at all menacing. Its colour was also mysterious. In the glow of the sunrays reflected in the window it appeared to be emerald green, but if he tilted his head, it was turquoise. If he moved slightly to the left, it was a brilliant royal blue; slightly to the right, it was a mixture of all three. He was sure it would complement Adele's colouring beautifully, since her eyes too appeared different under different conditions – rainy days, sunny days, if she had just awakened, or was going to sleep. He could hardly wait to show it to her. Just then he saw her emerging from the pharmacy, and he was gesturing to her to come to him when he heard the tinkling of a bell attached to the dress shop door.

A silver-haired woman dressed in pale lavender was opening the door. John was about to say to her, 'I know it's late, but could we have a look at this dress in the window?' when she looked directly at him and said, "You and your wife are welcome."

They entered the shop as quickly as possible. The little bell tinkled happily behind them. Adele's eyes shone once again as she tried on the beautiful dress. It fitted her perfectly and John prepared to pay, standing at the bow window and looking out at the shimmering light reflections dancing across the surfaces.

"What a magical evening this is for us," he remarked to himself.

Just at that moment, Adele appeared at his shoulder and joined him in looking out. The lady in lavender smiled. Suddenly, it seemed to both of them that Marija had appeared under the light. Adele turned and saw the lady raise her hand in a brief greeting, but when she turned again to the window, Marija was gone.

John looked for the till, but the shop was so antique that the cash was kept in a closed wooden box. As he paid the lady in lavender, Adele took a last lingering look around the beautiful shop. On a tiny rail against the far wall, she saw a little black dress in a fine silk. It was quite short – shorter than anything she would normally wear – but it was in the exact style that John preferred on her. The silk brought out the creamy colour of her skin, the natural gold highlights in her hair, and her neat waist and slim legs. She held the dress against her to check the size.

"John, what do you think?"

Her husband was amazed that she had the courage to even consider a little dress in that style. "We'll take it with the multi-coloured one, if you please!" he said quickly to the lady.

She smiled again and directed her attention to Adele. "You carry yourself with such grace, and you are going to be beautiful in both dresses. It's always the case that it's not the dresses that are beautiful, but the woman who wears them."

Adele flushed with pleasure at these words, and John added proudly, "Absolutely true."

They left the shop, thanking the kind lady who had assisted them, and hurried back to the hotel, delighted not only with what they had bought, but with the way their new clothes made them feel. By now, as the sun began to descend, the light from the sky gradually waned, gently touching the tops of the buildings with a soft, amber-coloured hue.

Adele was still puzzling over the fact that she was sure that she had seen Marija twice on the street. *Is it possible that she was guiding us?* she thought, but she put it to the back of her mind while getting ready for the evening ahead.

13

The Concert

Adele and John took more time than they had ever taken before in preparing for the evening. Luckily, Adele had packed beautiful patent leather shoes that she rarely wore. But for this occasion, they suited perfectly and matched her new dress. She brushed her hair until it shone, and she felt that John saw and appreciated this.

They left their room in an animated mood and cheerfully entered the Hall of Four Chandeliers. It was aptly named, since hanging from the ceiling were four glittering crystal chandeliers. A platform for the performers had been erected at the far end of the hall. The audience sat in small groups around little tables and were being served aperitifs by staff in black tuxedos. The gentlemen and ladies were dressed elegantly. In their new clothes, John and Adele felt at ease in the presence of the other guests. Completing their assignment for the day meant that they were beautifully attired. They were shown to a table just in front of the stage and found that their names had been written on place cards. A server offered golden, effervescent Prosecco in fluted glasses, and wished them a pleasant evening.

"What do we know about the Stradivarius violins and cellos?" asked Adele, looking at the concert programme.

John took out his smartphone and searched the internet. "Incredible!" he exclaimed, attracting the attention of two elderly ladies. Then he whispered, "Listen: 'The market value of a Stradivarius string instrument can reach hundreds of thousands or even several million... They are so unique that they are given names, and only the most famous performers can afford to buy them. Normally, they're leased.'"

Adele opened her eyes wide. "Oh, really? It's interesting that—"

She was in the middle of her response to John when she was interrupted by enthusiastic applause. Four musicians – three men and one woman, all dressed in black – entered the hall, carefully carrying their precious instruments. The quartet was composed of three violinists and one cellist. As soon as the applause stopped, the musicians started to play the first piece in the programme: Ludwig van Beethoven's 'Serioso'. The ferocious opening alternating with a soft, light melody enchanted everyone in the hall. As the music climbed to its crescendo, the audience at first felt immense tension, were then thrown into the depths of despondency, and finally were brought to a state of exhaustion. After several moments, an unexpected tranquillity descended on them, bringing with it a feeling of optimism and relief. Everyone present was overcome by the transformative power of this striking composition. The technical expertise of the musicians was equally impressive. Not a single sound was audible in the hall, apart from the music – no whispering, no coughing, no swallowing. It seemed that the audience had even ceased to breathe.

John found the music inspiring. It transported him to a world of imaginary delights, just like when his mother had read him fairy tales as a child. In this state of reminiscence, he admired the graceful shapes of the musical instruments, as well as the faded colours of their old wood. *The master craftsman who made them long ago must have been very gifted*, he mused. He imagined an old master in his workshop somewhere in Cremona, gently touching the wood, and working like a magician with his tools, ready to give birth to a new violin. *It's intriguing to imagine how such masterpieces of craftsmanship and precision could have been created. These instruments were never intended to be put in a glass case in a museum. They are works of art that still serve their purpose: after all these years, and in spite of their fragility, they still produce an incomparably beautiful sound.* The professor of economics within him had already calculated the investment value of such an instrument. *Its price will never go down, and the investment risk is very low compared to other options on the market.*

Preoccupied by his calculations, John suddenly realised that Beethoven's dramatic composition had ended. There was a slight pause, and he looked at the programme. Wolfgang Amadeus Mozart's Prussian Quartets was the next piece to be played. As this uplifting music started, John turned slightly towards Adele. She was completely absorbed. Her gaze was fixed on the cello, but she was immersed in her own thoughts; lost in another world. Not wishing to disturb her reverie, John concentrated on observing the musicians, who were performing this well-known composition with new energy. *How well trained they are!* he thought. *Compared to the three-hundred-year-old instruments, the musicians are like children just beginning their lives, but in reality they are mature professionals. They cradle their instruments so carefully and gently, like parents clasping a weeping child.*

He leant back in his chair and relaxed, inspired by his fresh insights, the good music, and the exceptional atmosphere of this distinguished hotel. He was very proud of himself for making the decision to book it without needing to be persuaded by Adele. Suddenly, he recalled the look in her eyes in the moment when he had suggested that they stay at The Park Hotel. Surreptitiously, he glanced at her, and he could not help smiling. As if illuminated by an inner light, her face was radiant in the dimly lit hall; even more so than her new multicoloured dress. *It's remarkable: money only has real value if it makes you happy!* Struck by this realisation, he also had to admit that this conclusion did not fit into any economic theory with which he was familiar. Darius's warning – that a life-affirming idea would not be very likely to change your life if you kept on following the same pattern – resounded in his head. All of a sudden John sensed a joyful lightness in his body and mind. He was determined to change his life… together with Adele. Then the powerful music brought his mind back to the present.

While the music had triggered philosophical streams of thoughts in John, Adele had given herself up to her inner feelings. The waves of music carried her through a limitless ocean of emotions: from anxiety and sadness to hope and light-heartedness, and then back again to deep desperation. This was followed, after an interval, by brave notes of struggle and resistance. At one point, Adele closed her eyes and felt as though she were moving against time. She was travelling to the very centre of her soul, where she saw a little girl lying in a meadow, looking at the vast, endless sky. That little girl was a bit frightened by this intimidating world of drama in music. At the same time, she was trusting and curious; her feelings swirling in resonance with the waves of music. After the majestic sounds of Beethoven, the joy of Mozart made the girl want to jump up and dance. Thrilled by this sudden impulse, Adele opened her eyes and looked at the musicians. The cellist attracted her attention as if by magic. She played intensely and passionately, embracing the instrument like a giant bird with wings. With every movement of the bow, the wings became wider and wider; it seemed to Adele that the cellist was about to rise up from the stage and fly, and only the weight of the cello itself was keeping her grounded. Adele was fascinated by this image, and by the strong emotions emanating from this woman. *I would love to involve myself in something that I could do with the same energy, passion and devotion as she does*, she thought, watching the cellist in admiration. *I wouldn't choose to be a musician, but I can do something else with equal passion. I can learn to know myself, as she knows that cello, and to create my own oeuvre in my life.*

This challenging thought came to Adele's mind just before she was overwhelmed by another wave of music that brought in new emotions. It now seemed to her that the music had become a kind of dialogue between melodies. The first melody introduced a theme, and the second complemented it, but added nuance in its own distinct way. In its turn, the first melody then repeated some notes proffered by the second, giving further approval and encouragement. The two melodies wove in and out of one another, moving forward in unison, and then apart, until at the conclusion they merged into one harmonious and joyful stream of sound. *This is so beautiful; it's like an intimate conversation between a man and a woman*, Adele thought. She looked at John, sitting at her side. *Why don't we communicate like this? Why can't we listen to each other and truly understand the real meanings that lie beneath the sentences we speak? Why do we allow our words to become like sharp arrows that wound us both?* Adele reflected in sorrow. The quartet continued to play, and the intoxicating pleasure of the music overtook her once again, and did not permit her any further melancholic contemplation. The strains of sadness were soon dissipated by an outpouring of gladness, like clouds penetrated by the luminous rays of the sun. Deep within the recesses of her heart, Adele's intuition told her, *But yes, it is possible for a couple to communicate like this: we can listen to and truly understand each other. That is why we are on The Road.*

The audience seemed to be affected by the profound emotion expressed in the music. Each person was lost in their own private world of memories, thoughts and dreams. The ascending rhythm of Maurice Ravel's 'Boléro', reaching its culmination, brought them out of their reverie like an early-morning cold shower. The entire room felt in good spirits. As the enthusiastic applause died down and people began to gather their belongings and take their leave, Adele and John proceeded to the door of the hall.

They were not long in finding the hotel's restaurant, for the pleasant scents of grilled steak with rosemary and thyme led them along a corridor to the dining room. Moving too quickly, John nearly collided with a young man and an older couple.

"Oh... please excuse me," he said automatically, turning towards them.

The young man was about to voice his annoyance, when his irritation was replaced by an expression of surprise and then by a smile. "Professor Ross, is that you?" he asked, doubting himself.

"Yes, of course," John answered, looking more attentively at the young man. Then sudden recognition spread across his face. "Oh, Aaron... I don't believe it! I didn't at all expect to see anyone I knew. What are you doing here?"

"I'm here with my parents for the concert. Let me introduce you." Aaron introduced his father and mother, explaining that John was his favourite professor at university. "And I'm equally surprised to see *you* here; you're almost like a different person dressed this way..." He then turned to Adele and bowed slightly. "Mrs Ross, you probably don't remember me, but I've met you at university several times."

"Of course I remember you, Aaron!" Adele extended her hand to him.

Aaron seemed unable to take his eyes off her. He continued, "You're looking very well, Mrs Ross. You are very elegant tonight."

Adele smiled, pleased by the young man's sincere compliment. "I should mention to you, Aaron," she said, "that John has spoken to me about you many times. He has told me what an excellent and hard-working student you have been."

"It seems we're all moving towards the dining room," remarked John, enthused by this unanticipated chance meeting. He looked at Aaron's parents. "Do you think we could have dinner together? It would be a pleasure to get to know you better."

Having agreed, all five went into the hotel dining room, chatting happily together.

14

After Dinner

Everyone had taken their time over dessert, and they were awaiting coffee and tea. The group was in that agreeable state of relaxation that only occurs in the evening, after a good dinner in good company. Everyone was alert – not at all sleepy, but at ease, ready for some interesting, pleasant conversation. The discussion had turned to popular artists and their work. At one point, John had briefly excused himself and left the table. Adele's heart sank when she realised on his return that he had brought along his poetry, and that he fully intended to read it aloud to the entire company during coffee. As he unfolded the papers on his lap, she laid a gentle hand on his wrist.

"Not here, John. You can read your poetry to me later, in the room," she said in a low voice.

John took no notice. "I had a flash of inspiration recently," he declared, a little too loudly. He could hardly contain his enthusiasm. "The words came to me like a bolt of lightning. They seemed to be imparted to me – I'm sure everyone will be very moved by what they hear from me tonight."

Adele made one more discreet and futile attempt to stop John's recitation from going ahead. "John, dear, listen to me for a second: a lot of people believe that the poetry we write ourselves is private. Perhaps our guests think that too. Let's keep it between us, all right?"

But her words had no effect on John. He was reading his poetry silently to himself as a dry run, preparing to make a good impression on his listeners. Adele sighed inwardly. It was clear that the reading was going to go ahead, and she could not in any way prevent John's embarrassment. She took a deep breath and folded her hands in her lap.

The server arrived with the coffee and the tea, carefully placing a blue porcelain cup and saucer before each person. By the time he had completed his circuit of the table and added the cream jug, the sugar, and the petits fours, John had availed of the chance to perfect his delivery. Now he was like a well-known actor striding onto the stage, awaiting the thunderous applause of admirers in the seats below him.

He began, "I'll take this opportunity to present my newest poem to you. I'm sure you'll enjoy it."

Aaron and his parents looked confused. They had no idea what John was talking about.

"Excuse me, Professor Ross," said Aaron. "What did you say?"

"This is something I do in my free time. I have a penchant for poetry, and it just seems to come to me. I'm often inspired... I'm one of the lucky ones."

When Adele heard that last remark, she coloured with embarrassment. This was going to be worse than she had imagined. She made another attempt, this time to try to distract the others. "Would anyone like another plate of petits fours? I can ask the server... they're really delicious."

But John refused to take the hint, and was in fact annoyed. "Please don't interrupt, Adele," he said, more sharply than necessary. "I'm ready to recite." And he began to read his poetry out loud, stanza by stanza, in an authoritative and dramatic voice.

Adele swallowed hard and gripped her hands even more tightly in her lap. Aaron maintained a polite silence. As the unsought reading lasted, his parents were hard-pressed to control their impatience and their boredom. They began to shuffle their feet under the table. They shifted in their chairs. Aaron's mother sighed slightly, while his father drummed his fingers softly on the white tablecloth. When the reading had exceeded a quarter of an hour, they looked at each other, and Aaron's father rolled his eyes upward to heaven. Adele was absolutely mortified. She signalled to the server to bring the bill for the bottle of good burgundy that John had offered during dinner. Aaron and his parents smiled at her in relief. John had not noticed any of this, and continued to read until the server touched his arm lightly with a black leather wallet containing the bill.

"Oh, what a pity," Adele remarked quickly, nodding at their guests. "We've run out of time."

"No worries!" John smiled cheerfully. "We can resume our poetry reading in the bar."

Aaron's father groaned audibly, and his mother gave her husband a jab in the ribs. She extended her hand to Adele. "It was lovely meeting both of you. What a shame that we have such a long drive home…"

"Oh…" John was disheartened. "But perhaps we can arrange an evening when we're all free, and I can read my earlier poems; those I wrote last summer…"

"Of course, of course…" Aaron's mother nodded quickly. Then she and her husband hurried away, with Aaron in their wake.

"Nice to see you again, Professor Ross," Aaron called over his shoulder. He could not follow his parents quickly enough.

John, in his turn, could not hide his disappointment. He was downcast. He had lost his audience and he felt let down. He had thought that his work would be received with amazement, or at least a general agreement that his talent as a poet should be more widely recognised. Instead, they had hurried off as if they had been told that a hurricane was approaching and their house would be blown away. He looked sadly at his papers, crumpled on the tablecloth.

Adele felt a rush of sympathy for him. "I think you read beautifully, John," she said soothingly.

"Do you really think so?" he asked, looking up at her.

"Of course I do," answered Adele, averting her eyes. "Let's go now and have a drink." She patted his hand and helped him up from his chair. They went to the bar. "What would you like, John?"

"The strongest whisky possible," he answered forlornly.

As he sipped his whisky he began to recover his spirits slightly. The old Scottish single malt, with its peaty aroma and taste, was a real delight. The pleasure blew his sadness away. He began to imagine himself at his own poetry reading. This was not a small gathering of unappreciative people at a dinner table; it was a grand international tour organised by a world-renowned publisher. The crowd thronged towards him as he stood at a large podium on a high stage. The pressure was so great that people had to be pushed back by four intimidatingly large security men in blue uniforms. They were armed, and had previously worked as professional wrestlers. The crowd ignored the restrictions on their approach to the podium and shouted that they wanted their volumes signed by the author. Naturally, these slim blue-bound collections of choice words would soon sell out, at an astonishingly high price that took even John's breath away, and as he sought to escape the crowd the publisher informed him that it would be absolutely necessary to reprint the volume several times...

Observing John nursing his whisky, Adele considered the

situation. *Perhaps he understands now that this literary path is not the path for him. This evening he must have realised for the first time that he really has no talent for poetry.*

John ordered another whisky for himself and a cognac for Adele. "It's really deplorable, the lack of sensitivity some people have to poetry. It's an essential art, and the ability to appreciate it is being lost in modern society," he mused.

Adele sighed and knew then that he had not understood anything that had transpired at the dinner table that evening.

"It's the responsibility of the poet to bring this literary sensibility back to society," continued John. "To bring it back to those who need it most: to those who are trapped in a world dominated by technology, by information, by artificial intelligence…"

He was lost in his own self-importance. Adele decided not to contradict him, though she recognised that this decision signified a lack of sincerity on her part.

15

At the Piano Bar

Leaving the bar, John and Adele went back to their room.

John looked at his watch. "It's still early, and a nice summer's evening. I wouldn't mind going for a bit of a walk," he said. "What do you think, Adele?"

"Yes, it's a good idea to get a little exercise after our dinner, and I can put on the second dress we bought today and then we can go dancing. We saw that piano bar this morning, do you remember?" Adele was delighted at the prospect of going out again, but she knew that if she showed too much enthusiasm John would change his mind, so she feigned indifference. "Of course, if you don't want to go there, it doesn't really matter…"

But even though John was not really looking forward to going to the piano bar, it would still give him the chance to stretch his legs and breathe in the fresh evening air. He put on his newly purchased blue shirt, and Adele put on her new black dress. They ventured out, enjoying the clear evening sky and the mild sea breeze blowing softly through their hair. As they walked down the street, John noticed that Adele still did not feel comfortable in her short dress and higher heels.

"Adele, you look great; don't be self-conscious!" he told her, trying to lessen her discomfort.

These words encouraged Adele and her step became smoother and more confident. The change in her demeanour did not escape John's attention. He admired her figure and the slight sway of her hips as she walked. He had to admit that Adele looked very attractive in her new attire.

They reached the piano bar and were lucky to get a table as soon as they entered. The cellar bar was not big: it had the capacity for about thirty people. The barman served drinks from a tiny counter, and only two musicians – a guitarist and a piano player – were on the small stage. Their music filled the cellar with rich, strong sound, and no other accompaniment was needed. This music brought those who wanted to dance continually onto the floor. The ambience was relaxed and unpretentious, and as time passed John and Adele began to feel more at ease. They watched the couples dancing to the blues music, and found the experience truly pleasant. The bodies of the dancers responded to each subtle sound. Their movements were light, graceful and synchronised, and held within them more than simple agility. Each dancing pair expressed their happiness at being together. It was also clear that everyone on the dance floor knew each other. They chatted merrily, sipping their cocktails, taking to and leaving the floor in a continuous flow. John was sure that anyone observing the dancers would be tempted to join them… if only they had the same ability and flair.

"John, shall we?" Adele looked invitingly at her husband.

John was not prepared to get up to dance, and her proposal made him nervous. For a second, he imagined himself on the dance floor among these experienced dancers, who would mock his efforts. He broke out in a sweat. "Sorry, I need to take some air." He headed to the exit.

This disappointed Adele, but she continued to admire the dancers.

Then, unexpectedly, a fair-haired man broke away from his group at a nearby table. He came and stood in front of Adele, extending his hand. "Madam, would you care to dance?"

Adele was caught off guard by this sudden invitation. She could not, however, resist the addictive rhythm. She nodded and smiled, taking the man's hand, and stepped bravely onto the dance floor, accompanied by her new partner.

When John came back, he was surprised not to find Adele at their table. His surprise only grew when he caught sight of her on the dance floor. *God, what an idiot I am – I should have agreed to dance with her!* regretted John. But right now, he could only observe his wife twirling happily with a man he did not even know. He sipped his beer and pretended that everything was all right. His eyes followed Adele and her dance partner. Her new dress and her confident movements impressed John. Other people were watching her too, and he could sense their admiration. *She really looks gorgeous*, he thought, joining proudly in the admiration of Adele.

The slow rhythm became more rapid, and this brought even more dancers onto the floor. It was evident to John that Adele could not manage this new rhythm properly. Compared to the other women, who followed their partners with ease and grace, Adele, though she was still having a wonderful time, clearly had no idea how to dance like this. She twirled in a particularly awkward way, waving her arms in the air, and at one point she nearly stepped on her partner's foot. It was only his swift and elegant turn that saved the situation. John's admiration turned to contempt. He ordered another beer.

That dance was the last one before the break. Flushed and excited, Adele returned to their table. "Oh, John! I had a lot of fun… shall we wait until the break is over and then dance together?" she asked. She looked happy, and John kept his mixed feelings to himself.

"That's out of the question, Adele! It's time for us to go! We need to get back to our hotel. We don't know what challenges are waiting for us on The Road tomorrow," he said sharply, and Adele had no choice but to accept the truth of what he was saying. John gulped down his beer and went to the bar to pay the bill.

The refreshing night air was bracing. John and Adele took their time walking back to the hotel. The streets were nearly empty, and from time to time they crossed paths with other late-night revellers. Adele looked at John, who was stumbling slightly after a few too many drinks.

"I'm all right!" he said, catching her look and rapidly correcting his posture to appear as upright as possible. He looked absurd, and Adele's concern turned to giggles.

Suddenly, two men appeared at the corner just ahead of them and began walking in their direction. Their quick steps echoed loudly in the street. Adele's muscles tensed, and instinctively she moved closer to John.

One of the men spied her anxious look. "Hey, lady, you don't look like you have much confidence in your partner!" he said. "You should come with us."

The men stopped nearby and looked at Adele and John in a teasing way. The smaller of the two stepped towards Adele.

At that moment, John took hold of himself. This scene, with two potential assailants, had an air of déjà vu about it. His dream from last night took shape in his mind. He was quite frightened, but his anger was stronger than his fear. He pushed the man hard who was approaching Adele and shouted furiously, "Get out of here! Looking for easy prey? This time you won't scare me!" he added incongruously.

The man lost his balance and fell down on the pavement. John gave him a menacing look.

The second man was trying to help his friend to stand, and held up his open palms towards John. "It's OK, calm down!" he exclaimed, attempting to settle the situation. "It was only a joke…" He pulled his friend to his feet and they moved off.

"What was the matter with him?" The words of the silhouettes moving away reached Adele.

"Forget it – did you see how he looked at us? He's a nutcase."

"But his chick was cute!"

John was still boiling with anger. Adele took his hand in hers, and felt it trembling.

"John, it's over now. Why are you still shaking? Are you all right?" Gently, she pressed his hand. "Were you frightened?"

"Everything is OK…" John breathed deeply. "I was worried about you."

"I understand. You wanted to protect me. It's true that they were pretty annoying, although, I must admit, not really dangerous." She embraced him, but remained puzzled by his behaviour. "Let's go back to our hotel. It's only two steps away."

As soon as they returned to their room, they went to bed. They were both tired after their extremely long day.

Just before falling asleep, Adele put her head on John's shoulder and whispered, "My Johnny… You wanted to save me from harm."

It was a long-forgotten sensation for John to feel Adele's head on his shoulder. He could not even remember the last time she had done that. She was already away in her dreams, and he remained motionless, trying not to wake her. A few minutes later, he too fell asleep.

16

Raising the Level of Honesty

The night was calm. John and Adele slept well and woke in good spirits. Their breakfast in the hotel dining room was excellent. They finished their warm pains au chocolat and drank hot coffee while admiring the charming interior. The high ceilings were decorated with intricate white plasterwork depicting baskets of flowers and fruit guarded by peacocks. The walls were covered in wallpaper patterned with branches laden with clementines on a soft gold background. Recessed wall panels held enormous mirrors. Reflected in the mirrors, the light from the large windows gave those enjoying their breakfast an impression of limitless space. The tables were covered in snow-white tablecloths, with a shamrock-green linen napkin on each plate. Adele glanced at John, who was sipping his coffee contentedly while gazing at the impressive decor.

"I see that you're in great form this morning, and that the prospect of our time on The Road doesn't appear to be troubling you any longer," she remarked cheerfully.

"Well, after we managed the shopping so successfully yesterday, every other task should be like a walk in the park." John smiled.

"Very funny! I loved the challenge, and the time we spent together. Now I'm impatient to see what the new assignment will be," said Adele enthusiastically.

"All right, let's see what we have there today," said John, and he checked his mailbox on his phone.

Adele noticed a slight shadow come over his face. "What is it? Is this another task that you don't like?" she asked.

"There's nothing there. Nothing at all."

Adele raised her eyebrows in surprise.

"There are no emails," John repeated. Looking at his watch, he said, "We have to check out in an hour. Let's hope we receive further instructions soon."

The couple returned to their room and started to pack. Adele looked for clothes suitable for the journey, putting on one blouse after another, each time asking John for his opinion. In the meantime, John kept checking his mailbox. There were no messages from Darius, Marija or Mary Catherine, and Adele's questions started to irritate him.

"It's silly to be so concerned about clothes when we still don't know where we're going. Perhaps we'll stay in this hotel!" he exclaimed.

"Have they forgotten us? Perhaps we should call them," suggested Adele, trying not to take John's criticism to heart.

"Oh… not right now. Let's check out and we'll see about it later," replied John. Tension was audible in his voice. He put down his phone and began to collect together the rest of his belongings that needed to be packed.

Five minutes later, the phone rang. It was Darius. John launched into expressing the worry he had felt without waiting to hear what Darius had to say. "Thank God it's you, Darius. We are in need of further instructions."

"John," Darius interjected, getting straight to the point without acknowledging John's stress, "do you have the map we gave you?"

"Yes, I've got it here." John opened up the map, a bit perplexed by Darius's manner.

"Just look at the area south-west of Newtown. At some sixty miles or so, you will see a cross marked in red pencil," instructed Darius.

John examined the map, and Adele joined him.

"Yes. I see it," answered John.

"That is Mary Catherine's house, Columbine Cottage. You have to get to it before sunset. This is very important!" emphasised Darius. "You must complete the last part of your journey on foot. So go to the town of Enna and leave your car there. Good luck with your mission! You will have further instructions later." And then Darius was gone.

Adele scrutinised the map. "I'm sure that cross wasn't there before," she said thoughtfully.

"You probably just missed it," said John. "Let's go and check out!" He was satisfied with the new task, since it seemed relatively simple, and was keen to begin the journey.

They left the room, paid their bill, and went to their car. As soon as John started the engine, he heard the trill of a message alert from his phone. "Let's see if there are any further instructions." He checked his emails again. To his great surprise, he saw only a poem, but no further information. "This looks mysterious," he said, handing his phone to Adele. "You can read it while I drive."

Adele started to read the message out loud. "It's a poem: *The Water's Wisdom* by Kotryna Lockhart."

Two lonely people, trapped in their routine.
Boredom their constant and unwelcome scene.
Then through the river's course they find
A magic that releases restless minds.

For in this river's ceaseless churn,
They hear a lesson they must learn:
That life's fast current cannot wait.
There's little time to hesitate.

So let the gurgling ripples animate their ride.
The water's crystal clarity will be their guide.
While bravely diving deep in searching for the truth,
The walls between them crumble and leave a golden proof.

"Oh, Kotryna Lockhart! Did you know she has Polish roots?" John was happy to demonstrate his extensive knowledge of modern poetry. "What an enigma... it's like a puzzle!" He was intrigued. "Do you think there's a hidden instruction in this poem?"

"I've no doubt, John!" exclaimed Adele, fascinated by the verse. "And we have to figure it out." She read the poem again and again, and then she smiled confidently. "John, I have an idea about what this poem may be telling us and what our clue is, but I want to hear your impression of it first."

John followed the directions on the ring road and turned the car onto the motorway.

Adele continued, "Which words from this poem seem to you to be the most important?"

"'River'? 'Crystal clarity'?" guessed John. "Or... maybe 'the truth'? Of course! The search for the truth, diving deep for the truth, because it sounds like that is the point of this poem! Do you think they want us to play the Truth or Dare game?"

"Well, I think that it's about the truth, too," Adele said with certainty. "But it's not a Truth or Dare game, since there's nothing about the challenge there. I suppose that what they want to tell us is that, on The Road, the truth plays an important role. So, perhaps it would be more useful if we were honest with each other?"

"But we are!" exclaimed John. "We know each other; we know everything about each other's lives, plans, finances, habits... we don't have secrets." When he uttered this last sentence, however, there was a note of uncertainty in his voice. "Of course, there are things that we *don't* tell each other, but they are rather unimportant, I'm sure..."

Adele's reaction was immediate. "Is that so? I'm listening!"

"Well... erm... for example, last week I ate the organic yoghurt you had bought for yourself, and I said nothing when you were looking for it," John tried to joke.

"Oh! I thought I had left it on the checkout belt in the supermarket... that's terrible!" said Adele, joining the game in the same playful mood. "Anything else?"

John thought for a moment. "All right, if you insist... about a month ago, I threw away a lot of your clothes hangers. You know – the ones that you cart home regularly from the dry-cleaner and then hang in every corner of our house?"

"Are you sure that you really threw them away?" asked Adele teasingly.

"Yes, I'm sure. I put them on top of the bin outside," John laughed. "Somebody took them."

"That was me!" giggled Adele.

"Oh, you're incorrigible! OK! The score is two to one. But I'm sure you have some more secrets." John was clearly encouraging the continuation of their game.

"All right, if we're speaking about throwing things out, I have to confess that two weeks ago I got rid of that invitation to the auto fair that you receive every year," Adele said in a guilty voice. "I knew that if you saw it, we would spend our entire weekend looking for a new car instead of visiting my mother as we had planned."

"I can't believe you did that!" exclaimed John, slightly angered.

"But you wanted to play this game!" said Adele defensively.

John said nothing and took the motorway exit towards Enna.

Adele turned to him. "So, are we still playing? It's your turn now."

"Adele, you know that you're very sociable, and that you love dinner dances, luncheons, family gatherings… but you also know that I always try to avoid them," John said slowly. "A couple of months ago, I declined an invitation from my colleague to take part in our university fundraising table quiz. I've turned down a few invitations like that, saying that you were ill and I had to stay at home with you."

John looked at Adele to see her reaction, but she did not seem surprised by his revelation.

"Well…" she said, dragging out the syllables, "I've done the opposite. I have to admit that I've invented some stories in order to arrange family meetings. Do you remember my Aunt Helena's visit last year?"

"Of course. She was so eager to chat with me, and followed me around everywhere. I found her behaviour really strange!" said John.

"That's because when I invited her to visit us, I mentioned that you missed her…"

"Impossible! She's the last person I'd miss: so boring. She tells the same stories about the neighbours over and over again as if they were of worldwide importance," complained John. "How could you tell her such nonsense?"

"John, I really wanted to see her, but she was afraid that you would find her a nuisance. So, I needed to persuade her to come. You know that I spent a lot of time with her during my childhood. She has no children and thinks of me as a daughter. Every time she comes, she brings me a nice present or even a little pocket money, just as she did when I was a girl. She is so kind, and after all, it was only a little fib."

"That's selfish!" exclaimed John, annoyed by the revelation.

"I didn't know that you were capable of such scheming," he added harshly.

Adele crossed her arms against her chest, as if to distance herself from his remarks.

John held back his increasing irritation and tried to remain engaged in the game. "I don't remember you ever sharing that money with me…" he joked.

Adele looked at him and blurted out, "So what?"

They fell silent. Both were now unwilling to take the matter any further. They had begun to feel unsettled and ill at ease with this attempt at honesty, which had turned into a pointless game they no longer wanted to play.

17

An Unexpected Turn of Events

John and Adele were coming into the town of Enna, and started to look for somewhere to park the car. They found a safe car park under a grove of trees at the entrance to the town, where they were permitted to leave their car for a day or two. They decided to have lunch before setting off on the walk to Columbine Cottage.

Enna had been a market town founded in the twelfth century. The couple found it pleasant to walk along its narrow medieval streets and twisting lanes crammed full of old stone houses with steep roofs for storing grain. They reached the town square, which was framed by quaint shops and small restaurants. A sound of rushing water proved to come from the swift current of a little river running through the centre of the town. It created a relaxed and refreshing atmosphere.

"This river reminds me of this morning's poem: *That life's fast current cannot wait. There's little time to hesitate*," quoted Adele. "Let's find a place for lunch."

They went into a quiet restaurant by the river and easily

found a table on an enclosed terrace with a nice view. Both ordered some simple snacks.

John looked out through the windows, feeling annoyed and drumming the surface of the table with his fingers. "*Boredom their constant and unwelcome scene,*" he said slowly, citing another line from the poem. "Adele, don't you think that that will happen to us if we continue this game?"

The quotation made Adele think for a moment. She then realised the true purpose of this assignment. She took a breath and looked at him. "John, you're right. We can't go on this way. Up to now, we've just been teasing each other. That's fine! But we haven't been speaking about the issues in our lives that really need to be addressed. We could do this exercise again, but this time more seriously. We can use the game as a way to allow each other to express the things that have burdened our hearts and minds…" she paused, "for quite a long time now!"

John looked at Adele attentively. Without waiting for his further agreement, she started to speak.

"Do you remember when we met for the very first time?"

John propped his chin in his hands as memories rose through his mind. His eyes softened, and this fact was not lost on Adele. "Of course I remember," he assured her. "You came into the university coffee bar, where I was marking the end of term with my first-year students. Quite by chance, one of the students sitting beside me left in a hurry. I might even recall her name… Yes, it was Lara. So, Lara left because she had something urgent to do, and since it was so crowded, the only free seat was at our table. Then suddenly you appeared, looking for somewhere to sit. So, I invited you to sit next to me." He could not conceal the pleasant emotions this memory evoked in him. Then he looked curiously at Adele. "What made you ask me about this?"

Adele shifted uneasily in her chair. Then she said in a low voice, "Well, our meeting was not exactly accidental… nor was it the first time I had ever seen you."

John opened his eyes wide in surprise. "What do you mean, it wasn't accidental? You've always told me that you had taken a shortcut through the campus and suddenly decided to have a coffee. And you had never been to that coffee bar before – wasn't that the case?"

"Well, that *was* the first time I had gone in, but I had seen you before on the campus."

John listened carefully, saying nothing.

Adele continued, "It was my neighbour, Lara, who helped me to arrange the meeting with you."

"I don't understand," John interrupted. "What are you trying to say? Lara was your neighbour?"

"Yes – we lived in the same building and were quite good friends at that time. The friendship lasted a few months before she married and moved away. We have not been in contact since," explained Adele.

John looked at her, seeking further explanation.

"One day, I was waiting for her at the main entrance to the university when you happened to be going out through the side door of the lecture hall. When Lara arrived, I told her that I had seen a young professor I thought was very handsome. After that, every time I met her after classes I kept an eye out for you. She knew it, and often teased me about you. After a while, she came up with a strategy she called 'How to Catch Your Man'. She really was a master of intrigue. In the beginning, I was very ill at ease with it and didn't even want to listen to her talk about it. But she was always saying that it was only a game and would do no one any harm. When I look back, I realise that she wasn't a very good influence on me, but I made the decision to take part in it, and I accept responsibility for that. I have always felt ashamed that I played that stupid trick on you." Adele sighed with regret.

John was listening intently. "So, what did you actually do?"

Adele passed her hand over her face. "Little by little, we formed a serious strategic plan to get me close to you in the coffee bar. So, Lara had to organise a gathering of students that would include you. Then just before I arrived, she would leave… and the rest you already know."

"And the book of poetry that 'accidentally' fell out of your bag? Do you remember 'When the Weather Clears' by Pasternak? What about your love for *Doctor Zhivago*? I've always adored Boris Pasternak, and my students at that time knew it… Was that also a part of your plan?" John asked, remembering the surprise he had felt at the happy coincidence that Adele had exactly the same interest.

"Yes… although years later, I really did start to appreciate Pasternak and his books."

"How clever of you," remarked John ironically. He felt embarrassed, and unsure of his reaction to Adele's admission. All these years he had been under the impression that it was he who had dared to approach an attractive young lady. He had found her radiant in her intelligence, but tactful, curious and delicate. He had very much wanted to gain her favour. He had always been proud of himself for taking the initiative, and now Adele's confession shook that pride. However, he had to acknowledge that he had obviously impressed her so much that she had decided to approach him in this devious but audacious way. He had always thought of her as unassuming and a bit timid. Clearly, she had hidden mysteries within her that still lay undiscovered. This idea intrigued him, and he made an effort to remain neutral in his reaction. "Adele, why didn't you tell me this earlier?"

"Well… you know, at the very beginning, when the direction our relationship would take was not yet clear, I didn't feel it was necessary to admit to it," explained Adele. "But later, after the little scheme had worked out and we were together, you told all our friends about the 'incredible story' of our meeting. I was reluctant to destroy that myth, and I didn't want to lose you. At the same time, I was really afraid that Lara would gossip to your colleagues and spread the word about how we had really met." She swallowed hard. "In all honesty, this little deceit has always upset me because it casts a shadow over the moment you first came into my life. Our relationship started out on the basis of an untruth. I did something to you that isn't consistent with the person I really am." She looked forlorn.

Ready to put aside any remaining confusion on his part, John replied, "Ad, it's all right: I understand why it happened, and in the end it turned out well. This story has a happy ending! It's all right," he repeated, reaching for her hand.

Their order arrived, made up of fresh bread in a basket, cold roast beef with horseradish cream, some pickles and green olives, and mineral water just out of the fridge, with moisture beginning to run down the side of its big blue bottle. As they ate, John was quiet and pensive, and Adele began to think that she had been stupid to reveal her secret. His silence vexed her, and she continued to reproach herself when suddenly John spoke up.

"Adele, since we're playing this game, I also have something to disclose…"

Adele's eyes widened in interest. She leaned towards him, her self-reproach replaced by curiosity.

"Do you remember when I was very angry with those two men in the street yesterday?"

"Yes, I do," confirmed Adele. "You were very brave in chasing them away. But I did find your reaction a bit extreme."

"It was," John said. "But there's a reason behind it all."

"What?" exclaimed Adele, surprised and a bit anxious. "Please tell me, Johnny!"

The server came to remove their plates. John asked her for some coffee for the two of them and then waited until she had moved away from their table. Adele could sense the rising tension in his body, certain that he was apprehensive about revealing something to her.

"John, it's all right. Just tell me! I'm sure that you haven't done anything wrong, and I'll do my best to understand whatever it is and your feelings about it."

"I feel so ashamed every time I think about it." John closed his eyes. His voice caught in his throat, and he took a deep breath. "It happened in Newtown when I was still a student. I was visiting the place with my best friend Steve during the summer holidays. Steve and I had a lot in common; we spent loads of time together, and had some fun." He smiled in remembrance. "But what happened to us in Newtown was serious, and it ended our friendship forever." His face darkened in distress. "One evening, we were drinking in a pub and stayed later than usual. I had passed all my exams and Steve was very happy with the sweet letter from his girlfriend that he had received that morning. We cheerfully emptied one pint glass after another, and when we left the pub, we were fairly drunk.

"We headed towards the youth hostel where we were staying, joking together in loud voices. At one point, I noticed two other guys directly behind us, but at some distance. I told Steve, but he didn't seem troubled at all. Suddenly they approached us very quickly, and a few seconds later they were breathing down our necks. One of the guys jumped forward and grabbed Steve's backpack. Steve turned around but was immediately punched in the face. He tried to push the assailant back, but received another punch from the second guy and fell down on the pavement. I rushed towards them and shouted that I would call the police. But one of the men pulled out a knife and threatened me. In that instant, all my courage evaporated. I knew I was in real danger, I was terrified, and my only thought was to escape. I ran as fast as I could in the other direction. I only realised when I was at a safe distance that I had abandoned Steve. I looked back and saw that the attackers were kicking him as he lay on the ground. Fortunately, a passing car stopped nearby, and the guys stole Steve's backpack, jumped over a fence and disappeared. Steve was still lying in the street. I ran back to him; saw that he was seriously injured and needed medical attention. The driver of the car took us to the nearest hospital."

John ended his story and Adele saw that he felt terribly guilty.

"What happened to Steve?" she asked cautiously.

"His condition was not as serious as it could have been, thanks be to God! He had some minor surgery, and was released from hospital after a few days. He recuperated at home." John sighed heavily. "But we couldn't remain friends afterwards. Our friendship didn't survive, and I really hate myself for abandoning my best friend in his hour of need."

There was silence. John continued to sigh, trying to relieve his inner turmoil.

Adele's feelings were mixed. John's account of his actions that night left her disappointed in him. After experiencing the attempted assault during her adolescence, her trust in any man had been based largely on his capacity to protect her. She had never had any reason to think that John would leave her to her own devices if she found herself in trouble. He had always projected an image of a self-confident, courageous man. He had also brought up Patrick to value those qualities. Could the reality actually be that John was a coward? She looked at her husband, who sat staring at the tablecloth, rolling his napkin between his fingers. *It's only now, after all these years, that I see that John is not as chivalrous as I thought,* she mused. *He behaves like a child in stressful, threatening situations... But despite all that, he overcame his fear and did his best to protect me last night. I need to be more appreciative of his genuine effort to change, and the trust he has placed in me, in honestly telling his story. It certainly wasn't easy for him. I have to be sympathetic and understanding.*

"John, it's clear to me that you sincerely regret what happened with Steve, and it's not for me to judge you for that," she said. "We can never predict how we might react in a real crisis. I'm glad that this game of truth has encouraged you to reveal your story to me. I hope it relieves your burden a little."

"You're right." John's expression was already less strained. "Thank you so much! I'm beginning to understand the importance of honesty between us. What happened just now is certainly no game."

Adele agreed. But at the same time, she felt that this exchange of honest feelings and true experience was not yet over. She still had something to say to her husband.

John asked for more coffee. Adele looked out at the clouds chasing each other across an azure sky. She watched the tops of the trees swaying in the gentle breeze from the Enna Valley, and decided that this was the moment to introduce the subject she had always avoided. John looked more relaxed after his release of emotion, and now was peacefully sipping his hot coffee.

Adele took a deep breath, as she usually did when preparing to talk about something important, in the hope that additional air might give her courage. Now she was more determined than ever to confront the issue. "About last night, John… at the dinner…" she started slowly.

"Oh, yes! Don't worry – the reaction of Aaron and his parents will not discourage me from continuing to write and recite my poetry," he replied at once.

Adele was taken aback. He had read her mind… the message did not transmit. She made another attempt. "But, John, I wanted to tell you the truth—"

"It's clear now what I have to do," John continued, without hearing her. After admitting his long-buried secret, he felt an indescribable lightness and an inflow of energy. The vision he had had of himself yesterday – that of a renowned poet – re-emerged and filled his mind. "A great poet has responsibilities!" He put his coffee cup down on its saucer with a decisive ring. "The ideas in my poetry must be communicated to and received by society. It's my mission in the world—"

"John, think about what you're saying," Adele interrupted, trying to bring her husband back to reality. Accustomed to viewing him as a respected economist, as well as a rational man with a critical mind, she was bewildered and irritated to hear him speak in such a childish way.

"Yes, Adele!" continued John, as though hypnotised. "I realise now that this, not economics, is my true calling in life. It is for me to bring this message forward. I'm surprised that I didn't realise it before."

His pathetic dream of a glorious literary career, along with his exaggerated self-confidence, seemed to Adele even more inappropriate in the context of his revelation about Steve, which she still found disturbing.

"Perhaps I'll leave the economics faculty—"

Adele could not stand it any longer. She brought the palms of her hands down hard on the surface of the table. "If you even *think* about leaving the university, you won't get very far... and you're *not* going to bring any message to the world, because your poetry is absolutely awful and no one will have the patience to listen to it!"

A great silence descended upon the table. As if awakened from a trance, John regarded his wife with amazement. He could not recall even one instance in their life together when she had spoken to him in that tone of voice. He looked at her as if he were seeing her for the first time. "You've changed," he said slowly. "You've never spoken to me like that before. It's as if you are a different person."

"Yes, well, maybe I am!"

"You've always loved my poetry."

"No, I haven't!"

"But you've told me many times that you loved it."

"No, I've always said that I admired the way you read it. I admired your persistence. I've never, ever said that I liked your poetry. John, I'm sorry, but I never did!"

"Never?"

"No, never!"

"So, you don't think I have any talent?"

"No, not for this."

"Are you sure?"

"Yes, I'm sure. I'm not an expert, but I don't think it's at all good."

John fell silent. Adele thought he was on the point of accepting the situation when his reaction suddenly took a turn for the worse. He looked at her with an angry cold regard.

"Well, I don't think you know anything about poetry. And perhaps you're a bit jealous. After all, you think you can dance, and last night you were like a flapping chicken on the dance floor!"

Adele was stung. This was an unexpected ambush on her self-esteem. "I'm trying to help you understand, to save you from being hurt by people being disappointed or bored by your poems, and in return you're making a personal attack! My dancing last night has absolutely nothing to do with your poetry or your reading of it in front of other people without their permission."

"Well, you danced in front of everyone last night and it was an embarrassing spectacle. Did you ask everyone's permission to do that?" persisted John sarcastically.

Adele tried, with much effort, to hold on to her dignity. John's words were so unfair that she was speechless. Tears gathered in her eyes and began to run down her cheeks. She swallowed a sob. "I don't understand you! Why do you want to hurt me like this just for being... honest? I..."

Her words choked her and she was unable to say more. She got up quickly from her chair and moved across the terrace towards the exit. But in her haste, she accidentally overturned her coffee cup, staining the linen tablecloth irreparably; the dark brown liquid soaking the pristine expanse of fabric. It was as if John's words had stained what had been a fair and balanced exchange of confidences. Events had taken a wrong turn for them both while playing this challenging and risky truth game.

18

The Golden Thread

John remained alone at the table. He was angry, and glanced around to check whether the other diners had taken note of their dispute and Adele's abrupt departure. *What kind of behaviour is that?* he thought furiously. *Humiliating me in a public place! Luckily, this restaurant isn't very crowded at the moment.*

He surveyed the room again, and noticed small groups of guests engaged in conversation or studying tourist brochures. There was, however, one couple in their twenties who had stopped eating their lunch and were staring at him, disturbed and embarrassed. John's face coloured, and he threw down his napkin. He rose from his chair, and then noticed Adele's mobile phone on the table. In her rush, she had clearly forgotten it, and this meant that he could not even call her.

He went to the bar and paid the bill. *It's absolutely irresponsible of her to behave like this. I have to get her to see reason.* He loitered for a few minutes near the restaurant's entrance, expecting Adele to return and apologise to him. *It's also unacceptable for her to speak to me as she did. She provoked me, and so I had the right to respond in the same way. And after all, she always reacts like this in a stressful situation: she runs off and slams the door!*

Leaving the restaurant, he returned to their car, sure that Adele would be there. Approaching the car, he saw no one. A fresh wave of anger rose in him. *What the hell is she thinking? That I'll wait here for her for the rest of the day?*

John weighed up the situation. It was already mid-afternoon and they had to get to Mary Catherine's cottage before sunset. He had no desire to abandon this venture; he wanted to go ahead with it. He looked at his watch. It was time to get on the road. If they did not, the sun would set and they would still be searching for Columbine Cottage. He decided that it was more sensible to look for Adele in the town than to wait for her at the car.

Enna turned out to be much larger than it had appeared on satellite navigation. The Old Quarter was full of narrow streets that led into squares and little parks, and then opened out into more commercial areas. In the first half-hour John covered a lot of ground energetically. He then found himself wandering aimlessly, peering into shops and coffee houses here and there, hoping to spot Adele. But all was in vain: she was nowhere to be seen. His anger became concern, and then anxiety. *What if I was really too aggressive in my reaction? What if I insulted her when she was only being honest with me?* he asked himself hesitantly. *Even if Adele had no right to speak to me in that way, she did not intend to hurt me. And I have to acknowledge that she was carrying out our assignment. We were asked to be more honest with each other. My reaction was too extreme – it* was *an attack!* He felt guilty. The only thing he wanted now was to find Adele and apologise to her. He started to speed up, but soon noticed that he was going around in circles in this complex town. He sat on a bench in a park and tried to control his rising panic. On autopilot, he took out his phone and checked his messages. The most recent one was from Darius. John called Darius's number.

"I'm listening, John." Darius's voice was calm, and John felt that he was giving him his full attention.

The relief of hearing Darius's voice meant that John held nothing back. He burst out, "Darius, I've lost Adele somewhere... in fact, I've hurt her by being insulting and rude, and now she's gone!" He choked. "I can't find her anywhere. I'm still in Enna, and we might be late for our appointment with Mary Catherine. Anyway, that's not the most important thing just now: I need to find Adele and to be sure that she's safe! This truth game went too far."

"In a partnership, truth is always the companion of love. It breaks down barriers, increases confidence, and reduces the distance between two people," Darius said quietly. He did not ask for any details of the argument; it was as if he could view the situation perfectly well using a crystal ball. "Remember that there is also a risk in telling the truth. You expose your vulnerability or your guilt to your partner but you cannot be sure that your explanation will be accepted or your vulnerability respected. Such moments bring many rewards, but also great stress. Both partners often feel the need to escape the situation, and the relationship may be on the verge of ending. But it is in this very situation that it's possible to see the strength of the golden thread that binds the couple together. If it is not broken, it always draws them back towards each other."

John clung like a drowning man to the sound of Darius's voice, and his words brought him back to himself. But his explanation remained unclear to him. "What do you mean by 'the golden thread'?"

Darius seemed to be holding the telephone receiver closer and speaking even more clearly. "The golden thread, John, is the subtle link that forms when two people are really drawn together and begin to understand each other. It remains the essence of their relationship. It can form in an instant, or over time. We never know exactly why or how that happens; it is a mysterious moment in which both partners know that their destinies are linked. The problem is that often people forget about this moment, allowing a situation to develop in which they neglect each other. That inexplicable moment is left to sink into the depths of their sea of memories; hidden and forgotten in their everyday life together. As time passes, the golden thread can seem to become ever more irrelevant and unimportant to the couple. Then the connection that unites them is no longer truly felt. Each partner begins to question why they chose to build a life together. Without that crucial connection, the partnership can become a set of chains that restrict the couple's freedom and stifle them. Failing to consider your partner's needs and feelings can damage or break the golden thread that is essential for a profound, true relationship. Once broken, it can be difficult to restore, but we won't discuss that just now..." Darius paused for a few seconds, then added, "From what you have told me, John, it seems that the golden thread linking you and Adele is still strong."

"But what can I do to find Adele?" John asked earnestly.

"Go back to the beginning of your relationship, find the moment when your hearts really met, and you will know how to call her to you. Be courageous and creative!" Then there was silence. Darius was gone.

John remained on the bench, staring, perplexed, at his phone. Slowly but surely, with each passing second, he felt his energy return, inspired by his conversation with Darius and in particular by his final words. In his mind he began to go over every little detail of his first meeting with Adele and their early friendship. These memories, he hoped, would provide him with clues that could help him to find her. He thought of that university coffee bar, but could recall nothing about it that might be of use to him now, especially considering what Adele had revealed about their first meeting. *Could something have happened in the moment when Adele first saw me on campus?*

Is there something I should take note of there? he asked himself. *But how could I possibly know what was significant there, since that experience happened only to her?* Rejecting that idea, he went through his memories once again, turning them over in his mind and his heart.

Suddenly, his eyes lit up. He took out his phone and checked the map of the town. Then he smiled. He knew exactly what he had to do...

19

At the Point of No Return

On leaving the restaurant, Adele walked at a brisk pace, without glancing left or right. Her eyes were so full of tears that she was barely able to see the pavement ahead of her. After some time, still breathless and blurry-eyed, she found herself at the edge of a green meadow surrounded by trees. Seeing a large stone, she sat; then broke down and wept loudly. All the unresolved sorrows and pain of her childhood – indeed, of her entire life – seemed to reawaken and come to the surface. Like a child unfairly punished, she felt them keenly.

"You have to be patient with your brother and your sisters," was the phrase that Adele had heard over and over again from her mother. "You're older and should have more sense. And you're clever, so you should know better. You're responsible for what happens to them. You need to set a good example for them."

Adele loved Eddy, Julia and Elisabeth and had sincerely done her best to take care of them. But the constant obligation of care imposed on her by her parents had been too much. It was very hard on a child who was only a few years older than they were. Her mother was involved in her artistic pursuits, her father in his business affairs, so they had had little time to listen to Adele, or to allow her to voice her anxieties. She had learned at an early age to keep her worries to herself, and to confront her problems on her own.

The soft, verdant meadow and the serenity of the swaying birches and weeping willows offered her a safe environment in which to cry with no one nearby. Eventually she stopped crying and, raising her head, took a gulp of fresh air. The release of emotion made her feel better. She felt stronger in body and mind. *It's happened again! Yes, again! Why is it that every time I try in all sincerity to do something good for someone, my efforts are rejected and every problem becomes all my fault? Why am I always considered a troublemaker when I am honest?* she thought.

Suddenly she recalled herself as a schoolgirl sitting in the corner of a corridor with her head in her hands. She was sobbing after a reprimand from her physics teacher, Mr Robinson. Adele had enjoyed physics very much. She spent considerable time on her homework and studied eagerly each detail of any given problem. On that particular day, during the lesson, the students had been given a test made up of problems set by Mr Robinson. He was strict and exacting, but Adele respected him for his clear explanations and interesting lessons. In working out the first problem, she had seen a fundamental error which meant that it could not be solved. Raising her hand, she brought Mr Robinson's attention to his mistake. She had expected her diligence and her knowledge of the subject to be appreciated by her teacher. But his reaction was so icy as to leave her hurt and bewildered.

"Miss O'Brien, mind your business and get down to your work," he said sharply. "We'll discuss this after class."

When the bell sounded and the other students had left, he looked at her with an air of criticism.

"It seems that you doubt my competence and want to damage my standing in front of the whole class. I will not tolerate such insolence during my lessons!"

Adele had been so shocked that later she was unable to recall anything that Mr Robinson had said after that. She had left the classroom terribly hurt, with an immense feeling of injustice, and after that incident, her passion for physics had faded away.

Recalling these painful memories, she felt the same sense of injustice regarding her argument with John on the restaurant terrace. *He has the problem, not me!* she concluded. *From the very beginning I have tried to be supportive of his creative writing because I know that his poetry is very important to him. But today I had no choice but to tell him how I honestly feel. He really has no talent in that particular domain. His determination to write poetry comes from the fact that he wants to be part of an artistic elite; a golden circle of universally admired talent. That is the real problem! He lacks self-esteem, and believes that if he receives recognition as a 'great poet' he will then have the status he deserves within that elite group. Even worse, he has always been convinced that he has a superior ability to write poetry, and that drives people away. They're disappointed or bored by what they perceive as poor content, but they are also often taken aback by his narcissism and arrogance in asserting his so-called 'talent'. I've been tolerant for many long years, but today he infuriated me!* Adele clasped her hands together in anger. *Even if he were upset about what I think of his poetry, that does not give him the right to humiliate me. I can't accept his disregard for my opinions and my feelings any longer. I need to stand up for myself. I have to put a stop to this behaviour!*

Standing up, she looked at her watch. It was time to start their walk to Columbine Cottage. Just this morning their journey had seemed so attractive, but now Adele was suffused with negative emotion and part of her was reluctant to continue it in John's company. Conversely, a strong internal vibration also made her want to stay on The Road with him in spite of this painful conflict. Still, she refused to give up her battle against his unacceptable conduct. *No, Adele! You've put up with this treatment long enough and too often. You know exactly where it will end. You will be thought of as the one in the wrong. John won't change. He has already forgotten about what he has done to you. He doesn't care about you or how he makes you feel!*

She recalled another situation that had happened the previous summer during their visit to the spa. She had chosen the Ayurvedic massage, described in the brochure as having 'a rejuvenating effect on the body and soul'. As soon as John had noticed this and had seen the price, he had looked sceptically at her, scanning her from top to toe, then had blurted out, "I doubt it'll help much; it's just a waste of money." She had had the massage in spite of his dismissive attitude, but his remark had wounded her. In addition, the fact that he had no regard for his implied insult of her hurt her even more. She had been so cast down that she had no longer had any desire to go to the theatre that evening as they had planned. Then, of course, she had been blamed once again. She remembered with chagrin that John had spoken of that incident during their morning meeting with Darius, Marija and Mary Catherine. He had attributed it to her lack of timekeeping.

Adele had an image of John still in the restaurant, sitting at the table in a state of fury and storing up an avalanche of reproaches to hurl at her. A surge of anger overwhelmed her. *I refuse to accept this from him any longer – he's really gone over the absolute limit!* she concluded. *I'll fight for my dignity, whether it threatens this marriage or not!*

Adele then made an impulsive decision. She would leave Enna by bus if it were possible. Departing the meadow, she started to walk back towards the town. She walked rapidly until she was in the centre, then asked a young man she met on the way where she could find the bus station. Determined to catch a bus and then somehow let John know of her decision later, she went straight to the departure area. She checked the timetable, looking for a coach that would take her home. The next was to leave in fifteen minutes.

Suddenly, her gaze was drawn to a small piece of paper pasted to a corner of the timetable. She looked closer, expecting a change in departure times, but to her surprise, she recognised John's handwriting. It was a poem:

Trapped by a poet's self-glory, dreaming of my Greatness,
In arrogance I forgot the danger we were warned of by the witch.
With trembling heart, as on our first date,
Once again, I'll wait for you on the bridge.

Oh, heaven help us! He is certainly the worst poet in the world, Adele thought with a sigh, but she felt her mood lift and could not suppress a smile. Nonetheless, her determination to go home did not lessen. *Does he honestly believe that he will win me back with this pathetic poetry?* she asked herself, still astounded by her discovery of this paper in a public place. But the words of the little poem touched her, and she read it through once more. Long-forgotten memories came to her mind. Instantly she was transported back to that day, and it was as if someone had gently strummed a hidden string within her heart. With its vibration, all her anger and sorrow vanished as if by magic.

She vividly recalled their first date. They had arranged to meet on the Nightingale's Bridge, which was popular as a rendezvous point for young people, couples, and visitors to the city. Its art nouveau architecture stood out in metal painted dark green, and was reflected in the rushing river beneath. Many people had liked to stroll or simply linger there. Adele had rushed to be on time, having been delayed by a sudden rain shower with a strong wind during which she had been forced to stop for several minutes and take shelter. The bridge had been deserted due to the heavy downpour, but the rain had started to ease off. Hurrying towards it, she had seen John standing alone, looking out for her. She had approached him. The poor man had been soaked to the skin. On seeing Adele, his face had lit up. Their eyes had met, and in that moment she had sensed his happiness at seeing her, and she had felt the same. All her life she had waited for a man to look at her in that way, and she had trusted him immediately. She had felt it, but could not have explained why. Their eye contact had lasted only a second, but she had savoured the thrill that had passed between them.

She had broken the silence. "John, you'll catch your death – come under my umbrella!"

He had then ducked underneath her little yellow umbrella. She had taken tissues from her bag and had tried to dry his face and hair. His expression had revealed that he had felt he was in seventh heaven. He had submitted to her efforts like an obedient child.

"Let's find somewhere to warm up," Adele had said, taking the initiative. "You're drenched – I'm sure you feel like a soggy sponge."

She had continued to comment on his appearance, until John had said good-naturedly, "All right, then. It's raining! I'm wet! I know!"

They had laughed and left the bridge.

At the first corner, they had noticed a tea room attached to an art gallery, and they had gone inside. The interior had been cosy and warm, with a little glowing lamp placed on each table. They had sat down and had taken off their wet things. The tea room had been filled with the scent of cinnamon. The server had brought a steaming pot of tea with ginger shortbread biscuits. The gallery had been holding an exhibition of art from the Ashanti Kingdom, but it had just closed for the day. However, some carved wooden statues and masks were on display in the tea room. Just beside Adele and John's table there had been a statue called The Witch of Destiny. Adele recalled word for word the English translation of the sentence carved on the witch's cloak:

Once you are caught up in vanity and arrogance, you are my slave forever.

This quotation had led them into an animated discussion of their opinions on its meaning. Adele had considered the words to be a warning, and argued that the artwork of ancient societies often contained the collective wisdom of the ages, to which modern society could lend an ear. John had thought of the quotation as a mere superstition. They had spent an excellent first evening together, which both had, in subsequent years, often recalled with great happiness.

Suddenly the realisation hit her. John had written this poem and left it for her to find because that first rendezvous still burned brightly in his memory, as it did for her. *I was mistaken in believing that he no longer cares for me! He really regrets his behaviour, and he is calling to me; I feel it…*

She was so lost in thought that she failed to notice that the bus she had intended to catch was pulling up to the stop.

"Madam, would you like a single ticket?"

She came to with a start, her recollections interrupted by the voice of the bus driver. She was silent for a moment. "Where can I find a bridge?" she asked him suddenly.

The driver's expression showed that he was taken aback by her strange question. "Well," he replied politely, "there's only one bridge in Enna…" He pointed straight ahead.

Adele hurried away in the direction he had indicated.

The driver began to wonder if he had done the right thing. *I hope she's not thinking of doing anything foolish*, he thought. He watched her rush away with a worried look in his eyes.

Adele was now running to the direction given by the driver. Within a few minutes, she saw the bridge rising in front of her. As she got closer, she spotted John standing on its arch and felt the same thrill she had experienced so long ago on their first date. She slowed her pace, but her heart was still racing.

John had seen her approaching from a distance, but he did not move towards her. He stood stock-still. It seemed to Adele that he was doing so in order to signal to her that he would wait for her until the end of time; that he would watch for her final step to be certain of her decision.

She came to him. They stood close to each other, face to face. It was then that they both felt the vibration of the thread that, on that other bridge, so many years ago, had linked them together. They were travelling on that vibration into their own universe, where neither time nor distance existed. The moment of their first meeting merged with their present one. They had found again the source of their relationship. As John timidly touched Adele's shoulder, she had no doubt that she wanted to continue on life's road with him.

20

The Road to Columbine Cottage

"John, what happened between us on the terrace was so hard to take," sighed Adele. "I was very hurt and I broke down completely afterwards. Sadly, I have heard insults like that from you quite frequently. I thought I could deal with them by just ignoring them and swallowing my resentment and pain. I believed that this was the right thing to do, and that I was strong enough to do it for the sake of our relationship. But I've realised now that it's a terrible approach to take. I can't save our marriage alone. The malice you directed at me today was so unfair I couldn't accept it. This time, I was ready to hit back at you; I was about to explode with all the anger that's accumulated in me over the years. I was even prepared to tear down everything we've built together and finish it…"

John was silent, listening carefully to everything Adele was saying. He wanted her to have the opportunity to express her emotions freely, without feeling constrained by any intervention from him.

Adele sighed again. "But your funny little poem turned everything upside down in me. It reminded me of something very important in our relationship, and what we nearly lost. This precious feeling of closeness and trust in you was stronger than my anger and my hurt." She looked into his eyes. "I feel quite overwhelmed, and I'm lost for words…"

"You don't need to say a word, Adele," said John gently. "I know what you mean – the golden thread that links us – and I see now how you feel. I'm really sorry for how I spoke to you. I am happy you're back, and I'm so relieved that I've found you."

They stood silently for a while; then John drew in his breath. "We should think about getting back on the road, Adele," he said. "It's already late afternoon, and we are meant to reach Mary Catherine's cottage before sunset… that is, if you still want to go on this journey with me?"

Adele smiled at him, and John smiled back and gave her back her phone. She checked the time. "You're right. We'd better get going."

They hurried towards their car to collect the essentials for their stay at the cottage. While waiting on the bridge, hoping that Adele would join him, John had studied the map that Darius had given them, and so now he felt confident about their route and could not wait to begin the journey.

They went through the town, and on the outskirts took a footpath up towards the mountains. The weak rays of afternoon sun filtered down in beams of coral light. But as time advanced, dark and gloomy clouds started to fill the sky, and the wind grew stronger. Adele and John picked up their speed. The wind blew even harder and the clouds moved closer and closer.

John stopped and took out the map. "I saw a shelter marked on here somewhere. Ah, here it is! We'll reach it in five minutes," he said. "The rain may be heavy. I don't want you to catch cold, and I don't want to arrive at Mary Catherine's cottage looking like a wet dog."

Adele thought again of that heavy rain during their first rendezvous on that bridge, so many years ago, and smiled.

They continued walking, and soon they heard the first patter of raindrops on the leaves above them. The shelter was just ahead. They ran and ducked under its roof. Thunder rumbled loudly and the rain intensified, but they felt safe. The shelter was a simple construction consisting of one wall and vertical poles supporting the wooden roof. A big table and a couple of benches allowed hikers to have a snack and take a break there. Adele and John sat down on one of the benches. The shelter's location afforded a panoramic view of the town and its surrounding valley. The contours of the multicoloured parks and houses were softened by the rain, and everything looked as though it had been painted in an impressionistic style, with barely visible brush strokes.

Adele looked at John. He seemed thoughtful and even melancholic. Perceiving the reason for his contemplative mood, she asked him, "Are you preoccupied with thoughts of your poetry, John?"

"Yes," John said curtly. "I'm beginning to realise that I'm probably hopeless as a poet, but it's not easy for me to accept."

"John, I spoke *so* unkindly on that terrace today. I'm sorry!" she broke in. "I didn't intend to hurt you, but I wasn't tactful and I should have been. Now I see why what I said made you so angry that you mocked me, but I had to tell you. Our game of truth encouraged me to do so, and I never expected our conversation to end so terribly."

"This has been a good lesson for both of us," John sighed. But a few seconds later he smiled and added, "But it has also given us the chance to learn to know and understand one another in a more significant way." He paused again. "After all of this, the fact that I have no artistic talent doesn't really matter."

"No – don't allow yourself to think for even one second that you have no talent!" pleaded Adele. As he had been speaking, she had been gazing at the landscape in front of them. The valley had suddenly brightened, lit up by the sun emerging from the clouds. The unexpected light reminded her of something. "John, listen to me: you could find another path; another way to express your creativity. Think of how beautifully you draw – remember the sketch you did when we were on holiday with Patrick at that little cottage in the woods? You have a natural flair for it; you do it with ease and are never pretentious about it. I still would like to have that sketch framed and put up in our living room for all our friends to see."

"That's good of you to say, Adele! I'm not so sure myself. We'll have to see…" John said, his melancholy dissipating and his equanimity nearly restored. "I don't wish to make any predictions as to my competence in drawing or painting… I might be trapped again in vanity by our witch." And he winked playfully at Adele.

Seized by a sudden impulse, she threw her arms around him and held him close, putting her face against his chest.

John was caught off guard by this spontaneous gesture of affection. He stiffened unconsciously; his body did not seem to remember how to respond to her. He felt awkward and foolish. He leant back and moved away a little, looking at the sky and then at his watch. "Ah… we should move on. The rain has stopped. Look – the sky has cleared," he said quickly.

"Yes, I suppose it has…" Adele was disturbed by John's instinctive movement away from her. He had clearly sought to avoid her embrace. She was confused and did not know how to interpret his reaction. However, she decided to put aside her clouded emotions in the spirit of continuing their journey. She wanted to preserve the happiness of their reconciliation.

They stood up. The fresh, oxygen-rich air of the mountains floated over them, bringing with it an aura of tranquillity. The life-affirming atmosphere kept them alert and ready to forge ahead. They walked along the path, which was now leading downhill. After a while, they entered a wood composed of birch, ash and alder trees. The treetops formed a green canopy against the sky, and beneath it they found themselves in comforting darkness. They followed a path of wooden planks set out among the trees. They stepped carefully through the brook, which rippled over rocks soft with moss, and from a distance heard cascading water. Within a few minutes, they came upon a magnificent waterfall, and stopped to admire it. Then they were plunged into the intoxicating scent of Scots pines. They continued on, and then came upon an intricately carved wooden bridge. A large bush of white Queen Anne's lace hung over it. Its blossoms brushed against their cheeks as they crossed the bridge. The sound of the gurgling water below chased after them, like a small child not wanting to be left behind.

As they left the forest, there were no more wooden planks on which they could walk. The way became muddy and slippery. John and Adele had to be careful of their footing going up and down along the path. At one point, John tripped over a rock, lost his balance, and landed sprawled in a swampy patch just beside the path. He sat up and looked around him, trying to figure out what had just happened. Then he glanced down and, seeing the state of his clothes, began to rock back and forth in a fit of laughter.

"What… John, are you all right?" Adele asked anxiously.

John still could not contain his laughter. "Yes, I'm OK," he answered finally, and breathlessly. "I'm just imagining the faces of my students if they saw their professor covered in muck. You certainly wouldn't need to worry that any of the girls would be attracted to me. They would never want to flirt with me like this!"

Looking at him flailing helplessly in the mud, Adele also started to laugh in spite of herself. "I have to admit, it *is* very funny. You're worse than a piglet on a farm." She reached for

John's arm to help him up, and then pulled up a handful of grass to clean the mud from his trousers. She admired the self-effacing manner in which he had handled his fall, as well as his ability to make fun of himself in such an unpleasant situation. She had not seen this side of John's character before; normally, he tried to save face. "Now we need to hurry! This time it's you who might catch cold," she said in a kindly tone.

They resumed walking, and after a short while they saw a white cottage in the distance. The hilly meadows surrounding it were full of columbine flowers, identifiable by their five pointed, deep violet petals that seemed to suggest the flight of doves. It could not be anything else but Columbine Cottage. Mary Catherine's little house stood on its own on rising ground surrounded by fine, tall trees. Those closest to the cottage were cedars, and to Adele they looked like sentinels guarding it from harm. The small windows reflected the evening sun. They seemed to wink and beckon the visitors forward.

As they came nearer, they saw Mary Catherine waving happily to them from the doorway. Adele and John came into the yard, and looked around curiously. In the centre there was a stone well, with a wooden roof to protect the purity of the water. Flower beds along the fine gravel paths led to the front door of the cottage. There was a little bench to the left of the door, handmade from oak. The wood had been bent by steaming and then stretched in order to accommodate the comfort of those wishing to sit on it. On the wide windowsills, Adele noticed an array of terracotta pots filled with various fragrant herbs. Some she recognised immediately, such as rosemary, lemon thyme, and clary sage. Others were not known to her, their leaves giving off unfamiliar but wonderful scents.

"Welcome. I see you've crossed the mountain road successfully!" exclaimed Mary Catherine.

"Successfully, in part," John corrected her, smiling and gesturing towards his dirty clothes. "We were caught in heavy rain. The path leading up to your cottage was quite slippery and covered in mud."

"Really?" Mary Catherine raised her eyebrows. "We haven't had a single drop here…"

John and Adele looked around again. There were indeed no signs of rain on the grass or the bench. The sun glittered on the windows.

"Come in!" Mary Catherine said. "I've prepared a room for you next to my tiny veranda."

They entered and crossed the large, comfortable living room. All the furniture – including the table, the chairs, the bookcases, and the chest of drawers – was also handmade. The couple saw no plastic or metal details. Everything was in fine wood, beautifully crafted, and perfectly arranged.

Mary Catherine showed them their bedroom. "John, give those dirty clothes to me. I'll wash them and find something clean for you to put on."

"Thank you, Mary Catherine. Luckily, I've packed a change of clothes in my backpack."

Mary Catherine opened the door to their bathroom. "It's quite a large Victorian bath, you know," she said rapidly. "Take your time. I'll have to leave you to bring a tea mixture to my neighbour just over the hill, as she has a cold."

"Oh, how wonderful to have a bath! I'll go first," said John, and he entered the bathroom.

Adele heard running water and John humming light-heartedly to himself. With this relaxed atmosphere and the strong scent of musk soap, she felt a desire to join him. She opened the door. Steam was rising, clouding a mirror hanging above the ceramic sink, and encircling John.

He looked at her in surprise as he soaped his neck and chest. "Hello – is everything all right?"

"Yes, of course," Adele replied, disappointed that his tone was not more welcoming. "I thought, perhaps—"

"I'll be happy to discuss anything you wish, a bit later. But for now, I just need fifteen minutes to relax and finish my bath."

She drew in her breath, taken aback by his abruptness.

"And please close the door after you! There's a draught coming through."

Adele turned quickly and left, shutting the door more firmly than was necessary.

21

Tuning Into the Power of Plants

John appeared at the door to their bedroom, dressed in soft cotton trousers and a chequered flannel shirt. He was holding his muddy clothes in his hands. "It's very kind of you to offer to wash my clothes," he said hesitantly. "I don't know how to repay you for all of your help."

"Don't even mention it," replied Mary Catherine warmly. "That opportunity to do something will come soon. How is Adele?"

"She's fine, but she's glad to have a rest. After today's trek, she's pretty tired. She had her bath after me and now she's stretched out on your soft bed."

"She well deserves a soft bed." Mary Catherine smiled. "By the way, Darius and Marija will join us for dinner very soon. Would you like to help gather some herbs for our meal?"

"I may not get it right," answered John, a bit embarrassed.

"Oh, you'll be a great help!" replied Mary Catherine. "You've done it all many times before," she added quietly, holding open the kitchen door that led out into the garden.

"Many times before... but many years ago..." John murmured to himself.

"Yes, John," Mary Catherine answered. "But you'll be surprised by all you will remember."

John looked at her. He had not realised that she had heard him. He took the flat basket especially made for collecting herbs that she offered him and followed her through the grass. Entering the small but well-tended garden, he caught the scents of tarragon and lavender wafting through the warm air. Mary Catherine walked beside him, carrying delicate garden shears. She handed them to him carefully, covering the blades and offering him the handle. She pointed to a beautiful flowering tarragon bush a few paces ahead, the scent of which he had caught on leaving the kitchen.

"Some tarragon, John, and then some parsley? Perhaps a bit of lemon thyme or coriander for the salad? Nasturtium flowers? You can decide. As you and Adele are staying the night, perhaps some lavender sprigs for the bedroom to help you sleep?"

John held the tiny shears in his left hand and approached the tarragon bush without a hint of uncertainty. He cut the sprigs in a practised way, ensuring that it was done evenly and at a slant. As he moved on to the parsley, he felt as though he were starting to say a prayer. He was a child of nine again, doing the same in the garden with his mother; sadly lost late that cold autumn to an uncontrollable pneumonia. He drew in his breath and tensed himself in anticipation of the old, familiar pain that always rose in his throat and spread to his chest, but it did not come. Instead he felt a strong warmth in his chest, which he found pleasant and comforting. He bent down to a lavender bush at ground level, carefully clipping the stems, when suddenly he sensed a slight movement in the bush. A tiny black-and-white paw appeared, before being quickly withdrawn. Mary Catherine laughed, but said nothing. Moments later, the black-and-white head of a little kitten emerged, slowly and timidly. He was a real baby. He gazed intently at John, waiting for permission to come all the way out.

John laughed. He knelt down and picked the kitten up, holding it to his chest affectionately. "You little scamp!" he said into the kitten's ear. "All scamps want to meet each other," he remarked to Mary Catherine, still smiling.

She put her hand on his shoulder as she sprinkled water from a watering can onto the rosemary in front of her. "He's afraid of the garden shears, and he's wondering if he can trust you," she whispered.

"Of course you can, little one. No one is going to hurt you." John held the kitten closer to his chest, and it gazed even more intently at his face, with curiosity rather than fear.

"It's hard for him to overcome his fear of scissors, since his ear was almost clipped when he was hiding in the rose bushes last week," Mary Catherine noted. "He is also afraid of water, and thus my watering can."

John laughed again. It had been a very long time since he had heard himself laughing as he had in his childhood.

"Maybe you can reassure him about the water," she continued, in a serious tone.

"Yes…" he began to reply, and then stopped in mid-syllable and took in his breath sharply. Flashes of memory were coming from even deeper levels of his mind. "Sorry, I can't…"

"It's important to put words to it," Mary Catherine said gently.

"It was a terrible experience for me," John began again, agitated. "I was only seven years old when that rowing boat overturned on Lake Ellyn. The boat kept covering my head as I tried to rise to the surface. I was running out of air… that was the most frightening thing I had ever experienced. Thank heaven the neighbour thrown into the water with me was able to lift the boat off my head. Only then was I freed, and I swam out." He fell silent. He had always pushed away memories of that day, fishing with his little school friend and the boy's father on a Sunday that had started with bad weather and an ominous yellow-grey sky. Now he struggled inwardly as he felt the old emotions rising in him again.

"If you think about the fear you felt that day, the lasting effects that it has understandably had on you, and the feelings that have stayed with you, you can better understand the fears of others," said Mary Catherine.

"Yes… yes, it's true: the effects of that accident have never left me." John was still trying to catch his breath.

"The pain of these memories has value if it helps you to understand the experiences of those around you," continued Mary Catherine. She paused. "Has Adele ever had an experience like that?"

"Not concerning water or a lake, but she has experienced overwhelming fear."

"As a woman alone?" asked Mary Catherine.

"Yes – a group of aggressive men roughed her up a bit," replied John. He was quiet for quite a while. "Up until now, I suppose I didn't really think about what damage was done to her that day and how it's influenced her behaviour ever since. I don't think I've taken it seriously enough. Reflecting on what happened to me as a child, I am beginning to better understand Adele's fears."

The kitten did not cease to be fascinated by John. He had given up avoiding watering cans and garden shears and had taken it on himself to wash the inside of John's ear with his prickly pink tongue. John's laughter filled the garden again as he and Mary Catherine began to walk back towards the kitchen door. She took the basket of freshly cut herbs from him. From among them she picked up a stem of slender green needles.

"Rosemary is the herb of remembrance," she said slowly. "Your mother would be very proud of all you remember of her herb garden."

22

An Awakening of the Senses

John entered the kitchen, following Mary Catherine and still in a daze after his turn in the garden with her, and her comments. They found Darius washing salad leaves while Marija and Adele worked beside each other at the hot range.

"Good evening, Mary Catherine, John! I hope you don't mind our intrusion in your kitchen," said Marija. "We took the initiative and started chopping onions. We still plan to have a vegetarian feast, don't we?"

"We do!" said Mary Catherine, looking at John and Adele. "If there are no objections?"

"We're just the guests," John replied dubiously, perturbed by the prospect of munching on salad all evening. After the long walk, he had worked up quite an appetite, and he was dreaming of a good, thick steak with green peppercorn sauce. But he decided to be polite and added, "I'm happy to try anything. It's been quite a while since we've had a vegetarian dinner, hasn't it, Adele?"

Adele was cutting the tomatoes and cucumbers on a wooden board, and seemed immersed in the preparation. Seeing John holding the kitten tenderly in his arms, she smiled. Approaching her husband, she put a piece of cucumber into his mouth. "Johnny, don't worry – you won't be disappointed. Come over here; we need your help!" Then she leaned against him and whispered in his ear, "Darius and Marija told me that I should be totally present while I prepare the food. In the beginning I couldn't understand what it meant, but I have been watching how Marija does it and I've tried to do the same. It's really enjoyable – try it! Just follow our lead."

John glanced at Darius, who was adjusting the heat under a steamer, as well as keeping an eye on something in the oven. Even though John was not very enthusiastic about taking part in preparing dinner with the others, he reluctantly put the kitten down and washed his hands. He then had a look around at what everyone was doing to see how he could help. The simplest task he could come up with was to put those dishes that had already been prepared onto serving plates or into bowls and then arrange them on the table. Mary Catherine joined him in doing this.

After a little while, they had raw and steamed vegetables, fruit, a pitcher of a fresh wild berry drink, and mountain spring water on the table. Soon the hot food was ready too. As John and Mary Catherine carefully arranged the last of the dishes on the table, they stepped back to admire everything that had been prepared. The dinner was ready. It looked to John as though it were fit for royalty. They had assorted salad leaves to start, dressed with walnuts and pomegranate seeds. The warm, dense rolls baked by Marija were expecting their dollops of thick, soft butter. Freshly gathered mushrooms in cream, cooked with tarragon and pine needles, competed for attention with aubergine slices sautéed in olive oil with cumin. A fluffy pilau rice had been placed at the centre of the table. Its steam gave off aromas of coriander, ginger and cloves, and its layers were full of crunchy almonds, plump raisins, and sour red cherries. Steam also rose from the hot Camembert cheese baked in breadcrumbs and bursting in creamy, saffron-coloured ripples from its golden crust. The scents of the freshly cooked dishes, combined with those of the herbs that had just been collected from the garden, filled the room and whetted their appetites. John could hardly wait to sit down and start eating, and stood near a chair, impatient for Mary Catherine to invite everyone to come to the table.

Finally, she did so. "Enjoy what you are eating, everyone, and savour it with your full attention."

As they began their meal, John and Adele ate more rapidly than everyone else. Everything on the table was as delicious as it looked. But soon they relaxed and started to appreciate every single bite.

John began to notice how colourful their table was. The palette seemed to cover all tones, from the deep red of the tomatoes to the orange of the carrots and peppers; the light green salad and dark green cucumbers; and finishing with purple plums and violet aubergines. Although he had placed the serving platters on the table at random, taken together they seemed to create an arc of colour. "Adele, look! Can you see the rainbow?" He nudged his wife gently.

Adele looked out of the window in front of her, which showed her nothing but the landscape in twilight.

"No – look at the table!" John pointed to it.

"I still have no idea what you mean," replied Adele.

"John, I can see that your sensory perception is very acute!" laughed Mary Catherine on hearing Adele's reply. "Once we begin to be more aware of what our senses tell us, we discover that the world is more colourful and multifaceted than we believed. We then constantly wonder how these nuances remain invisible to others." She put grated carrots, sliced red onion, and strips of cucumber on her plate and added some green lettuce with dressing. She stretched out her arm and with her fork speared a cherry tomato from a plate at the opposite side of the large table. Her movements were fluid and slow, and her supple gestures seemed like dance moves.

Mary Catherine's words impressed Adele, and she decided to concentrate more on her senses. She started with a piece of watermelon. Slowly, she put it into her mouth, exploring how it melted and released its juice. Then she took a mint leaf, smelled it, and chewed a small piece. "Oh, it tastes like sangria to me!" she exclaimed in surprise.

"Really?" Darius joined in the game. He picked up a piece of onion and put it in his mouth, then ate a strawberry. His face stiffened in a sour grimace. Then he laughed. "It reminds me of some bitter pills I had to take when I was ill as a child. My mother used to give them to me, along with strawberry jam."

Everybody started to taste different combinations of food and share their feelings and memories. Even the same combination could arouse different sensations and images when tasted by different individuals. Some of them recalled meals eaten during their childhood, or berry-picking in the summer. Others remembered pleasant evenings with friends at the table. This sensory game ended as naturally as it had started. John had taken a portion of several dishes and had eaten his fill. But he did not feel that he had overeaten. He had a sensation of lightness within his body.

"Every other time I have had vegetarian food, I've had a sense of not having eaten enough. But tonight, I really enjoyed my meal," he said, satisfied. "Did you use any special ingredients?"

"Yes. We used Himalayan pink pepper, herb salt, some good olive oil, some other seasoning…" Marija smiled and paused. Then she continued seriously, "And some love, some goodwill…"

John looked at her as though he thought she was making fun of his question.

Darius took note of his expression and added, "What Marija

has just said is literally the truth. When you are preparing food, your thoughts, your attitude and your emotions contribute much to the end result. We all enjoyed preparing our dinner together tonight and we put a lot of positive energy into it. That is why it was so delicious and nourishing."

"Yes, absolutely delicious," remarked John, setting down his fork and knife on his plate. "I'm in no need of anything sweet."

But Adele was still finishing her meal, delighted by the taste of roasted pineapple slices soaked in fragrant coconut milk and flavoured with lime. The responses of Marija and Darius to John's questions triggered memories in her. She thought about their own kitchen, their cooking, and the way they organised and ate their meals. Usually, it was Adele who prepared everything. She rarely did it with John. She could count on one hand the number of times they had made their dinner together. She had to admit that creativity was not the reigning principle in their kitchen. She knew a limited number of recipes by heart, that she had learned from her Aunt Helena or her grandmother. In sum, Adele could prepare a meal almost automatically, while watching television or talking on the phone. The majority of the time, it was a routine task that she performed without much pleasure. *It's quite clear that food prepared automatically is eaten automatically as well!* she concluded. In fact, it was not unusual, later in the evening, for John to actually ask her what they had eaten earlier. This really annoyed her and made her feel that her efforts were unappreciated. On reflection, however, she had to admit that John might have been sincere in asking that question. She smiled to herself.

"Is it possible to put our intentions into the food we are preparing?" asked Adele. "What I mean is, can I influence someone's behaviour or well-being through the way in which I prepare their food?

"That is something that you can experiment with yourselves," Darius answered, putting the ball back into Adele's court. "All that aside, let's go out and build a fire."

Working together, they quickly cleared the table, tidied the kitchen, and went outdoors. In the back garden, there was a circular stone firepit. Darius and John went to the woodshed and retrieved some wood to make the fire. Mary Catherine brought five Irish wool plaids, and everybody sat on tree trunks placed around the fire. The night was beautiful and calm. The sky was studded with stars, and the flames threw out tiny sparks that seemed to fly towards them. All five sat in silence and enjoyed the warmth generated by the flames. The plaids were not needed yet. Adele, who usually felt the cold, left hers to one side to enjoy both the heat of the fire on her face and knees and the cool of the night on her back. John stretched out his legs in contentment. Occasional distant sounds – a dog's bark, an owl's hoot, and the soft calls of other nocturnal birds and animals – reached the cottage. The trees and bushes rustled soothingly. Darius put some more wood onto the fire. Flames caught the dry log and the strong scent of pine pervaded the air. Darius moved closer to Marija and put his arm around her shoulders. Marija leaned into him and rested her head on his chest. At that very moment, the kitten approached Mary Catherine, jumped up, and curled up on her lap. He was warmly welcomed by the affectionate caresses of his mistress.

Observing those around him, John somehow felt ill at ease. *Have they forgotten us? They're so relaxed, they seem to be in a world of their own. What are we doing here? Are there going to be any more assignments for us?* he thought. He stole a glance at Adele, who also seemed slightly perturbed. The silence started to irritate him. He coughed and looked at Darius. "Well, it's been a long day, and not an easy one, but luckily, we've overcome all our difficulties, haven't we, Adele?"

John glanced at Adele again, expecting her agreement. She looked him full in the face but did not respond, so he continued.

"Since we have rediscovered what brought us together in the first place – that is, since we have found each other again, so to speak – I can't imagine what else there is left for us to do. So, I'm assuming that our journey on The Road has been completed?" Then he added, in a low voice, "Because we are soulmates once again."

"Actually, you are now in the middle of The Road," Darius pronounced calmly.

Adele and John looked at each other in confusion.

"In a partnership, it is also necessary for each person to go on a journey of self-discovery." Darius paused. "You say that you are soulmates. A meeting of minds and hearts is essential, but the union is not complete until the bodies have met too."

Seeing the disconcerted expressions on their faces, Mary Catherine intervened. "You know, the Irish philosopher John O'Donohue wrote that the body is the home of the soul. It has its wisdom as well as its own memory." Softly, she started to sing a Celtic melody. Once she had finished, she continued, "Our bodies accumulate both good and bad experiences during our lifetime, and those experiences sometimes prevent us from coming together completely. Think about giving the best of yourself to the other person. Your most loving thoughts, your most profound touch…"

Adele shifted uncomfortably. It was clear that this topic troubled her. She passed one hand over the other repeatedly, and tipped backwards the trunk on which she was sitting. Finally, she asked, "When you speak about the bodies meeting… hmm… I mean… that is, do you mean… physical intimacy?" She looked at Darius, then at Mary Catherine, and then turned to John, expecting his support.

But annoyance darkened his face. He seemed to be asking her, *Why have you raised this subject?* He crossed his arms over his chest and, as if trying to defend his dignity, said firmly, "I don't believe that this is a subject that we should continue discussing. The physical side of things is a private topic. If there are other things to be discovered on The Road, that's all right!

We'll carry on. But what happens in the bedroom should remain a matter between the two people involved. That's it!" He sat back with his arms still crossed and looked upward, indicating that for him the subject was closed.

Although John had been prepared for a negative response, nobody seemed to be in the mood to debate this question, and thus lose the serenity and stillness of this beautiful night. No one except Adele, who stared reproachfully at her husband, disappointed by his curtailing of any development of the topic. Despite her unhappiness, as soon as John realised that he had achieved his goal of closing the discussion, he visibly relaxed.

Marija extended her hands towards the fire. It had already started to burn down: its heat had diminished and its light had begun to dim. The stillness of the night seemed to deepen. All the nocturnal animals and birds who had been keeping company with the group seemed to have gone to sleep, and those who normally scurried about in the morning had not yet awakened.

John yawned and turned to Adele. "Ad, I feel exhausted; can we hit the sack?"

She sighed but said nothing. John and Adele then got up from their places and thanked Mary Catherine, Marija and Darius. After wishing them all a good night, they went back into the house.

23

Stinging Nettles

John and Adele walked through to the guest bedroom. They were enveloped again in the fresh night air flowing through the slightly open window, and the soft scent of lavender.

John undressed quickly. As he drew back the finely woven linen bedsheet, an image of his grandmother putting him to bed as a child came to his mind. In an instant he recalled the handmade bed linen that she would bring as gifts on her visits. "This feather pillow is calling my name, Adele," he said. He got into the bed and settled in, relaxed and comfortable. "I'll be in the Land of Nod before you know it... Ad, are you coming to bed?"

Adele heard him almost at a distance as she entered the bathroom. When she emerged a few minutes later, John was sleeping like a baby. He was taking up most of the bed. She did her best to find some space for herself without waking him. She curled up close to her husband. But, although she was extremely tired, she could not fall asleep. The past few hours had been one long emotional roller coaster, and the events of the day revolved in her mind. John sighed in his sleep and turned his back to her, leaving a larger space for her in the bed. This did not, however, add to her comfort. In fact, it had the opposite effect. She now felt abandoned.

Don't allow your imagination to run away with you! she reproached herself. *You must try to chase away this feeling. It has no foundation. Be reasonable: you have nothing to worry about. John is just sleeping; he's tired. And anyway, today was wonderful! We confronted a lot of difficult aspects of our relationship, and now we're close... closer...* The word repeated itself, and then faded from her mind. Suddenly, she was not very sure of how close they were. Two contrasting images appeared to her: John caressing the kitten, pressing him affectionately to his chest, and then John in the mountain shelter, stepping back from Adele's embrace. *What's going on?* Her resentment exploded inside her. *Do I need to magically turn into a kitten to earn my husband's affection?* The absurdity of this idea lessened her anger and nearly made her laugh out loud. Her worries seemed to recede. She turned in the bed and looked out of the window. The night held promises. The bright stars winked at her and then became blurry. The light from the sky covered her in its warm, shining veil. Her breathing became deeper. Her eyes closed. Distant, calming voices from the firepit smoothed her passage to sleep.

The morning dawned clear and sunny. Adele entered the kitchen with John.

Darius was mixing dough for the breakfast croissants. "I'll make you some tea," he said. "But in the meantime, perhaps you would like to go into the garden with Marija and Mary Catherine to pick some blackberries?" He pointed to the bushes, laden with fruit, that lined the outer stone wall of the garden.

Adele went out the kitchen door, moving towards the bushes. "Good morning," she said to the other women, and then took the basket that Marija offered. She popped a few of the juicy berries into her mouth, laughing as their colour stained her lips and chin.

"What a child!" John muttered from the door in an exasperated tone.

Adele advanced further and further into the thick bushes, catching her long, wavy hair on some nettles growing beside the blackberries. The thorns scratched her left arm as she withdrew the basket from the prickly plants. Glancing at the very few berries she had collected, she approached Marija timidly and said, "I'm sorry, Marija, that I couldn't do this more easily. I haven't many berries here. I'm so sorry that I don't have more." The embarrassment she felt at her lack of skill in picking the berries showed clearly on her face. "It is a very small amount for such an effort."

Marija, who had been gathering mint leaves, stood up from her kneeling position. Adele's face reddened as she gazed at the scratches on her arm and tried unsuccessfully to pull the nettles from her hair.

Marija put her hand on Adele's arm and said soothingly, "Don't worry, Adele, you've picked quite a lot – more than enough for all of us. Many thanks."

Adele looked at her basket once again, and it seemed much heavier. The basket was full of fruit. Marija passed her hand gently through Adele's hair but, curiously, after this delicate touch, the nettles caught deeply in it seemed to have multiplied and her general appearance to have worsened. The nettles were embedded. They were caught all through her hair. As the full sun reflected the lighter strands of colour within Adele's locks, the snarls and tangles were clearly evident too.

Beside Marija, Mary Catherine had been silently immersed in her gardening. Now Marija turned to her, and Mary Catherine handed her a neat blue packet containing what appeared to be a roll of bandage and a coil of white surgical tape. Marija pressed lightly on Adele's arm, which had been scratched in the bushes, and it then began to bleed profusely. Marija tapped on Mary Catherine's waist as she examined the contents of the bandage packet, and Mary Catherine drew a larger, heavier packet from the pocket of her apron. Both packets were wrapped in blue linen. Marija nodded, and then called to John, who was avoiding the blackberry-picking by playing hide-and-seek at the side of the garden with his new friend, the little black-and-white kitten.

"Come, John! Darius, John is coming into the kitchen to wash his hands." And Marija led the way to the kitchen door. As she passed Darius, she signalled to him, and he motioned to Adele to come in. Her left arm was still bleeding profusely.

"How strange," Adele remarked to Darius, as he held the kitchen door open for her. "It doesn't hurt at all!"

John followed, not really aware of Adele's injury until they faced one another in front of the kitchen sink. He reacted badly. "Look at the state of you! Could you not just pick a few blackberries?" he reprimanded her, raising his voice.

Marija advanced quickly towards him, holding out the two blue packets.

Darius cleared his throat. "If you would be kind enough, John, to take these packets to your bedroom, you will be able to look after Adele properly there."

"What's all this?" John asked.

"Some bandages for her arm, and a new boar-bristle brush for her hair," answered Marija.

"So, I'm supposed to attend to these scratches instead of eating my breakfast?" he replied, annoyed.

"Brush out her hair, John," Marija said softly. "Brush out all the nettles caught in her hair."

"I can do it myself," declared Adele, her face flushed again as she noted John's irritation. "I'm sure I'll manage... he won't have to—"

Darius lifted the palm of his hand in a call for silence. "Don't stress, Adele. John will do it for you," he said, quietly but firmly. "And meanwhile, we will finish preparing the breakfast."

John and Adele advanced slowly to their bedroom, John carrying the two blue-linen packets. As soon as they entered the room, he threw down the packets angrily. They made a sharp clacking sound as they hit the floor…

Adele sat up in bed and looked around. John was still sleeping. The window shutter was moving in the breeze. She approached it and closed the clasp to hold it in place. In the half-light of early morning, she looked closely at her hands and left arm. There were no scratches, there was no arm wound, no bleeding, and no nettles caught in her hair.

"I've only dreamt it," she sighed with relief.

Still caught up in her dream, she could not fall back to sleep, and so she decided to take some fresh air. As she went out of the cottage, she saw Marija sitting on the little oak bench. She was still wearing the light blue jean jacket that she had worn the previous evening, and Adele thought that she had probably not slept at all. But regardless, she looked as fresh as a daisy.

Seeing Adele, Marija invited her to sit down next to her. "Can't sleep?" she asked softly.

"Not really," answered Adele. "I was tired and fell asleep rather quickly… but then I had a strange dream…"

"Would you like to tell me what it was about?" Marija asked.

Encouraged, Adele recounted her dream in all its detail and high emotion, as though she were still feeling the prickly thorns on her skin. "It's nonsense!" she exclaimed when she had finished. "I know it was only a dream, Marija. But I feel terribly hurt by John's coldness!"

"That's not surprising," Marija said thoughtfully. "We all carry hidden wounds within us. Sometimes they start to bleed." A few seconds later, she continued, "The deepest wounds are inflicted by those closest to us, and so only they can help us to heal fully and effectively."

Marija spoke for a little while longer, and her kind, rhythmic voice calmed Adele. Both women watched the white mist which was rising from the valley as the new day dawned. As the light broke over them, Marija's face looked as though it were dissolving into the air.

Looking at her, Adele remembered something. "Marija, could I ask you something? When we were in Newtown, it seemed... I mean... I thought that I saw you twice... Were you really there?"

"Hmm... I don't know." Marija smiled intriguingly. "You could ask Darius. He says that in a quantum world, objects can be in several places simultaneously." She patted Adele's shoulder. "You could still sleep for a few hours, if you'd like to. It's best to go back to bed now before the birds start their morning chorus."

"You're right," said Adele, and then she yawned. "I'm sure I'll fall asleep easily." She touched Marija's hand. "Thank you!"

She returned to her room and slipped silently into bed. The morning birds were already beginning to cheerfully greet the rising sun, but they did not disturb Adele, who, with each breath, moved deeper into sleep. At one point, almost fully asleep, she vaguely perceived fragments of conversation, probably coming from the veranda.

"It is clear that they both feel it."

"But they are not fully aware of the importance."

"That's why they have to go there."

"Are you sure that Christos... his therapy...?"

"There's no doubt that they need it." Marija's voice was clearly recognisable. She seemed to have just joined the conversation. "They have to connect with each other."

Still groggy, Adele was unable to follow the conversation any further. The words merged and lulled her back to sleep.

"Both exercises appeared in Adele's dream, but neither was

completed by John," said Marija. "He hasn't learned to touch her with compassion or to be gentle and soothing. Do you both agree with me?"

"Definitely!" confirmed Mary Catherine.

"This is a real obstacle for them on their Road," observed Darius. "Let's see how we're going to proceed…"

24

The Roadworks

John opened his eyes and looked around. He needed a few moments to get his bearings, and then he remembered what had transpired the previous day. Adele was still sleeping. John stretched his hand towards the night table to check the time on his mobile.

"It's almost ten!" he called out. He noticed that an envelope had been slipped under the door, and got out of bed to pick it up. Opening it, he read the note he found inside. "Adele, wake up! Look at the time!"

Adele awakened by John's voice, slowly sat up in bed and stretched.

"Look – we already have a new task." John put the letter in her hands.

She leaned against the pillow, yawned, and started to read the letter out loud without fully taking account of its meaning.

FOLLOW THE ROAD AS INDICATED ON THE MAP

UNTIL YOU REACH THE WELLSPRING OF LIFE.
FIND CHRISTOS. HE WILL GIVE YOU FURTHER
INSTRUCTIONS.

Below the message there was a map with directions. Adele did not bother to study it. She yawned again. "Christos... that name means something... hmm... can't remember."

John was already dressed, and he urged Adele to hurry. "Adele, I can still smell coffee – perhaps we're not too late for breakfast?"

They entered the main room and saw that the table had been set. A pot of coffee and a purple plate of etched glass laden with freshly baked croissants had been placed at the centre of the table. Mary Catherine was busy preparing something. The black-and-white kitten followed her every step with his head up, obviously looking for attention and food.

"This is not for you! It's for our guests to take on their journey. Yours is right there," said Mary Catherine playfully, pointing to a small bowl in the corner. Then she turned and saw John and Adele. "Oh, you're already up – good morning! Sit down at the table and help yourselves. I'll join you in a little while."

The couple sat down and poured themselves some coffee. Its scent was irresistible. *It must contain some of the magic ingredients that Marija mentioned yesterday*, thought Adele.

"Mmm... this croissant tastes wonderful!" exclaimed John. "Adele, try one! I'll bet you've never eaten anything like it."

Adele, who usually preferred bread and butter at breakfast, ate a tiny piece of the large croissant, which was still warm. Then she ate another, much bigger piece. Soon the entire golden crescent moon had disappeared into her mouth. "They're incredibly delicious. I didn't realise I was so hungry," she said. "You get all the different flavours in proportion: sugar, sour yeast, melting butter..."

"Darius would be very proud to hear it," said Mary Catherine,

143

who was approaching the table and had obviously heard Adele. "He started preparing them yesterday evening and finished in the morning."

"That's funny!" remarked Adele. "I saw him mixing dough for croissants in my dream last night."

"Darius is so fond of croissants that I'm not surprised he can make them in other people's dreams!" exclaimed Mary Catherine.

John and Adele laughed and continued to eat. Mary Catherine filled her cup with hot coffee and sat down on a chair close to Adele.

"We've found the envelope," John said, ending the happy morning's small talk and getting down to business.

"Oh, yes. Before leaving this morning, Darius asked me to put it under your door," answered Mary Catherine. "I'll drive you to Enna and you can continue along the indicated road."

"This place we have to go to, The Wellspring of Life… what is it exactly?" John asked, with some trepidation.

"It's a natural mineral wellspring. Many years ago, a few affluent families from Newtown built a health spa there in the countryside. It offered treatments based on the special healing properties of the local mineral water. Later, it ran into financial trouble and went bankrupt. It was abandoned for many years. But recently, the old buildings were renovated by a community group very engaged in promoting natural health remedies. The new spa was named The Wellspring of Life. It has now become a well-known venue for therapists practising alternative healing methods, and for those offering meditation techniques, relaxation, yoga, Zen and so on. They have excellent swimming pools and saunas. I'm sure you'll enjoy it," Mary Catherine said encouragingly.

"So, it seems that your wish to spend time in a spa has been granted." John turned to Adele.

"That's great!" said Adele, delighted by the idea. "But what are we going to do there? Practise yoga… or Zen? Has this anything to do with yesterday evening's conversation by the fire?"

Mary Catherine leaned towards Adele. "Be patient – you'll know very soon. You'll be pleasantly surprised." She almost whispered the last sentence.

John was already studying the map and paid no attention to their conversation.

Time pressed on. Mary Catherine brought John his clean clothes and handed a lunch basket to Adele. All three stood at the door. For the last time John caressed the kitten, who looked at him with big, longing eyes, ready to follow his new friend. Then John glanced at the garden, remembering the evening before, and the same wave of pleasant warmth filled his chest.

"Mary Catherine, thank you for everything. I felt so at home here," he said sincerely, putting his hand on his chest. "And all these plants… they're special. I'd like to cultivate some like them at home."

"If you truly mean that, John, don't delay – do it as soon as possible," said Mary Catherine. Looking at Adele, she added, "It's always like this: once you have made a decision with your heart, act on it immediately. Otherwise you start to hesitate, and afterwards you regret that you haven't done anything."

Adele embraced her. She shared John's emotion on leaving the cottage. She was also pleasantly surprised by what he had just said.

Mary Catherine's tough little jeep brought them down to Enna quicker than they had expected.

"Good luck! Keep a close eye on The Road… and take care of each other!" Mary Catherine blew a kiss, waving goodbye as she drove away.

John and Adele felt a bit strange being on their own again with so much uncertainty ahead of them. But that uncertainty also inspired them to move forward. John started their car and left the car park, following the directions on the map.

"How long will it take us to get there?" asked Adele.

"It's not very far, but with the local roads it may take a couple of hours," answered John.

They fell into silence while enjoying the picturesque valleys and small villages on their route. The sunlight was quite strong, but its rays were dimmed by wispy white clouds curling across the sky. The fields were a lush dark green and the trees were in full splendid foliage. A little girl, playing outside her cottage, waved to them as they passed.

Although concentrating on the road, John noticed Adele's thoughtful expression, and felt that she had something to say. "Adele, are you thinking about our stay in Mary Catherine's cottage?" he asked.

"Yes. You seemed to be having a wonderful time there," she began. "I noticed that you were remarkably different in that lovely cottage: your childish laughter; your relaxation. You were like a spool uncoiling; you let everything go. I saw your passion for plants, and the way you caressed the kitten—"

"Roadworks ahead!" John interrupted, reading the road sign aloud. "Sorry, Adele, what did you say?"

"I said, I saw how you can be passionate and tender," Adele continued, "and I can't understand why you behave differently in regard to me. I had a very odd dream, you know; the kind in which you start to wonder if it's real or just your imagination." She paused. "It's not easy for me to talk about this, but since yesterday, I think there is increased honesty between us..."

"What do you mean exactly?" John asked. His voice betrayed tension and some defensiveness.

"I mean..." Adele stopped, holding her breath. "You avoid physical contact with me."

A sign reading 'Diversion' appeared ahead. There were heavy maintenance vehicles on the road in front of a bridge over the river. The bridge, probably damaged by flooding from the heavy rain the day before, was closed. John took the detour indicated. Another road sign appeared: 'Attention! Narrow Road.'

"John, you avoid physical contact with me," repeated Adele.

At long last, John responded. "No, I don't! But I really felt uncomfortable with Darius and Marija snuggling up by the fire; I didn't find it necessary to display affection in front of everyone gathered there."

"But what's wrong with that? You didn't hesitate to demonstrate your affection to the kitten!"

"That's different! He's just an animal; it's not embarrassing to touch him. It's not a public display of affection. But what you are talking about concerns privacy between two people," asserted John.

"Then our understanding of privacy is different, John!"

"Of course I consider it inappropriate to talk about what happens in the bedroom in front of others. Honestly, yesterday I was annoyed by your attempt to start this discussion beside the fire…" John paused. "Well… I'm not unaware of the fact that we have some problems in… hmm… our sex life. But that's normal – we aren't like people in their twenties, who can be turned on in the blink of an eye. We can solve our problems on our own!"

Having driven on a rocky path for some time, they finally reached an asphalt road. But a few hundred metres further on, it ended in a curved gravel road. John missed his turn and nearly drove off the road. He slowed down. The car crossed a cattle grid put down to prevent the animals in a nearby field from leaving their enclosure, and then continued on to join an even narrower road. Down the hill, within moments they were immersed in a dense mist rising from the river. John had to be very careful in order to stay on the road.

"Maybe we *can* solve our problems," mused Adele doubtfully. "But it's not only about our sexual relationship. There are times when I simply need you to be physically close to me and to feel that you accept me. I don't think that you're fully aware of how important this is to me." She looked attentively at John. "I'm not sure that you like my body. Do you? I'm not sure that you find me attractive. Do you?"

John's discomfort reached its limit. "Adele, you must be mad to ask me questions like this."

"Then can you explain why you didn't want to have a bath with me yesterday? And why, earlier in the day, you avoided my embrace in the shelter?"

John braked abruptly to avoid a collision with some cattle that suddenly rushed onto the road. He closed his eyes under the strain. "No, I can't, Adele… I don't know why…" Opening his eyes, he looked at her. "Adele, it's dangerous to drive and talk about this at the same time. Just let me get on with it!"

For quite a while he drove very cautiously and in silence. Adele wound down her window, and could hear nothing but the buzzing of bees in the clover, and lambs bleating as they lifted their heads towards the car. They passed a ramshackle shepherd's shelter, then another cattle grid, and finally left the pastures behind them and reached the main road. This diversion had lengthened their journey by at least an hour. Moreover, John could not identify either their location or their destination. The satellite signal was so weak that the navigation was not working.

"Adele, we need to stop somewhere and figure out where we are. I'm quite tired, and I also think that it's time to have a snack," he said.

They continued along the unfamiliar road until they saw a filling station. They pulled in and stopped. There was an empty picnic area behind it. John and Adele sat down at one of the wooden tables and opened Mary Catherine's wicker basket. Inside she had packed two ripe red apples, some fresh rye bread, a piece of cheddar cheese, some celery sticks with carrots and tomatoes from the garden, and home-made mayonnaise with fresh dill. A large packet wrapped in a linen napkin proved to contain a chocolate cake, still warm from the oven. Mary

Catherine had also included a bottle of home-made lemonade with mint leaves.

"She went to a lot of trouble. She's so thoughtful," exclaimed John.

The two began their lunch.

"Coming back to what we were saying," Adele took up the subject again, "I doubt we can resolve this problem ourselves. Johnny, I don't blame you, but I'm sure this current task is somehow related to our difficulties in this area."

"And *I* have huge doubts as to whether I want someone interfering in our intimacy and teaching me what to do." John stood firm. "It's gone too far now and it's time to stop."

In silence, Adele ate the sandwich she had made with some of the Cheddar.

"Adele, I need some coffee. Do you?" asked John.

"No, thanks!" she said curtly.

John stood up from the table and went to the shop in the filling station. He looked around. Something about it seemed familiar. Suddenly, he saw the funny little piggy bank on the counter. He took his coffee, paid for it, dropped a coin into the piggy bank, and went back to the picnic area. "Adele, look around you!" he said in surprise. "This is exactly the same filling station we visited three days ago."

"Hold on… so, we've just made a loop and now we're back where we started?" concluded Adele. "That means that if we stop our journey now, it will be as though we haven't moved forward at all."

John sat down again. He really hated the idea of consulting anyone about their intimate life, though it was not yet clear whether Adele's presumption about the purpose of their destination was correct. He had little self-confidence in this domain. But when he thought about being locked into this starting position, he felt the frustration a gambler might feel on throwing unlucky dice and suddenly realising that he was right back where he had started with no cash, no promise of a loan, and no chance of winning. John looked at Adele. She was silent, but he felt that it was very important to her to go on with the task in hand, and she was determined to do so. He also understood that if they stopped now, they would still be a couple in trouble, in spite of the three wonderful days that had already given them so much. Now it was for him to make his decision. John took the map and studied it. He easily identified the filling station, and from there their destination. It was thirty minutes' drive away.

"Let's continue on our road towards this Wellspring of Life," he said.

They finished their lunch and got back into the car with the intention of going forward, despite any obstacles they might encounter or any apprehension they felt.

25

The Wellspring of Life

As the couple prepared to recommence their journey, John was conscientious this time about ensuring that the car had all the petrol it would need before they set out. They encountered nothing on the road to hinder their progress. In a quarter of an hour they reached a bridge and crossed the river. They were now in open countryside, where the sky met the earth without obstacle. Eventually, in place of the fields of grazing cattle they had seen on the far side of the river, they began to move through a more wooded landscape, dense with high pines and verdant meadows. John and Adele sensed the essence of nature breathing on them. In time, they arrived in a small village and saw a sign indicating 'The Wellspring of Life Retreat Centre'. They left the village, and further on saw an old, established park. John parked the car just at the entrance, and the couple followed a footpath to the retreat centre reception. They had instant admiration for the way in which the centre's buildings appeared to be in complete harmony with their natural surroundings. Adele noted also that the period buildings had been well integrated into the more modern structures. The fusion of old and new had created a centre that was visually appealing as well as ingeniously practical.

On entering the reception, they found themselves in a large hall with tall windows shaded by roller blinds of bamboo. Soft lighting and subtle music promoted an atmosphere of relaxation. Ficus plants and palm trees in big containers decorated the space. The far wall was made entirely of glass. Water cascaded down it from the ceiling to the floor; then fell into a stone groove that fed into a pool full of water lilies. To John and Adele's left hung a wooden panel bearing a long list of the activities and treatments available at the centre. They approached the panel and consulted it. The treatments were divided into three groups: 'Body', 'Mind' and 'Soul'. Some, like aromatherapy, saunas, aqua aerobics, Thai massage, yoga, and cognitive behavioural therapy, were familiar to the couple. But others, such as, mindfulness sessions, touch therapy, sound healing, and laughter meditation, were completely new to them. Both were curious about these and wondered what their purposes or methods could be.

Having read the list, the couple went up to the reception desk. There was no one there, but when John rang the bell, a woman wearing a white T-shirt with 'The Wellspring of Life' written on it appeared from a room off to the side.

"Good afternoon. How can I help you?" she asked kindly.

"Hello. We are here to see Christos," said John, a bit embarrassed by the fact that he did not know more about the purpose of their visit.

"Dr Christos Anghelos?" asked the woman.

"Probably, yes…"

"Have you made an appointment with him?"

"Well, it's complicated…" John was not keen to explain the situation, and added in an uncertain tone, "It was someone else who made – or, rather, had to make – this appointment for us…"

152

"That's all right. Don't worry," the woman assured him gently. She seemed well accustomed to visitors saying that the reason for their visit was complicated. "You are…?"

"The Rosses," said Adele.

The receptionist looked at her register. "Yes, here you are – everything has been arranged," she confirmed. "Dr Anghelos will see you straight away. Please come this way."

They followed her, and soon arrived at double doors with a brass nameplate reading 'Dr Christos Anghelos'. The receptionist wished them a good day and returned to her desk. John and Adele each began to wonder if they were in fact prepared to go ahead with this meeting. But before they could consider that question any further, someone inside the room opened the doors.

A man of about sixty stood in front of them. He was of medium height, and had a slim but solid build, greying hair, and a beard. His sparkling hazel eyes belied his true age. "Please come in." He gestured towards the room and, when John and Adele entered, introduced himself. "I'm Dr Christos Anghelos, the medical director and a therapist here. Please, call me Christos."

He shook hands with each of them, and immediately Adele felt a sense of warmth coming from him. His touch was soft but strong, and he emanated an unusual positive energy. All three took a seat around a low table.

"So, John and Adele, you're very welcome to The Wellspring of Life. Darius and I arranged your stay here, and I have really been looking forward to meeting you. I am so glad that you've been able to come."

"Thanks, Christos." John paused. "But honestly, we're a bit ill at ease, since we don't know what will be expected of us here."

"Don't be at all stressed. All will become clear very soon," Christos assured them. "First, feel free to unpack in your room. Then I would recommend that you try our saunas. Afterwards, please come back to me for massage at seven o'clock this evening. Everything in your own time…"

John and Adele took their leave and went back to reception to check the location of their room. They learned that the centre's hotel was on the other side of the park, facing the river. They collected their suitcases from the car and took the path across the park. It led along an avenue lined with plane trees. After that, they gradually descended through differing levels of flowering plants on either side. Each level had its own variety of flower. There were blue geraniums, yellow petunias, and hydrangeas in every hue imaginable: snow white, indigo, violet, maroon…

In contrast to the nineteenth-century buildings of the retreat centre, with its marble columns and classical white balustrades, the hotel was modern. It was also practical, unpretentious, and very comfortable. There was a small interior bar, and several guests also sat out in the open air, enjoying their refreshments in the warmth of the late afternoon. John and Adele's double room was not large, but it was full of light, with French doors opening onto a balcony with a splendid view of the river valley below. They arranged their belongings in the wardrobe and stretched out on the champagne-coloured satin bedcover, putting soft teal cushions under their heads.

"What a pleasure it is to put the feet up after such a long and difficult drive," sighed John.

"You deserve it," said Adele, turning towards him. She started to collect imaginary specks of lint from the fabric of his shirt with the tips of her fingers, and then brush it gently with her palm. John did not move. After few moments she added, "I wonder what awaits us here? Is it going to be pleasure or pain? Christos really didn't explain very much or give us any details."

"I see no reason to worry… that is to say, so far!" John replied, still completely relaxed. "A sauna and a massage might be just what we need."

We need much more than that, thought Adele. This called to mind her dream of the previous night. She remembered John's look of irritation, and his rapid refusal when Marija had asked him to brush the nettles from her hair. And even now, when he was so physically close to her, Adele was not sure that he was fully present. She did not have the impression that he was at all pleased to have her lying next to him. She was painfully conscious that the honest questions she had put to him in the car a few hours earlier still remained unanswered.

They did not stay very long in their room, and instead made their way to the sauna and bathing area. There were two large swimming pools: one indoors and the other outdoors. Most of the saunas were also situated in the open air among the trees in Nordic-style wooden cabins. Narrow stone paths wound through green lawns coloured by tiny yellow-and-white wild camomile flowers. Thin, wispy smoke rose from the small cabin chimneys, disseminating the pleasant scent of burning pine wood. Adele and John walked around, exploring the area and wondering which sauna to choose. Then they came upon one cabin which was much bigger than the others and, judging from the number of hooks on its outer wall, designed for a larger number of people. A framed notice at the door specified the scheduled times of 'guided sauna ceremonies'. The next was due to start in ten minutes. The name of the sauna, The Spirit of the Wood, told them nothing at all about what went on inside.

They were hesitating at the entrance when suddenly a young black man, accompanied by two dark-haired, kind-faced women in their thirties, approached them. The man had deep-set eyes of a striking golden colour, and a gentle smile. "Please don't feel at all uncomfortable. You're welcome here," he said with a slight French accent. Then he opened the doors. "Would you like to come in?"

Attracted by the warmth, John and Adele decided to go in, hung their bathrobes on the hooks, and entered the sauna. Inside, they saw a cast-iron stove, with an ample compartment for stones, attached to one of the walls. Wooden benches lined the other walls; some already occupied by guests waiting for the ceremony to begin. John and Adele walked over the wooden slats covering the floor and took their place on a bench. Adele looked around her. Small windows, perhaps meant to conserve heat, let in sunlight. The wooden ceiling was so low that she could nearly touch it. A dozen bath brooms were propped up on a shelf near the stove. Made from the branches and leaves of various trees that had been dried and tied around a wooden handle, they gave off a delicate but intoxicating scent. A big wooden ladle hung on the wall next to the shelf. Other guests continued to enter the sauna, and soon all the benches were filled.

The young man then rang a copper bell that was fixed to the door. "Hello, everyone! I'm very glad to welcome you to The Wellspring of Life," he said. "My name is Aliou, and together with Rebecca and Judith, I will guide you through this ritual dedicated to the spirit of the wood. To bring the essence of the wood forward, we will have four elements: stone, water, fire and air. They come together here in our sauna. I'll begin with the marriage of fire, stone and water." He took the wooden ladle, scooped water from a big barrel, and lifted the ladle solemnly with both hands. Then he poured the water over the stones that had been heated by the fire. It evaporated at once in a steamy fizzle, followed by a wave of warmth that enveloped the participants. He poured a second ladle of water onto the stones… then another… and another…

John felt the almost unbearable heat rushing towards him. His skin reddened, and although he was finding it a challenge to take a full breath, the sensation was a pleasant one. He began to sweat profusely, and his perspiration cooled him down. His breathing deepened. He touched Adele's knee, and looked at her. He knew that his wife was unable to tolerate heat well, and normally avoided extreme temperatures. Delicate tendrils of her hair were adhering to her damp forehead, and her face already had a high colour. "Do you feel all right?" he whispered.

Adele smiled, took his hand and squeezed it encouragingly.

The overwhelming heat diminished gradually. Aliou continued the ritual. "Now we'll add to this symphony the fourth element: air. But just before that, I would like everyone to choose a certain type of wood. With your eyes closed, you'll be able to concentrate more fully on your sense of smell. I will approach each of you to give you the opportunity to breathe in different tree essences. Please choose the one you like the most."

As the participants closed their eyes, Aliou took one of the bath brooms, immersed it briefly in the water, and held it above the hot stones. He then shook it slightly. A light, familiar aroma caught Adele's nose.

"Birch!" announced Aliou, and then he brought the broom close to each person's face, letting them enjoy its scent for a moment. "Lime!" he continued in the same way. "Oak! Walnut! Maple! Juniper! Now, please let Rebecca and Judith know which tree essence you preferred."

John spoke first. "Birch," he said, with no hesitation.

"Lime," Adele announced firmly.

"Oak."

"Birch."

"Birch."

"Lime."

"Juniper."

"Maple."

The other participants were equally certain of their choices.

"Now open your eyes and lie comfortably on your bench. You will soon sense the presence of the tree you have chosen. The spirit of the tree makes itself known by means of its movement in air, its scent released in warm water, and its touch through the broom," continued Aliou.

He then poured a few more ladles of water onto the stones, and all three guides began the second part of the ritual. They picked up the bath brooms and approached each participant one by one, according to the wood they had chosen. Aliou came to

Adele and, with great energy, started to wave the broom above her body. She felt a gratifying heat descend over her back, arms and legs, and inhaled the sweet aroma of lime. It seemed to her that the wood was transferring its strength and vitality through the air which gently caressed her skin. Then Aliou asked for permission to tap her with the broom. Adele nodded. The direct contact with her body intensified the sensations even more. As she opened her mouth and took in her breath, her lungs started to fill with the warm essence of the lime tree. An exhalation of relief came from deep within her chest. Aliou moved on to another participant, and Adele looked at her husband. Judith was skilfully manipulating the birch bath broom, carefully pressing and tapping his back with it. John's body was bright red, and some birch leaves were sticking to his wet skin. He looked like Tarzan in a primeval forest. Adele giggled.

John reacted with a wide smile. "Fantastic! Never felt anything like this in my life!" he declared.

At the end of the ceremony, Aliou advised the participants to go one by one under the waterfall that simulated the tropical rainforest with showers of cool water. Rebecca and Judith then brought each of them a glass of fresh Wellspring mineral water.

26

Getting Closer

Having rested on the terrace for a little while, John and Adele went to Christos's office for their seven o'clock appointment. They found him reading at his desk. He took off his glasses and invited them to sit down at the same low table.

"How are you?" he asked calmly. His eyes sparkled as if he already knew the answer.

"I feel really good," answered John. "I'm totally relaxed. I feel so light that I wouldn't be surprised to find that I've lost a couple of kilos. And I'm breathing more deeply in this pure, fresh air."

"And you, Adele?" Christos turned to her.

"I'm very well. I'm still filled with the warmth of that sauna. I feel at one with my body, and in harmony with the beautiful natural environment here," Adele said quietly. Looking through the window at the trees with their leaves swaying in the breeze, she smiled. "I feel as though I'm sixteen again."

"The benefits to the body of this type of sauna are remarkable," began Christos, and he proceeded to outline all the advantages of the treatment they had just experienced.

"Aliou and his team seem very knowledgeable," said John.

"Yes, and I was really surprised that I was able to put up with such intense heat. I usually can't bear it at all," added Adele. "I didn't think I had that ability."

"In fact, in general we know little about the abilities, capacities and limits of our bodies," responded Christos. "We dress our body in clothes, we protect it from heat and cold, and we move about, according to society's customs and rules concerning what is acceptable or polite. But our bodies actually have unbelievable cognitive, as well as communicative, capacities. That is to say, the body can acquire knowledge and then pass it on through the messages it gives us. It's a pity that we are so ignorant of this that we cannot utilise it to its full potential. In particular, our skin is very receptive to touch. Through this sense, we are able to convey information that cannot be communicated verbally. As a newborn baby, we experience touch through our mother's caresses. In time, as we develop and learn to speak, we come under the impression that we have advanced in knowledge and thus become more intelligent. But sadly, in early childhood we leave behind the language of touch." Christos placed his hands on his knees in a gesture of conclusion, then stood up. "Silent communication through touch cannot be learned through discussion. We discover it for ourselves in a practical way, and you both will have that opportunity very soon."

He invited the couple to follow him, and they all left the office together. They went down a set of stairs and approached a sign indicating that this was the holistic treatment section. A large screen presented information on the therapies available: hot stone massage, Tibetan sound therapy, Ayurvedic massage, detox wraps, acupuncture, aromatherapy, salt therapy, deep relaxation and so on. John and Adele entered a round hall with walls in soft pastel colours. In the middle there was a fountain surrounded by marble statues in the style of ancient Greece. Several corridors in light wood set out in a sun-ray pattern led off the hall. The two accompanied Christos down one of the corridors, and he stopped in front of a door marked 'Rose Room'.

"Here we are," he said, opening the door and allowing them to enter the room.

The walls were a soft pink, and the room's delicate floral scent matched its name. There were no windows and the light was dim. John was surprised by the absence of a massage table of the sort normally used in wellness centres. In place of this was a high futon in the middle of the room. Covered with a crisp light olive-green sheet, it had several fig-coloured cushions placed on top of it. It was surrounded by shelves of rolled towels, as well as baskets filled with bottles of oils and lotions. Candles placed in small alcoves created an intimate, relaxing atmosphere. The soft sound of Indian flute music floated across to them.

"Are you going to massage us one by one, or both at the same time?" queried John, a bit confused by what appeared to him to be an unusual interior.

"Not at all," Christos answered enigmatically. "The purpose of this practice is to awaken your sensuality through your mutual interaction. My presence will not be necessary." He smiled. "You are going to massage each other, in order to practise communication through touch, but first I'll give you some direction. Is that all right?"

Adele and John looked at each other dubiously. In no other spa they had ever visited had they been confronted with such an odd proposal. They stood in confusion for a few moments. But their beneficial experience in the sauna and the excitement of a venture into the unknown inspired them to take the leap. They felt that they had no reason to distrust Christos or to decline the therapy.

"I would like to explain one of the basic exercises of touch therapy," continued Christos, in the absence of any objection from Adele or John. "One of you, the receiver, lies on the futon, and the other, the giver, sits next to the receiver. Once the receiver feels at ease and is ready, the giver starts to glide over the receiver's skin with the palm of one hand." Christos raised his right hand and moved it slowly through the air. "Be gentle, don't rush, and find the rhythm that pleases your partner the best. If your hand is dry, use oil or lotion. Pay attention to every part of the receiver's body. Do not feel that you ought to skip over intimate areas, but don't focus on excitement. If it happens, don't worry – it's natural; just continue. Once you finish one side, ask the receiver to turn over and repeat the process. Then switch roles."

While giving his instructions, Christos observed John and Adele carefully. Their initial embarrassment had changed to curiosity. John looked as if he were trying to memorise what Christos was saying. Adele, in contrast, was not paying much attention to the actual words; she seemed to understand intuitively everything that he was trying to illustrate with his gestures.

"And the most important thing you need to keep in mind during this practice..." Christos stopped to be sure that his words would be heard and understood. He looked intently at Adele and John. "Be fully present in your role as giver and as receiver. When you are the giver, do what makes your partner feel comfortable. If you are not sure how they feel, ask them. As receiver, don't hesitate to say if you like or dislike something that the giver does."

The couple remained silent, expecting other instructions to follow.

"Any questions?" asked Christos. "Fine. You have ninety minutes for this practice. Afterwards, you will still have time for dinner. You are safe here. Nobody will observe or disturb you. And... you both need to be totally naked. Enjoy each other's presence. I'll see you tomorrow after breakfast." He then took his leave.

As the couple reflected on Christos's explanation, they were taken aback by the fact that they had to massage each other. At the same time, they were more intrigued than confused. The positive energy suffusing their environment was very encouraging.

Adele approached the futon hesitantly, but after gathering her thoughts for a moment, she decided to leave her inhibitions behind and to be the first to dive into the lake. "All right, then. If you don't mind, John, could I start out in the role of the giver?" she proposed. She knew that it was up to her to begin the exercise in the best possible way for them both. "Could you undress and take your place?" she asked gently.

Normally, John would have considered this exercise to be a clear intrusion into his comfort zone; however, he also wanted to be consistent with his decision to continue on The Road. He undressed quickly and lay down. He felt the soft cotton sheet touch his chest, belly and legs. The room was sufficiently warm and he had no sense of discomfort without his clothing. He heard Adele undress and approach him. She knelt close to him, rubbed her hands together, and then put her palm on his back.

"My hand isn't too cold?" she asked, uncertain.

"No, it's fine. It's warm and soft," John assured her.

Encouraged, Adele started to move her hand gently along his back, shoulders, arms, sides and buttocks. She also caressed John's neck and head. He felt her knees touching his hip, and the warmth emanating from her body was very pleasant.

"Mmm… that's very good…" murmured John.

When she reached his legs, he asked for some oil to make her touch smoother. Adele opened several bottles to let him smell the oils, and he chose eucalyptus. She warmed the oil in her hands and continued to massage his legs. Although it was not a taboo for them, they rarely undressed or appeared naked in front of one another. In the dim light, Adele began to view John's body differently. She saw it as powerful and attractive. Moreover, through her touch, she discovered its vitality and sensitivity. It seemed to her that her hand and his skin communicated with each other. Adele began to enjoy her role as the giver.

When John turned, their eyes met. This intense eye contact excited John even more than Adele's nakedness. "You look lovely, Adele," he said, looking at the glow of the candlelight on her rosy skin. Her graceful seated pose reminded him of one of the Greek statues he had just seen in the round hall.

"I like looking at you, too, John," she replied.

He closed his eyes, ready for his next portion of pleasure. Confidently, she touched his chest and leaned closer to him, moving her hand along his arm. He felt her soft hair brush against his skin. As she touched his face, John could still smell the scent of lime from the sauna within the strands of her hair, mingled with the eucalyptus on her fingertips. She put her hand back on his chest and moved down, reaching his pelvis and thighs. When she leaned forward to touch his calf, her breast glided briefly over his stomach. John sighed, delighted... but this confused Adele. On the one hand, she wanted to proceed with the massage and give herself over fully to the exercise. On the other hand, she began to think that continuing would excite him, and she was certain that that would spoil everything. Her touch became less attentive. She began pressing his skin with her fingers rather than her palm; in fact, barely touching him at all. All she wanted now was to finish as quickly as possible. Her anxiety meant that she was less present in the moment, and John was conscious of this change. Her increasingly cautious and almost imperceptible touch broke the rhythm they had established, and was not what he had been expecting. It started to irritate him.

"I preferred the way you were doing it earlier," he said, not at all attempting to hide his disappointment.

This sounded like a criticism to Adele, and after a few more half-hearted and uncertain gestures, she finished her part of the exercise.

Then it was John's turn to be the giver. He stood up, switching places with Adele. The dissatisfaction that he felt following the unexpectedly hurried end to his massage had not extinguished the overall sensation of well-being throughout his body. Adele lay down on her stomach with her arms crossed under her forehead. John made himself comfortable next to her and looked at the clock on the wall.

"Adele, relax. We have enough time for you. I'll do my best," he assured her. He put his hand on her back. "Would you like some oil or lotion?"

"No, I don't think so," answered Adele.

The warmth of his palm was soothing, and she stretched out her arms along her sides. John started to move his hand confidently across her shoulders. Rhythmically he massaged her back, arms, neck and head, but Adele felt that he was following his own plan of action and not paying any attention to her body's reaction. The pressure was fast and hard, while she longed for him to slow down or even pause for a moment with his hand on her shoulders to caress them gently.

"John, could you go a little slower? And try to listen to my body," she said.

This surprised John, as he was sure he knew how to do the exercise correctly. He made an effort to go slower, but then, unsettled by Adele's remark, he stopped and hesitated; unsure what to do next. He then continued timidly with her legs, though Adele preferred a deeper stroke.

"Now you can press harder," Adele said, trying to guide him.

John interpreted this to be the exact opposite of what she had just said she wanted. Totally confused, he felt that his efforts were unappreciated and she was just nagging him. His stomach muscles tensed. Adele turned over, and he looked at the graceful contours of her body, which he found more and more appealing. He touched her breast and pressed gently, but even though she said nothing, John sensed that he was disappointing her once again. Although she was physically close, he felt that she was withdrawing inwardly from him. He felt offended, and so carried on with the exercise without any real motivation. When he finished, she thanked and hugged him. Her sincerity emanated true warmth, and his defensiveness softened. He relaxed, watching Adele delicately rearranging the towels and the bottles of oil and lotion she had taken from the baskets. She was still naked, but her smooth, confident movements showed that she was feeling at home after the hour or so they had spent in the room.

At home, John mused. *We have nothing like this lovely ambience at home. Our bedroom is basically a sleeping area. We make love there only occasionally, and sadly, it just happens without any special preparation. It's really a pity.* He tried to imagine Adele lighting candles and preparing their bedroom for something special to happen that evening. No major expense or rearrangement would be necessary for this. *There's nothing complicated that we need to do. It's simple, really: establish the mood, and good intentions and sincere effort.*

They took their time dressing and went on their way, looking for the dining room in pleasant anticipation of their dinner. They walked down a long passage with high windows looking onto the park. The opposite wall was hung with photographs of people of all ages, genders and ethnicities. Most were practising meditation, yoga and dance. Others were having dinner together, or merely in conversation. John and Adele were drawn to the photos, and stopped to look at them in detail.

"Everyone in each photo seems to radiate a kind of inner beauty," Adele said slowly.

"That's probably because they feel happy and at ease," remarked John. "Let's go for our meal."

At the end of the passage was the entrance to the dining room. It was comfortable and spacious, and was serving a buffet supper. There were still quite a few people at table, despite the late hour. They chatted quietly while eating, with little desire for attention from the staff, and no wish to disturb other guests with boisterous behaviour or loud voices. It appeared that no one, including the staff, had any concern for clock-watching. John and Adele recognised some of those who had been present at the sauna treatment, who said hello and wished them a good evening.

The last meal the couple had eaten had been Mary Catherine's picnic, so they filled their plates generously at the buffet and found a table. Although the ambience was pleasant, they ate in silence. The tension between them was palpable, and both acknowledged it inwardly.

What's happened? thought John. *We had an extraordinary experience in the sauna. Hmm... I must admit, it's true that the massage veered away from what was expected, but that is no reason to be downcast. I honestly found it pleasant, and I think Adele did as well. If we're not able to figure out what's gone wrong between us, we'll most likely be trapped right back where we started, and that defeats the purpose of going on this journey.* "Listen, Adele – I'm sure that you feel the strain between us, just as I do," he said resolutely. "We need to talk to get to the bottom of all of this. It seems that we have different needs in our physical life together, but during our time on The Road we've worked hard to communicate with each other in a more honest way. If we've managed to do that so far, surely we'll be able to overcome this difficulty too, and..."

"Become closer?" Adele finished his sentence.

"Indeed." John swallowed hard and coughed. He was clearly struggling to find the right words to express his thoughts on the matter.

Adele knew that her husband had something important to say, and she attributed his hesitation to a desire not to hurt her. She waited.

"The massage exercise was a real surprise to me," continued

John. "It was so pleasant to be together in that lovely room, naked. It was so new to me. I loved it when you were sitting close to me and caressing my body. But at a certain point, I felt that you were detaching from me. It was as if you were trying to escape from the situation, and I just cannot understand why!"

Adele listened attentively. She was grateful for the sincerity evident in John's question, and conscious of the fact that this was the right moment to express to him her long-held concerns and fears about their physical intimacy. It would not be easy, but she was prepared. "John, I enjoyed being with you, too," she said. "When I touched you, I put all the tenderness and love I could into it."

"Yes, Adele. I really felt it," said John, deeply affected by her candour. She had come to him with a conscious intention. It was not just a gesture. He could not recall her ever before having linked her love for him with her touch in precisely that way.

"But all of a sudden, I felt that you were interpreting my touch as… sexual." She sighed.

"That's natural!" exclaimed John.

"But not for me!" argued Adele. "I don't want every single touch to lead to sex! And it's always been like this. Sometimes I'm afraid to show you my full affection: if I cuddle up to you, you either avoid me or become aroused. Why can't we simply embrace and stay like that? Why can't we just enjoy each other's presence?"

Unwittingly, they had begun to raise their voices. John then realised that the guests at nearby tables would be disturbed by their loud conversation. "If we go on like this," he said more quietly, "we'll not only interrupt their dinner, but the other guests could also easily overhear our conversation. We should go back to our room."

They finished their dinner without dessert, left the dining room, and took the path through the park back to the hotel.

John took up the discussion again. "Adele, I want to understand what you need, but you have to believe me when I tell you that it's nearly impossible to know what you really want. I'm not a mind reader! I tried hard today to please you, but your remarks nearly did me in."

"But I was just telling you how I felt in response to what you were doing! And Christos told us that that was very important," Adele said defensively. "I didn't feel that you were paying much attention to what I liked."

"I did my best!" retorted John. "I told you how I felt as well. It should have been easy for you to see what was pleasant for me; what was making me happy. But even after so many years together, you still have no idea!"

"Well, frankly, that was not an appropriate place for us to begin having sex. It was meant to be an exercise to increase our awareness of the importance of touch in our relationship."

"All right, that might have been true. But it isn't the first time that you've reacted to my excitement by withdrawing from me. Can you imagine how I feel when you suddenly become distant and detached?"

Adele continued along the path in silence. She felt keenly the injustice in John's reproaches. She remembered other times when she had yielded to his advances even when she was tired, had something urgent to do, or was simply not in the mood to make love.

"I don't have the impression that you really care at all about what I want," John blurted out angrily. "Sometimes I think you have no interest in sex. You're as cold as ice!"

"I'm never cold to you!" cried Adele. Her voice caught in her throat. "You're wrong to tell me that." Her lips began to tremble and her eyes smarted with tears. She walked away quickly, intending to keep her distance from John. But in the darkness, in stepping off the path she did not see a small bench just to the left of it. She knocked against it hitting her shin very hard. Adele cried out in pain and, crouching down, put both her hands on her throbbing leg.

John caught up with her. "What's happened, Adele?" he asked, frightened.

Adele was weeping. John had no idea if this was due to the pain in her leg or his hurtful remarks. He knew that his last reproach had been an exaggeration; one rooted in anger rather than reality. He felt ashamed. She let go of her leg, but then put her face in her hands. She looked vulnerable and in despair.

John squatted down beside her and took hold of her hands. "Adele," he said, kindly but firmly, "we need to get back to the hotel to have a look at your leg. Are you able to walk?"

She stood up, teetering a little, trying to keep her balance. He assisted her in taking a couple of halting steps. Holding on to his arm, she continued to walk. The pain lessened as they slowly reached the hotel. In their room, John looked at Adele's leg closely. It was a bit swollen and bruised, but it did not seem that a doctor would be needed. In the darkness of the park, this little accident had terminated their discussion, and neither of them had any desire to return to the subject for the moment.

While Adele was in the shower, John turned back the quilt, unfolded a blanket and sat waiting for her. When she reappeared in the bathroom doorway she had a tube of cream in her hand.

"I found this mint arnica cream in my vanity bag. Maybe it could help."

"In any case, it won't do any harm," agreed John. "Lie down, and I'll apply it."

Adele stretched out on the bed and closed her eyes. John took his pillow and put it underneath her leg for support. She felt him touch her leg with attention and tenderness. The cream had a cooling effect and gave off a pleasant aroma of mint. The pain diminished more and more with every touch as he delicately massaged her whole leg. He did not ask any questions, but it seemed that his hands had found the best way to relieve her pain. It was not only his gentle physical touch that she experienced, but also the compassion, kindness and sincere regret flowing from his heart and through his hands.

John covered her with the blanket and she turned onto her side, ready for sleep. She heard him going into the bathroom. When he returned, he slipped underneath the bedclothes and embraced her, putting his arms around her waist. Adele was unprepared for this gesture of affection, since each of them usually fell asleep in their own corner of the bed. If she ever tried to move closer to him, he complained that he did not have enough space and could not sleep. Now was a perfect opportunity for Adele to claim the same... but all of a sudden, the words that Marija had spoken, early that morning as they had sat on the bench, rose in Adele's mind. *When a man's heart starts to open, he becomes very vulnerable. Give him all your love and support in that moment.* Those words had a special meaning now. Adele took the decision not to get tangled up in the past, but to go forward into the future. She felt happy in John's embrace, and fell into a soothing sleep.

27

Celebration

"Your roses are magnificent, Mr Gruber!" John exclaimed, drawn in by the beauty and variety of the flowers growing in the side garden of a local florist.

"I'm happy to hear it, sir," replied the elderly gardener, pleased by John's compliment. "Especially from a man who made the effort to come to my shop so early in the morning. You are obviously in search of something special."

"You have it! I'd like to make up a bouquet for my wife," John explained. He turned and paused, looking around him in admiration. In this little plot, every millimetre of space had been utilised to advantage and everything his gaze fell upon seemed through its colour, form and grace, to be calling for his attention. He gestured to the left and then to the right. "But it's so difficult to choose which flowers to include. Everything that you have grown here is really impressive."

"You're lucky to see them now, just as they've been awakened by the sun's rays. All of these flowers are at the peak of their beauty at the moment." Mr Gruber guided John through carefully planted sections of many different blooms in glorious full flower. "Here are my tiger lilies, with the trumpet lilies beside them. In the wild, they are normally found in the forest. Now, they are just starting to reveal their fleur-de-lys shape. The orange-red stamens inside their blooms attract the morning insects with that dizzying scent."

John took a deep breath, inhaling their perfume.

His guide walked on, occasionally touching a flower delicately with his gnarled hands. "Have a look at these gorgeous gladioli. Once cut and put in water, they continue to blossom, opening their buds one by one over an entire week or even longer. Wonderful miracles of Mother Nature, aren't they?"

Mr Gruber continued to lead John through his garden, allowing him to view at his leisure all the colourful inspiration that the natural world had to offer. They made a complete circuit of the garden until they arrived back at the roses. John stopped and stood in front of them.

"It appears that you've already made up your mind, sir," remarked the gardener, noticing at once the admiration in John's eyes. He smiled. "Roses are the best choice for a cherished woman."

Several minutes later, John was earnestly pedalling uphill the bicycle that he had borrowed from the hotel earlier that morning, with a splendid bouquet of roses in its basket.

In the hotel, the morning sun had already begun to filter through the curtains. Adele opened her eyes and noticed that John was not in the room. There was, however, a piece of paper on the bedside table. It read:

Good morning, Adele! Don't worry; I'll be back soon.
Yours,
J.

She smiled, pushed the bedclothes aside, and sat up. To her

surprise, she felt no pain in her leg. Moreover, she could hardly remember which leg she had hurt yesterday. They both looked and felt completely normal. The bruising was gone.

She stood up, went over to the French doors leading to the balcony, and opened them. A warm, invigorating breeze caressed her neck and cheeks. She looked down at the rippling sky-blue water of the hotel's outdoor pool and felt an instant desire to plunge into it. So she changed into her bathing suit and left the room.

The water in the pool was very clear, pure and refreshing. Its calm fluidity enveloped her body. Adele felt like a dolphin in its element. There was no one else around, and so she felt free to swirl and splash like a child, first diving down and then coming to the surface, allowing her body the liberty to make whatever movement took her fancy. Then she floated on her back, absorbing the tranquillity offered by the water and contemplating the tops of the trees in the nearly cloudless sky. She was completely relaxed, but at the same time acutely conscious of her immersion in the present moment. *This moment is so precious*, she thought. *The time I have spent on The Road has been one of mixed experiences. There has been pain as well as pleasure, difficulty as well as discovery; I have learned to trust and I have also distrusted… but I have never before experienced such intense moments of peace within myself, and I have certainly never felt such a genuine connection with John.* Remembering his embrace the previous night, just as they began to fall asleep, she felt a pang at his absence. Missing him, she left the pool and hurried back to the hotel room.

On opening the door, she heard running water in the bathroom. When she entered the room, she took in her breath sharply. There was a large bouquet of freshly cut apricot-coloured roses in a vase on the desk. Adele could not recall the last time she had received flowers from her husband for no special reason. John came out of the bathroom to find her standing stock-still, staring at the roses.

174

"John, they're so beautiful," she whispered.

John was embarrassed. He wanted to reply nonchalantly that he had found the flower shop quite by accident while cycling that morning. But he soon surrendered to Adele's penetrating gaze. "I thought about you… I wanted to do something nice for you, and please you with a little gift. I…" John stopped short and looked at his wife. With her wet hair pushed back off her face and drops of water still clinging to her cheeks, arms and shoulders, she looked as fresh as the roses. He picked up a folded towel from near the bed, approached her, and gently wrapped it around her. He took her in his arms. Their foreheads touched.

"Thank you, John." Adele kissed his cheek.

There was a pause. They could hear the wheels of the room service breakfast trolley squeaking along the corridor outside. The china cups and saucers produced a playful clattering sound.

"Well, wherever you found these roses, I suppose you're hungry after that 'secret mission.'" Adele smiled.

Breakfast was served in the large morning room which gave onto a sunny terrace. The menu was extensive. A smiling young sous-chef was preparing omelettes, while a stout blonde woman flipped blueberry pancakes on a grill. The couple asked for omelettes with Gouda cheese, diced yellow and red peppers, sautéed onions, and courgettes. The kitchen wizard cooked them up in an instant, working with two frying pans simultaneously. Adele grated some black pepper and herb salt over her omelette, while John sprinkled his with fresh parsley. They also took a platter with a bowl of raspberries and strawberries, and some honeydew melon with lime. A silver plate of hot buttered toast and a pot of coffee were their final choices before they staggered out to the terrace to find a table.

Over his omelette, John began to recount in an animated voice everything that had transpired during his morning cycle. "I left very early, and you know well, Adele, that I haven't been on a bike in a quarter of a century, but I persevered. I had a fair few obstacles to overcome: the road was very stony and I almost came off quite a few times, and then the road led into open countryside with fields of lettuce and cabbage. Then I got lost. Finally I saw a handmade sign advertising flowers, and that was what I had been hoping for, but I made the turn too early and ended up in a mucky farmyard, facing a man stacking hay with a pitchfork.

"I said, 'Good morning, sir! Do you have any flowers?'

"'Flowers?' he asked, looking quite puzzled.

"'Yes – do you sell flowers?'

"'No! I'm a pig farmer.' He paused. 'I could sell you a piglet.'

"Then I thought, *That wouldn't fit into a vase...*"

"Why didn't you try it?" Adele laughed, glad to listen to John's story and to see the happiness on his face. It occurred to her that in watching and listening to John, she now had the most essential information about the whole universe that she really needed that morning. They were immersed now in their own world, instead of breakfasting over breaking news on the television. Their usual monotony was being broken.

Engaged in this lively exchange, they had not noticed that Christos had come to the table and taken his place on an empty chair in front of them. "Good morning to you, Adele! Hello, John! I hardly recognise you: you are very different compared to the couple I met yesterday."

"Good morning, Christos!" they replied, surprised by his sudden appearance.

"This place is so unique; really special. It's hard to stay indifferent," offered John, as if trying to justify his good mood.

"We're both enjoying the sunny morning and the beautiful natural surroundings," added Adele.

"Wherever we are, we are still under the same sun. It appears to us, it shines on us, it warms us, no matter what our mood may be. The only difference is in us and how we see it," replied Christos, philosophically and enigmatically, looking up at the sky. "In any case, I hope that you keep this positive mood and celebrate this new day. Let yourselves be happy, and even a bit like children, if you wish. Oh – I spoke with Darius this morning, and he told me that he wishes for you to stay here until tomorrow. So, the entire day and the night belong to you!"

"That's good news! We've really enjoyed our time here," exclaimed John, and he looked at his wife. "Haven't we, Adele?"

"Absolutely! Christos, can we try another massage?" asked Adele.

"It's clear that you found it beneficial, Adele." Christos smiled sincerely. "Of course you can continue with this practice. It's very important for your relationship. But today I would like to propose that you join this morning's sensual dance session."

"That could be really interesting!" exclaimed Adele. "John, do you remember the photos that we were looking at yesterday? Some of the people in them were probably part of that dance session. As soon as I saw the looks on their faces, I thought that I would like to do something like that with you. Let's try it out… if…" She looked at him, and suddenly felt herself swallow the end of her sentence. Their visit to the piano bar in Newtown had come into her mind. She recalled the elation with which she had begun to dance, how that feeling had persisted, and then how she had been hit with John's hurtful remarks the following day. Even though they had now overcome that situation and she had forgiven him, his biting sarcasm about her dancing had exacerbated her lack of confidence. Another negative word from him on the subject would rub salt into that wound. Her sudden change in expression indicated all of this as she felt her enthusiasm dissipate.

At the same time, John was equally lost in thought. *If this dance session had been suggested to me a week ago*, he mused, *I would definitely have refused it outright. It would have been enough to put me in a bad humour for the rest of the day.* This present proposal was completely unexpected, and he struggled

177

with his instinctive opposition to it. Looking at Adele, he noticed immediately that the sparkle of exuberance had gone from her eyes. In its place he saw the shadows of disappointment and doubt, and he understood for what reason they had appeared. He also realised the fragility of the moment, and how much this new, brittle bridge between them depended on his decision. *I have no right to extinguish the sparkle in her eyes*, he decided. *In the end, apart from old fears and unfounded prejudices, I see no reason why I should reject this suggestion.* "Yes," he said, and he was surprised by how easily he blurted out the word. The sparkle in Adele's eyes reignited and became a flame, and he was sure he had said the right thing. "Let's go ahead with it!"

"Everything that is worthwhile in life takes a bit of courage," said Christos. He leaned across the table and put his hand on John's shoulder. Then he looked steadily at them both and, before taking his leave, added, "I wish you good luck!"

Inspired by her husband's unexpected consent, Adele practically flew as she took off in search of the dance studio, pulling John in her wake. He knew he stood no chance of escaping what he felt was sure to be an intimidating activity. Even though he sometimes gave in to Adele's demands for him to dance with her during a party, a wedding reception, or any other occasion, he had hated dancing. Ever since his teenage years when the girls had mocked him at the school dance, John had been convinced that he had no talent for and no capacity to enjoy dancing.

Following the signs guiding them to the sensual dance class, they reached the hall on the second floor of the centre. The participants' sandals and spa slippers were placed in a row at the entrance to the room, and so the couple also took off their shoes. They stepped inside the hall and the warm wooden floor gave a pleasant welcome to their bare feet. Three of the walls had large floor-to-ceiling windows looking out onto a beautiful view of the park, so that standing in the middle of the hall created an impression of being in nature. There was no furniture; nor anything else that could disturb free movement. This rendered the room full of space and air. Some couples moved together to the rhythm of the Brazilian bossa nova music coming from the speakers attached to the wall. John felt ill at ease, and did not know what to do or how to do it. *Should I move around too, or should I just stay still?* he thought. Seeing his embarrassment, Adele took his hands and they started to sway slowly.

"Good morning!" a joyful voice sounded as the music stopped. It belonged to a graceful, elegant lady in her fifties, wearing a grey linen dress and heart-shaped amber earrings. It was clear from her demeanour that she would be leading the session. "Welcome, everyone, to this sensual dance session for couples. My name is Ann, and I'll show you how to feel free within your body, and how to allow it to move spontaneously, while setting aside any preconceptions, rules or courtesies. If you've already learned some classical or modern dance, forget about it. You won't be needing that here."

"And what about those who haven't learned or can't dance at all?" asked an elderly Asian woman.

"Forget that, too – especially that!" answered Ann. She beamed, launching cheerful laughter among the participants. "You're born to dance; just believe in that!"

When Adele saw Ann smile, it triggered a sense of déjà vu within her. She was certain that they had met previously somewhere. Suddenly she recalled a couple dancing to the blues music in the piano bar in Newtown. The woman had electrified the atmosphere, and every person there had wanted to dance with her. Adele had no doubt that Ann was that woman.

Ann finished her introduction and put on some soft instrumental oriental music. "Now, I would like each of you to look for your own spot in the hall. Find the place that suits you best, and then close your eyes," she said.

The participants dispersed around the hall, each person seeking the spot that would make them most comfortable. Adele and John split up: Adele found her place close to a window, while John preferred to remain in a corner.

"Be aware of your breath: feel how the air moves through your lungs and fills your whole body with energy. That energy flows down and reaches your belly, hips and thighs. It descends further, to your feet. Now become conscious of your feet as they make contact with the earth. Feel the earth, its vibrations, and then another flow of energy streaming upwards. The two energy flows meet in your body, and create waves that power all of your cells. Remain motionless for a little while, and then allow your body to move when it's ready. Don't feel the need to rush. Take your time. Try to sense how your body responds to the music. Keep your eyes closed. Allow your body to move, but remain within your chosen space."

John did what he had been asked to do. He stood still for rather a long time, but it seemed to him that no impulse to move had sparked within his body. He opened his eyes slightly and looked around. Nearly everybody else had begun to dance. He closed his eyes again, continued to breathe deeply, and waited, but in vain. He simply could not get started. All the movements he could think of seemed artificial and pretentious. He opened his eyes once more and saw Ann standing in front of him. "Sorry; I can't seem to do it…" he stammered in frustration.

"Don't worry – there is no wrong way to do it. Just trust yourself. No one can dance like you can!"

John was struck by these simple words, which seemed to sweep away his reluctance to move. Ann looked intently into his eyes. Her gaze was so persuasive that he suddenly felt his body filling with the relief and tranquillity that self-confidence brings. He closed his eyes once more and relaxed. At a certain point, his body moved as if it were being propelled by a wave of sound. At the beginning, his gestures were timid and cautious, but with every successive musical note he became braver and his dance more expansive.

The music's slow rhythm shifted. It was now faster and more powerful.

"Now, let go, everyone! Set yourselves free!" Ann encouraged the dancers, moving towards the centre of the hall with energy and grace.

The beat of the drums made it impossible to remain motionless. In common with the other dancers, John let himself go with unrestrained spontaneity. He did not care how he appeared to the others, and he began to enjoy each moment, imagining himself as a neutral observer in his own body. Then he thought of Adele. He opened his eyes slightly and searched for his wife among the dancers. Adele shook her body energetically, letting her loose hair fly, her hands and hips drawing invisible pictures. *Wow! She moves with the life and strength of a lioness!* John thought, surprised. When he closed his eyes, the image of Adele dancing gave him another burst of energy. His entire body brimmed with the vibrations emanating from the depths of the earth, and started to resonate with the simple and elemental music.

"Stop!" Ann cried out suddenly. The music came to an abrupt end. "Remain in place with your eyes closed, and pay attention to what is happening inside you."

Though the music and the dancing had ceased, John still felt a powerful surge of energy moving through his body. His mind had been emptied of thought. Silence reigned as he stood still. He had no sense of time passing and no idea how long he had been standing there – perhaps it had been a second, perhaps a minute, perhaps an hour. It did not matter: his feeling of contentment spread until the warmth of it infused his face and made him smile.

The music started up again, and this time it was serene and peaceful. A woman's soft voice began to sing a gentle, calming mantra.

"Let the energy you have gathered spread outside the

boundaries of your body and fill the space around you, within the reach of your hands," Ann continued. "Imagine that you are inside a big ball of energy. The surface of this ball forms the boundary of your personal space. Take note of it as a part of you. Enjoy this energy and the light it brings. Now, open your eyes and start to step forward very carefully, still holding on to this feeling of your new frontier in space, and when you are sure you can manage it, let yourself move freely across the hall."

The dancers started to advance slowly, but with each new piece of music their movements became more generous until they danced confidently across the hall, respecting each other's personal space and avoiding any collisions. Even though each person had his or her own way of dancing, the overall effect was one of coordinated harmony.

Ann's voice floated through the air. "Next, approach your partner and continue your dance together. Do so without touching each other. Choose a distance at which you are able to feel the space occupied by your partner, sense this space and its vibration, and take your cue from the music. Allow it to guide you."

John and Adele approached each other. The instant Adele reached her husband, she experienced a warm, pleasant feeling rising through her ribcage. She was certain that this sensation had been brought about by the vibrations streaming from John, and she could not contain her smile, putting into it all the tenderness she felt for him. At that moment, John also sensed a rush of some sort of energising force in his chest. The light in his eyes was his response to Adele; no words were needed. They were both surprised by how easy it was to sense the other's presence without physical contact. They could even anticipate what gesture the other was about to make.

"Now connect with each other by extending your index fingers," said Ann. "Just a light touch; don't press hard. Continue your mutual dance. Lead, and let your partner lead you."

John moved carefully towards Adele. She felt his gentle touch on her fingertips. This reminded her of something she had experienced many years before, and the memory of it came flooding back to her, as clear and vivid as the night it had happened. She was lying in her hospital bed, exhausted and weak after having given birth to Patrick. It had been a difficult birth. Still semi-conscious from the drugs she had been administered, she had no idea that someone had approached her bedside. Then she had felt a soft touch on her hand. Dizzy and disoriented, even with her eyes closed, she had known that it was John. This was the same loving touch that she was now feeling on her fingertips. She could not remember if, until now, John had touched her again in that way since that night. Once their son had come into their lives, they had focused on giving him all of their attention, care and love. And as time passed, they had neglected to cherish their own relationship, and had detached from one another. Now, with their fingers joined and their bodies moving as one, Adele did not want to feel distant from John any longer; not for a single moment in the rest of their lives.

Her remembrances ended abruptly and she was pulled back into the hall as Ann said, "Embrace each other with the same intensity and attention that you felt on your fingertips. Put the joy of this moment into your dance."

The poignant, heartfelt lyrics of Joe Cocker singing 'N'Oubliez Jamais' filled the hall. The song's reflections on anger, regret, and the desire to find a way out of life's labyrinth touched John profoundly. Tenderly, he pressed Adele to him and caressed the back of her neck. "Adele, it feels as though the music is flowing from my heart," John whispered in her ear.

Adele raised her head, and he saw that her eyes were full of tears, but tears of joy. She put her head on his chest and they continued their dance.

Once the song had ended and the music had stopped, a

deep, meditative calm descended on the room, and all remained still and silent.

"Never forget this moment!" Ann pronounced each word carefully. "Remember the sense of connection that you have experienced today, both within yourself and with your partner. If that is important to you, practise it. Be sensitive to each other. I'm very glad to have guided you on this journey this morning. Thank each other, and... *n'oubliez jamais!*"

"Adele, thank you. I enjoyed the dance, and it was so surprising; especially dancing with you. I feel lighter and life feels less complicated," said John, hugging his wife tightly.

"So, should we continue to practise this dance as Ann suggested?" she teased.

"Why not?" replied John, in the same light-hearted mood. "This could be one of our future projects..."

They went over to Ann to thank her personally and to take her number; then they returned to the hotel. After the morning's intense practice, they needed to shower and change before going on with the rest of their day.

"There's still some time until lunch. I'd like to stretch out on the bed for a bit. I'll wait for you," said John, drying his wet hair.

Adele nodded and disappeared behind the shower curtains. Within a few minutes, Adele emerged from the bathroom, wrapped in a large towel that reached her knees. She went to the window and then made a turn, asking John playfully, "What do you think of my new outfit? How short should my skirt be? Like this?" She lifted the towel a little. "Like this? Or like this?" She moved the towel higher. Her slender, tanned legs were shown off to perfection by the white Turkish towel.

John smiled at her, enjoying this little performance. He could not remember the last time she had been so at ease and full of fun. He reflected that such radiant spontaneity was inherent in a person's character and could not simply be acquired. Adele certainly had it. She approached him and began to tickle him.

He started to laugh loudly, just as he had in Mary Catherine's garden, and snorted uncontrollably.

"Adele, stop! No... no... it's unbearable! Stop it! If you don't, I'll start reading my poems again."

"Your poems! They should be banned under the Geneva Conventions as a crime against humanity."

"Fine! Then you'll be punished by being kissed to death." John drew her towards him, trapped her arms by her sides, and peppered her face, neck and head with short, intense kisses.

This provoked explosive laughter in Adele. She escaped his hold and grabbed a pillow to defend herself. Then suddenly she dropped the pillow, took his face in both hands, and kissed him passionately. "I think we're going crazy, John," she whispered, looking into his eyes.

"If this is what being crazy means, then I'm happy to stay that way."

He embraced her gently, and she pressed herself as close to him as she could. Their bodies intertwined and fell into fusion, as if they had been Rodin's inspiration for his *Eternal Springtime*. Adele felt John's excitement, but this time it did not embarrass her. Her body naturally accepted this appeal coming from her husband, and she responded with a wave of passion. She could feel the same tenderness and attention from him as she had felt during their dance, and she allowed herself to be uplifted by the surge of love. They made love with their eyes open, like two clear skies facing each other. There were no clouds present; just two infinite spaces able to see the very depths of each other's souls. The rays of sun coming through the window played on their naked bodies and merged with the light in their eyes. Their barriers dissolved and faded away. They were no longer just spouses; they were lovers meeting again after a long separation.

Afterwards, they remained quiet and lost all sense of time. The silhouettes of the trees outside their window began to appear on the curtains and throw their shifting patterns onto the wall.

"Adele, I think we still have time until..." began John, looking at his watch, "until *dinner*? Wow!" He sat up to look again at his watch, his tousled hair standing on end. "How about dinner with champagne?"

"That's an excellent idea!" Adele replied, kissing him gently.

28

The Gathering

It was evening, and the windows on the upper floor of the Couples' Counselling Office had already been lit up for a long time. Mary Catherine, Darius and Marija sat comfortably in large, upholstered antique chairs at a round table in the middle of the room. A big semicircular lamp hung from the ceiling, casting a stream of warm light over them. The pleasant scent of clove-and-cinnamon coffee permeated the room. All three were deeply immersed in some inner contemplation, but at the same time one could feel that they were fully present and mutually connected. To an outside observer, it would have seemed that the most important part of their conversation was taking place in silence, because they appeared to communicate without many words. It was only the occasional exchange of a phrase or two that revealed the topic of their discussion.

"They have taken on quite a lot on an emotional level," said Mary Catherine. "And despite the fact that some of the tasks and their experiences were very challenging, they have managed to complete them well."

"The activities which concentrated on bringing them closer are essential to their partnership," Marija added thoughtfully. "They could help to inspire them to do more together in the future. It is also crucial that they both reflect on why those experiences were necessary for them."

"We have already seen what can happen when a couple's experiences and emotions on The Road are not followed up with awareness and attention afterwards," mused Darius.

"Yes – I'm sure you remember that young couple who neglected to follow through with what they had learned," sighed Mary Catherine. "They dissipated much of the positive energy they had accumulated during the programme. For two weeks they were very enthusiastic, telling their friends and family about their 'adventures' on The Road, instead of identifying the shared values within their relationship, as we had hoped. And so the benefits of their time with us were lost…"

"In this present case, the couple needs to develop a new view of their partnership," said Darius. "It could be a challenge for the husband – he's rather strict and conservative and finds it difficult to accept something new, whose purpose he doesn't comprehend."

"But his wife could help him to accept new ideas," remarked Marija. "As I see it, she is more flexible in unfamiliar situations… but she needs a gentle push to get started."

"I wonder if Dirk could help them?" Darius reflected thoughtfully.

"Dirk?!" exclaimed Mary Catherine, as if she had been pulled sharply out of her meditative state by Darius's suggestion. "He can be so academic; I remember the last time we had him in our company, I was struggling not to fall asleep…"

"Well, yes, he can be too theoretical," agreed Darius. "But if the topic of discussion is well defined, he is an excellent problem-solver. You have to agree, at least, that he is a very good abstract thinker. That is what this couple actually needs now: a fresh perspective that will allow them to see their partnership in a more neutral way from the outside, and not to be bound by the stereotypes they've formed during their life together."

"And in that life together, they've often ignored and suppressed their own desires and talents," added Marija. "That will be our next focus within the programme."

Darius, Marija and Mary Catherine fell into silence, perhaps continuing their communication in some unknown dimension, while remaining receptive to any solutions to come. After some time, they looked at each other and smiled.

"I see that we are all in agreement as to the next stage for John and Adele," Mary Catherine concluded happily. "So, the magical journey continues…"

Darius extended his hands, let out a breath, and brought his hands back down onto the arms of his chair. "All right, then. Now it is up to Providence alone to decide if this course of action is in line with her plans."

The stars, suspended in interest through the skies just outside the windows, darted back into the clouds as the three voices faded into the night.

29

Tracing Your Own Path in Life

The splashing of someone taking their morning swim just under their window woke Adele and John from a sound sleep. They glanced at each other and grinned, knowing that neither of them had any desire to quit the bed immediately.

After another half-hour, Adele languidly poked her head out from under the duvet and reached for her phone. "I suppose it's time to start our day."

"Hmm, I wonder what our assignment will be today?" said John, gently smoothing his wife's hair.

"Whatever it turns out to be will be fine with me. The most important thing is that we'll be doing it together," replied Adele, and she snuggled into him.

At that moment, the hotel room phone rang, and John took up the handset. It was Darius. Having learned that they had both slept well, he requested that they be at the reception desk in two hours, ready to leave The Wellspring of Life. There, they would be given further instructions.

The usually white light of summer appeared golden to John and Adele as they took a last look, from the balcony of their room, at the river valley below them. They were already well prepared for the continuation of their journey. Just before closing the door, Adele bade a final farewell to her apricot roses. A card had been left beside them, addressed to the thoughtful housekeeper, in the hope that the roses would bring the very same happiness to her.

Five minutes later, they were standing beside their cases in the foyer, waiting for the next part of The Road programme. Suddenly, Marija appeared at the glass doors leading to the park. She waved to the couple and pushed open the doors to enter. After greeting them both, she went immediately to the reception desk to arrange for their cases to be stored safely for a few hours.

Adele approached Marija. "I'm sorry, Marija, I'm a bit confused. What's going to happen now? We expected to receive instructions from Darius."

Marija smiled. "You will come with me, Adele. We can stay here, or walk around and do a bit of casual coaching for your future. But John will go on his own to meet with a friend of ours."

"A friend of yours? Does your friend need help? What will they do there?"

"Don't worry, Adele," Marija reassured her. "They will work well together. It's a special project, and you and I will spend some nice time together as well."

John, meanwhile, had taken a seat in an armchair at a little distance from them. He appeared completely relaxed.

Adele approached him, still somewhat puzzled. "John, dear, Marija has explained to me that you're doing a special assignment today with a friend of theirs. Is it all right with you if I stay with Marija and you go off for this project?"

John smiled. "I'm open to anything – anything at all."

Marija laughed as Adele stared at him.

John could see that his wife was taken aback, and his laughter mingled in the air with Marija's. "What's the matter, Adele? Don't you usually find me easy-going?"

Adele suppressed a smile as she struggled to come up with a suitable response.

Just then, a tall, distinguished-looking man with greying hair, dressed in a bright turquoise linen shirt, appeared at the glass door. He gestured to Marija. She rushed to the door, opened it for him, and kissed him on the cheek before taking his arm to bring him over to introduce him to Adele and John.

"John, Adele, I would like you to meet Magnus."

"Pleasure to meet both of you." Magnus spoke with a slight Scandinavian accent. His deep blue eyes were striking in their intensity, and it seemed to Adele that those eyes could penetrate her mind and read her innermost thoughts, but in a welcome and pleasant way.

We all have thoughts and dreams that we would like others to be aware of before we are obliged to make them known by speaking out. This is a positive feeling, she thought suddenly.

"Well," Magnus exclaimed, bringing his hands together in one short clap, "we had better get cracking! The day is advancing. Come along, John."

John grinned and hopped up from the armchair, like a little boy expecting his birthday cake in the next room. He gave Adele a quick kiss and whispered in her ear, "Everything's good. I'll be back soon." Then, waving goodbye to Marija, he followed Magnus out of the reception door and through the park.

Adele watched regretfully as the two figures disappeared into the distance. "What will they do, Marija?" she asked softly.

"They have a programme for this morning, but we have one too," Marija replied kindly. "Come – the day is sunny and beautiful, and we should be out in nature."

She led Adele out through the glass doors and up towards the limits of the park, where there stood a line of maple trees, their five-pointed leaves glittering in the sunshine and waving in the gentle wind. As they walked, Marija steered their conversation towards Adele's professional activity and her future aspirations, and how she thought she might achieve them. Circling the park, in the shade of some chestnut trees they came upon a wooden bench attached to a wide table. Marija was carrying a basket. She had prepared a little picnic. They had fresh parsley soup from a thermos; French bread, still warm and spread with creamy salted butter; and a lemon cake drizzled with lemon juice and icing sugar. They drank home-made elderflower cordial and melissa tea from Marija's garden. As Marija cut into the cake, Adele breathed in the fresh citrus aroma.

"You make the most delicious things out of the simplest ingredients!" She smiled. "I might even try to make some of your recipes. In fact, I am going to try to remember everything I've encountered with the three of you on this journey. I'll miss you when we're back at home."

Marija laid a gentle hand on Adele's wrist. "Yes, the time has passed very quickly, Adele. I will miss you too."

There was a long silence as they both looked up at the sky, watching the birds spinning above the trees overhead.

Adele took another forkful of cake. "I don't think that what I make will be half as good as yours!"

Marija looked at her intently. "Is there something that you feel you do really well; perhaps even a bit better than you have seen others do?"

Adele thought for a moment. "Well, I think I am quite good at supporting people; at helping them through difficult periods in their lives, and building up their self-esteem. I was really involved with my Aunt Helena when she had a fall and injured her back. I also helped her to see that she could regain her strength and confidence by continuing to work on her physiotherapy. I was very responsible even as a young child, and did my best to support my mother when she needed help. When

I became a mother myself, I tutored Patrick because he wasn't very disciplined in his studies or interested in school. I knew that a strong secondary education was essential for him to have a life he could enjoy. He has graduated from university now, and is very enthusiastic about international law."

"And did his father also tutor him? He's a professor."

"No, not often!" Adele smiled. "John had less patience with him than I did."

"And yet you are often hard on yourself for having given up your own studies. In our conversation you have compared yourself to John and described yourself as not very academic, not very intellectual, not very capable of logical thinking. Yet you tutored and guided Patrick throughout his school years. That is very impressive!"

Adele took a deep breath. "Thank you, Marija."

Marija sliced some more of the lemon cake for Adele, and poured out another two cups of melissa tea.

30

John

John and Magnus had arrived. It had been quite a walk, and John, unaccustomed to exercise, was a bit breathless. Magnus led him into a large, bright space that happened to be a living area as well as a workspace. It appeared to John to be almost empty, and surrounded on all sides by windows extending from floor to ceiling. The room was in the shape of a great barrel, and canvases hung on the curved walls. Most of them were completed paintings, but some appeared half finished, while others were totally blank. Magnus was clearly not interested in material possessions. Aside from a few items of clothing folded carefully on a shelf or hung from wooden pegs, and some pieces of hand-thrown pottery in a tiny kitchen space at a little distance from the door, everything in sight was associated with oil or watercolour painting. On entering the space John felt as though his mind had been plugged into a source of energy previously unknown to him.

"Sit down, John. Would you like a coffee, and perhaps some

cheese on toast?" Magnus produced crusty brown bread that he sliced and placed under the grill of his little cooker. As it toasted, the aroma of roasting sesame seeds filled the air. Removing the golden-brown toast, he placed thickly cut cheddar on it and then, taking a pestle and mortar, ground up some herbs and sea salt and sprinkled this on the hot bread and cheese. "Hope this is all right," he remarked to John. "The saltiness of the herbs complements the creaminess of the cheese."

Magnus added fresh apple slices sautéed in butter to the plate, along with some still-warm vanilla sponge cake sprinkled with cinnamon. He then prepared two large mugs of hot, freshly brewed coffee, swirled with cold cream he had retrieved from a metal ice bucket on the floor. John found it all delicious.

"The mind works at its best when nourished, and so does the body." Magnus smiled as they had their lunch in a leisurely manner. Eventually, Magnus pushed his plate away. "Have you finished, John?" he asked, with the air of someone who had prepared a surprise.

"Certainly have."

"Well, then, look up!"

"Look up?" asked John, confused.

"Sure, look up – what do you see?"

John did as he was asked. The table at which they were sitting was situated underneath a huge glass skylight. The summer stretched out above them in its full glory.

"Out we go!" Magnus opened one of the floor-to-ceiling windows with a flourish. There, set up in the corner of a well-tended little garden, were two wooden easels with blank canvases. Next to them was a folding table with a tray containing glasses of water, palettes, a myriad of paints, and a basket of eggs.

John stared curiously at the eggs. "We have already eaten."

"These are for mixing in the natural manner; the way it was done in medieval times," answered Magnus. "They also used beetles and snails for colours such as blue, purple and orange, but I don't have the heart to dispatch the poor creatures. So, I ask you again: what do you see when you look up?"

"Clouds," answered John simply.

"Yes, clouds," said Magnus, with encouragement. "But describe them. What is happening?"

"Well..." John hesitated. "Some are in full sunlight; some in shadow. Some are bright white; some are light grey; some are a bruised purple – carrying rain, perhaps, for this evening."

"Yes – go on!"

"Some look as though they have a very thick, fluffy texture, while others are almost like flimsy, torn fabrics."

"Good!"

"The ones just above us appear to be illuminated from behind, as though by a lamp. But the ones above the trees over there appear flatter, with no inner light."

"What about the sky?"

"Hmm... the parts above us are a brilliant, opaque blue, while the edges at the horizon have amethyst hues. The skies to the left over those hills are lilac or violet."

"Do you think you could show it?"

"*Show* it?"

"Show these effects on a canvas."

"A what?"

"Watch this!" Magnus put a paintbrush into John's hand and looked up at the clouds directly overhead. He began mixing paints on a wooden palette. "Now dip your brush into the paint and manipulate it to show what you see."

With some hesitation, John dipped the brush into an azure paint and dabbed it gently onto the canvas. In time, he was barely conscious that Magnus was pouring milk into some oil and breaking an egg from the basket. His concentration was focused exclusively on the sky and the effects his brush and paints were creating on the canvas. He had entered another world. But at the same time, he felt curiously at home. The effort he made to represent accurately what he viewed was not too difficult for him. The brush seemed to be an extension of his hand, rather than an awkward tool he was being forced to manipulate. He watched in fascination as the landscape around him began to take shape and the varied hues of the glorious sky were represented under his hand. The canvas had been as white as the new-fallen snow he had loved to tramp through each winter as a teenager with his golden retriever, Finnegan. Now it was filled with his vision of what he saw and sensed around him. His face flushed with pleasure, and he felt anew the extraordinary energy he had experienced on first entering Magnus's studio.

"I feel as though I'm soaring through this landscape on a magic carpet! I'm under its power, moving through the sky..." John could not contain his amazement. But then his old self intervened and the energy subsided. "I hope I'm not wasting your canvas, Magnus. I really don't know what I'm doing... I probably don't have a clue. Maybe this is no good?"

"We won't even consider that. Your instinct will guide you. We all must develop self-belief, John, for it is on this self-belief that the direction of our lives is built."

The two were silent for a while.

"Would you like to take a break and drink another coffee?" asked Magnus, surveying the work that John had completed.

"No..." John paused. "I have another hill and a cloud to finish."

He only needed a bit of guidance on using the marker pencils on the canvas, and how to best mix the colours. Magnus was amazed at the speed at which John worked. He had prepared two canvases in order to teach John the fundamental techniques for painting in oil and in watercolour, but John seemed to know instinctively, without much direction, exactly what he wanted to do in each blank space.

Magnus came over to John's canvas again. "Wonderful,

John!" His admiration was sincere, and John was ready to admit that he had painted a very fine picture indeed.

"Can I take it with me, Magnus?" he asked.

"Of course, John. But not now, I'm afraid. It needs to dry for a few days. I can ship it to you later," responded Magnus.

John sighed with disappointment and took several photos of his painting with his smartphone.

Eventually, the men left Magnus's studio and made their way back to the hotel. They followed the same road they had that morning, but it seemed to John that the world had somehow changed. It appeared more colourful, more vibrant, and there were so many aspects of the environment surrounding him that he had never previously noticed. Contours, proportions, perspectives... nothing was static; everything was in a state of flux, as part of some mysterious process. It was a constantly changing kaleidoscope of contrasts: light and shadow, stillness and movement, order and chaos... For John, it was clear that the smallest blade of windblown grass was not less important than the tallest tree in this process, and that it merited the same attention from him.

Approaching the hotel, they found Adele, Darius and Marija chatting on the terrace, and joined them at their table. John felt so elated after his painting session that he was unable to curb his enthusiasm. He immediately began to talk about his unanticipated encounter with the world of visual art, and proudly showed everyone his photos of the work he had done.

"How did you do this in such a short time?" Adele wondered aloud, looking admiringly at her husband's picture. "I feel as though I'm flying through your sky. Your painting is remarkable, John."

"Absolutely true," confirmed Magnus, smiling. "I have given painting lessons to many, but it's rare to meet someone who has such a strong sense of how to represent what he sees. It is as though he has been an artist all of his life. The only thing I needed to do was open the door and allow this painter to come out and paint. It was my pleasure to do that for you, John."

"I never had any doubt that you have talent!" exclaimed Adele. Moved by Magnus's words, she embraced her husband. "I always knew that you had a true gift for discerning nuances in colour." Opening her bag, she took out a narrow wooden box. It had a sliding cover with a shamrock carved on it. "John, this is for you." With a shy smile she handed the box to John, and it seemed to him that she had started to blush a bit. "I found this in The Wellspring of Life craft shop. I hope I've found exactly what you might need…"

John was curious. He pulled back the sliding cover and saw two fine paintbrushes lying on tiny wooden supports. They had delicate lacquered handles and copper ferrules. Both were made of soft bristle: one round with a needle-shaped tip, and the other square and flat at the end. John grinned happily.

"The woman who sold it to me said that you can use the needle-shaped brush for more detailed work. The flat one is for larger strokes," explained Adele with enthusiasm.

"They're just right, Adele," whispered John, touched by this unexpected present. He kissed her.

"That's an excellent gift for a beginner," confirmed Magnus, taking the box from John and looking at the paintbrushes.

John's mentor was evidently very pleased with that morning's work. He spent several minutes commenting on John's painting, as well as giving him some professional advice on particular artistic techniques and materials.

Once Magnus had finished his explanation, he approached Darius and they began speaking together in low voices. "I think, Darius, that this part of the work has gone very well. Another milestone has been reached. Are you satisfied?"

"Oh, yes," replied Darius, shaking his hand. "We're very satisfied."

Magnus then turned to say goodbye to everyone. "Keep up

200

the good work," he urged, looking at both Adele and John. He then left the terrace.

The remaining four sat in meditative silence for a moment.

"I see a lot of happiness in your faces," said Darius, leaning towards John and Adele. "You seem much more at ease with each other than when we first met." After a pause, he added, "As you have probably guessed, you are now approaching the end of The Road. Will you both be ready to return home?"

This simple question was so unanticipated that neither John nor Adele could answer it straight away. They looked at each other, perhaps trying to imagine their future life at home.

"It's strange, but for some reason I feel at home *here*, on The Road," said John thoughtfully.

"Yes – being on The Road with John comes naturally to me now." Adele took up his reflection. "I'm already accustomed to this sense of having a new and interesting challenge every day…" Suddenly, the light in her eyes dimmed. "But I'm not very sure if we'll be able to maintain this spirit of adventure when we're back at home. Will we manage to remember everything? We'll have the same old walls, the same old habits, the same old routine. So how can we bring something new and inspiring into our day-to-day life?"

"The most important thing to understand is that you already have this 'something new and inspiring' within yourselves," answered Darius. "The changes that have taken place within you will continue to influence your lives. But you have a point, Adele. With the same walls around you, and the same routine, the experiences that you have had on The Road may begin to fade, bit by bit, from your conscious minds. That is why it is crucial for you not to lose your momentum. Each of you could begin by initiating some changes, no matter how small. For example, when you return home, look around carefully. Perhaps you, John, are unhappy with the way in which things are arranged in your living room. If so, don't hesitate to discuss it with Adele and consider moving them straight away!" Then he addressed them both. "Also, take a good look at your domestic arrangements with new eyes, for this is the environment in which your partnership exists. If your old routine is not serving you well, change it. You will be surprised by how these minor modifications trigger a sequence of new ideas and solutions. Take each day as an adventure."

"But we understand each other well now. We've overcome obstacles in our relationship and solved our problems!" exclaimed John, who disliked the idea of altering the home they had built up together over the years, or changing their established habits. "Why can't we simply be with each other..."

"...and live happily ever after?" Marija finished his query.

This light-hearted question made everybody laugh; even John.

"Good point, Marija!" remarked Darius. "I have no doubt that the prince and the princess lived happily ever after, once they had accomplished all of their heroic deeds. But the fairy tales do not tell us how hard they toiled in order to remain happy together for the rest of their lives. Building a partnership is a process. If you don't continue to make an effort, you will risk losing everything that you have achieved together. The experience that you have gained on The Road is very valuable, but you will both face other challenging situations, and you won't be given any solutions for them. You need to develop a method – that is, a multipurpose toolbox – which can be used to approach any problem that you have as a couple. A partnership is most effective when both partners act as a team, in unison and in harmony – as a whole, so to speak. With their own structure and their own meaningful reasons for being together, the couple do not close themselves off from the rest of the universe. Instead, they remain in tune with the ever-changing external world, while at the same time resisting threats to their partnership. These can, for example, take the form of negative views of your partner, financial difficulties, serious illness, or criticism of the choices that you make as a couple. You need to remain as a whole to withstand these destructive forces. Remember, it is not for anyone else but yourselves to determine why you are together."

"Darius, could you explain what you mean by this 'whole'?" asked Adele, struggling to understand this intriguing and abstract expression. "I seem to remember you mentioning it on the first day we all met."

"Even though it sounds theoretical and vague, in fact, viewing a couple as an integral whole may have very real and practical results," said Darius. "I know someone with a great capacity for abstract thinking. He is also able to analyse and explain very complicated concepts. Your next mission is to meet him and discuss this issue. You will find his name and address in these papers. He is expecting you straight away."

Darius gave them some printed pages bearing a university crest. They contained a list of professors by faculty. One name was highlighted in bright orange.

"'Professor Dirk Engelmann, quantum physics'," read Adele out loud.

31

Adele

"I didn't at all anticipate that we would continue our adventure by visiting my world of academia," said John, evidently pleased as they headed towards their destination.

"That world may soon become familiar to me too," Adele said slowly, testing her husband's reaction.

John's eyes widened. He looked at her in surprise, and for an instant nearly forgot that he was driving, and so obliged to hold the steering wheel tighter. He remained silent, waiting for further explanation.

"I think I'd like to start studying again," continued Adele.

"What? Are you serious?" exclaimed John, incredulous and still having difficulty focusing his attention on the road. "Our son has already finished his studies. Don't you think that it's too… I mean, taking up study again after so many years will be quite difficult. How much have you thought about this? Are you sure you need to do this in your life?"

"John, I understand your reaction, to a certain point. Perhaps you think it's too late for me to resume my studies," answered Adele directly. "But it's not a question of need: I *want* to do this. I was surprised too when I realised how much I would like to do it. I have to tell you about my conversation with Marija this morning." Adele paused to think, sorting through the sequence of thoughts she had had that morning. She wanted to choose her words carefully. "You know, when I learned that we were going to spend some time apart today, and then when I saw you leaving with Magnus, I began to panic. Up until that point, we had been taking part in every assignment together, and the separation was so unexpected that I honestly thought we had done something wrong." She passed her hand through her hair, still trying to manage her compelling emotions. "Then Marija invited me to have a walk in the park with her. We had a long talk that concerned my feelings about myself, my aspirations and what I am doing with my life. It became clear to me that I was making some assumptions about my role in our marriage. I know now that they were based on outdated stereotypes of what a good partner should be. I thought it necessary and natural for me to give up on my career ambitions for the sake of a stable family life. I thought it was normal to make these sacrifices in order for us to have a life together. I had always been convinced that it was my own decision to put aside my hopes of a serious profession so that I could support your ambitions and success... but deep in my heart, I resented it. Often, when we argued, I would call you 'Professor'. In actual fact, I was jealous – that nickname was sarcastic and unkind on my part. You didn't deserve that, because you have worked very hard to achieve your position and your academic recognition. In addition, you love your job and are really involved in helping your students to understand and appreciate classical economic theory. They also clearly value the efforts you make on their behalf..."

John listened carefully. Adele's honesty moved him deeply. He had known at the time of her graduation, as well as during their marriage, that she had been keen to continue her studies. But when, due to a barely insufficient mark in one exam, she was not accepted early on for a highly competitive master's programme, she had been so upset that she had made herself ill. Later, after Patrick's birth, further study had been put off indefinitely by both of them, and it had never been discussed since that time. Now, with some shame, John had to admit that he had never encouraged his wife to try to take up her studies again. In reality, her giving up her career had suited him. She had remained at home, looking after Patrick and taking only occasional work covering for university clerical officers who had fallen ill or taken personal leave.

"During our conversation, Marija helped me to look more closely at the desires I still have for my life. She guided me towards an understanding of the real reasons behind my past choices," continued Adele. "And then it suddenly hit me that giving up my studies and any hope of a professional career had nothing to do with a sacrifice for you. It was my fear of failure and lack of self-confidence that was preventing me from achieving my goals. The roots of that fear seem to go back to my schooldays... But anyway, over the years, I kept hiding the real truth from myself. I invented various reasons to justify not taking any action, and sometimes I blamed you, John, for not having achieved my dreams."

Having said this, she swallowed hard, but John's attentive look urged her to go on.

"During this morning's session with Marija, I realised that the fact that we are in a partnership for life need not block any fulfilment of my aspirations. What is more, the happiness that comes from me achieving my personal goals will bring more life and joy into our relationship – that was confirmed for me when I saw your shining face after your painting activity with Magnus. Of course, that was *your* success, but I was also very pleased, and so proud of you. I feel that your new-found talent has brought fresh energy into our relationship, and I could sense that energy breaking down my own barriers, allowing me to have the courage of my convictions to realise my dreams." Adele took up the papers that Darius had given to them. "As soon as I saw this university crest, I was sure that it carried a personal message for me. This is my chance, John. Nothing is going to stop me from taking up my studies again. I couldn't care less what anyone else's view might be. Other people's opinions are of no consequence!" With a look at her husband, she added, "Except yours, John…"

"We've arrived at the university, Adele," said John, turning into a narrow street with stone walls on both sides and touching her knee gently. "Take a chance on this, Ad… but what we need to do now is look for Professor Engelmann's office."

They left their car in the car park, tucked away behind green hedges, and walked through the extensive campus grounds. Eighteenth-century buildings surrounded a central square, which had been beautifully set out with great attention to the placement of trees and shrubbery to permit pleasant walks as well as easy access to all parts of the university. A tall church tower in grey stone rose above all the other buildings in this quaint academic enclave. As the couple entered the square, the bell in the church tower rang out for four o'clock. A sign in front of them indicated by means of arrows the directions to take to the university's main buildings: the dean's office, the lecture halls, the library…

"Look, Adele – you'll see that, as in most universities, each department has been named after a distinguished academic in that field: Charles Darwin, who developed the theory of evolution; Herodotus, the ancient Greek historian; and Jean-François Champollion, the French philologist who deciphered the mysterious symbols on the Rosetta Stone."

"This is the way to go," said Adele, pointing to the arrow marked 'Maria Goeppert Mayer'. "She was the second woman after Marie Curie to win the Nobel Prize for physics! Do you know her name, John?"

"Hmm... no, I don't think I do... But in any case, Adele, I'm sure that you'll be the next to win it."

Smiling at each other, they followed the path to the Goeppert Building and the Department of Physics. This too was an eighteenth-century building, but modern laboratories had been added on as an annex. The Goeppert Building looked more extensive compared to the other buildings they had just passed, and it appeared that physics was considered a principal discipline within this university. They went through an ancient wooden archway and found themselves facing a small courtyard of paved stone. From there a number of smaller entrances led to different sections of the department. Each had a sign indicating its particular branch within the field of physics. Quantum physics was the fourth door, and on entering it was not difficult to find Professor Engelmann's office. His name appeared in black on the door, which was slightly ajar. Adele knocked, and the two inched into the room. It was quite spacious, with a high ceiling, and it was full of an enormous number of books and files. They were heaped everywhere: crammed into bookcases, piled up on tables, stuffed into pigeonholes, squeezed into filing cabinets, falling from the windowsills, and even stacked on the sliding ladders which were designed to reach the upper shelves. On a large, windowless wall opposite Adele and John there hung a huge blackboard. A pulley attached to the wall moved the sections of this blackboard ever higher as the occupant of the office covered it with equations. On the adjoining wall hung portraits of famous physicists. In the far corner of the room, a man was sitting at a big desk, looking intently at three computer screens. He was dressed in a green knit sweater and soft brown corduroy trousers. His long, curly grey hair fell down over his shoulders.

"Excuse us, but we would like to talk with Professor Engelmann." John addressed the man from a distance.

The man spun around in his chair, lowered his horn-rimmed glasses, and looked at the intruders. Without any introduction he launched into speaking, as if he knew exactly who his visitors were and why they had come. "Ah, yes… you must be wanting my opinion regarding your book about the holographic effect on a black hole horizon. As a book for the general reader, it's rather good, but I must say that you've omitted some essential aspects related to the entanglement and entropy of black holes. You concentrate your analysis too heavily on the energy conservation principle. You've made it central to your presentation of this phenomenon, but the *information* conservation principle is even more fundamental for holographic effects—"

"I'm sorry to interrupt you, Professor," John said politely, after recovering from this barrage of information. "But we're not here about any book. Darius sent us."

"Darius?" asked the professor distractedly, apparently trying to find the space in his mind that was reserved for that name. "Oh, *Darius*! My close friend. I got a message from him this morning. So, I assume that you are the couple about whom he wrote?"

"Yes," confirmed John. "We want to learn from you about the principles of partnership, and to ask you about our partnership in particular."

"*Your* partnership?" the professor exclaimed, staring at them and raising his hands in amazement. "But I don't even have any idea who you are! Darius is full of surprises, as usual," he muttered under his breath.

"We thought that we were going to have a discussion with you about the theoretical notion of a couple in a committed relationship," interjected Adele. "Darius told us that you are a recognised expert in abstract thinking. We don't really want to discuss the details of our life together, but we'd like to understand more fully the idea of a relationship as a complex unit, with the partners connected and not considered as two separate entities.

I presume that each structured unit can be seen as a whole – that is to say, that it acts in harmony. Is that correct?"

John turned to Adele, completely lost, and gawking at her in confusion. His expression indicated that he had no idea of the meaning of what she had just said.

"Bravo, dear lady! I'm sure we'll have an interesting discussion. We can make this a *Gedankenexperiment!*" exclaimed Professor Engelmann excitedly, his eyes flashing with inspiration. "However, please bear in mind that I'm not an expert in human relationships. But we know that objects in nature are complex and that their behavioural patterns repeat, and therefore perhaps we can apply that model to the way a human relationship functions."

He jumped up from his chair and gestured to Adele to sit on one of the armchairs arranged around a low table in the centre of the room. It seemed as though he had completely forgotten about John, who moved behind them mechanically and sat on a rung of a nearby ladder. In trying to resurrect from his memory his meagre German vocabulary, the only thing John had understood in this discussion so far was that the complicated word '*Gedankenexperiment*' which had been used by Professor Engelmann literally meant 'thought experiment'.

"So, let's assume that we have a Whole," began Engelmann, walking slowly from one side of the blackboard to the other.

An image appeared in John's head of a huge bubble floating in the air above them.

The professor continued. "Let's assume also that we have to find a means – that is to say, a tool – that will allow us to examine or measure this Whole."

John's bubble floated lazily in the air, and he imagined himself with a big wooden ruler in both hands, trying to measure it.

"Yes, a tool…" Engelmann mused.

"But this tool could destroy the Whole during our analysis," said Adele hesitantly.

"That's correct – it could!" Engelmann rapidly caught hold of Adele's statement, encouraging her participation in the discussion. "And we don't want the integrity of the Whole to be in any way damaged."

"Just as we don't want the integrity of a human relationship to be damaged," Adele added.

"In this context, we say that an observation can modify the phenomenon. This is Heisenberg's uncertainty principle," Engelmann concluded, without acknowledging Adele's last observation.

"Uncertainty principle?" John was rudely awakened from his dream.

"Yes, of course!" Engelmann looked at him as though he had just seen him for the first time. "I hope you are familiar with this principle?"

It was clear to Engelmann from John's reaction that he was clueless.

"Poisson brackets? Does that mean anything to you?" Engelmann tried once more.

"Well, '*poisson*' means 'fish' in French…" John tried to demonstrate some knowledge, but when Engelmann rolled his eyes helplessly to the ceiling, he understood that his attempt to enter the discussion had been in vain. He felt like a student sitting an exam who had no comprehension of the question on the paper.

"Professor Engelmann, we're not physicists," said Adele. "Could you please use simpler language?"

"Well, I'll try…" Engelmann scratched his head and paced silently back and forth in front of his desk. A few moments later, he resumed speaking. "So, turning back to the main point of our discussion, our Whole can be seen as a structured and dynamic object. We want to examine it without breaking it into pieces." He looked at Adele, who was following his reasoning attentively. "In order to describe our Whole, we have to start by fitting it into some kind of reference system within a space."

"So, in the three-dimensional space of our world, it would be logical to start with three perpendicular axes, wouldn't it?" asked Adele.

"Yes, that's possible," the professor acknowledged, and he drew three axes on the blackboard, designating them as 'x', 'y' and 'z'.

John's bubble was still revolving inside his head, but now three arrows had appeared and were piercing it.

"Now we have to define what each axis represents. Take note: we don't want to break our object into pieces, or it will lose its essence." The physicist examined his graph, trying to assign a precise meaning to each axis.

"So, can we characterise our object on the basis of how it acts in the surrounding world?" asked Adele.

"Oh, yes, excellent – that's a very good approach!" Adele's idea had obviously inspired Engelmann. "We'll call the y-axis 'object's activity in surrounding world'. Or, we'll make it simpler and call it 'the way it functions'." He then added the word 'functioning' beside the y-axis. "Now, we have to properly define the x-axis. This will represent the construction of the Whole: the foundation; the way it is set up or structured," he mused.

"Then, we could simply call it 'the structure'," suggested Adele.

"Certainly, that's what it is," agreed Engelmann, and he wrote 'structure' beside the second axis. "So, then, how can we characterise the z-axis? Our Whole is dependent on the external world, so it must be linked to it. Why not call it 'the link'?" He wrote 'link' beside the z-axis. "Look at this! Our Whole has come alive," he announced proudly, delighted with this new discovery.

Meanwhile, John's bubble had started to pulsate.

At the same time, Adele stood up and approached the blackboard. "I think something is still missing…" she ventured, and then fell silent. An image of her physics teacher, Mr Robinson, who had been so unfair to her, suddenly appeared in front of the board, preventing her from moving forward. She turned, and looked timidly at Professor Engelmann. He gave her a look of encouragement, and gestured for her to come up to the board. The image of Mr Robinson vanished, and she stepped up decisively, picked up a piece of chalk, and drew a circle at the point of origin where the three arrows met.

"Brilliant! You're very skilled, dear lady!" exclaimed the physicist. "What will we call it?"

Adele hesitated a moment, but then confidently wrote 'coordination' near the point of origin.

"This is marvellous! We have just produced a new method that allows us to analyse the Whole without breaking it up. Now that we have given it a precise definition, I hope that this model will also prove useful in regard to your partnership," concluded Engelmann. "Your abilities in abstract reasoning, madam, are very strong. I would encourage you to begin a suitable degree programme at our university, and you will certainly have my personal recommendation."

"Thank you very much, Professor! You have given us a lot to think about and a direction to take," Adele said sincerely.

On hearing the word 'us', Engelmann glanced at John with pity. In that instant, John felt his bubble explode into watery smithereens.

"It has been a pleasure to meet you!" Engelmann shook Adele's hand enthusiastically. Then he shook John's hand out of politeness and, after bidding them goodbye, returned to his screens, adding, "Please give my best regards to Darius."

John and Adele nodded and closed the door quietly. They left the building and went out into the square. John could not conceal his rising irritation.

Adele took his hand and looked into his eyes. "John, please don't be annoyed. It's been a wonderful day..."

"But I spent the entire time in that office having no idea what the two of you were talking about! Was that just a little piece of theatre? Was it meant to mock me? I understood nothing, and so I was completely ignored! I felt like an idiot," John snapped resentfully. "Of what possible benefit was that absurd conversation?"

"But our conversation was very important, and the principles we discussed can be applied to a couple's relationship," insisted Adele.

"What did that discussion have to do with couples? Nothing was said about a bubble – I mean, a couple," continued John, confused by his Freudian slip.

"Listen to me, John," Adele interjected. "Professor Engelmann has just shown us how to grasp the notion of the Whole. That was our purpose in coming here to meet with him. We will benefit from his knowledge in making efforts to reflect together on the mechanics of our relationship – that is, how it works."

John listened to her, and did not open his mouth once.

"In addition, taking it from this angle, we can use this method as a toolbox to analyse anything at all. Let's take this tree." She pointed to a yew tree in front of them. "It has its structure: for example, its trunk, roots and leaves. The tree's activity – that is, its function – is to grow and to spread seeds. It has to grow tall in order to access the sun's rays. Its structure therefore has to be adapted to this purpose. If the trunk is too thick, the tree will probably exhaust all of its energy in maintaining its width, and then it will have nothing left in its upper branches to allow them to reach for the sun. Its roots have to be strong, but they also need to be open to receive water and minerals. It's clear that the roots are the yew's link to the earth: the bigger Whole with which the tree is connected."

As John listened to Adele, those tiny droplets began to come together in his mind and re-form into the big bubble.

She continued to set out her explanation. "So, in this Whole we call 'the tree', it is this invisible genetic programme that brings together – that coordinates – everything that happens in that tree. It keeps all the tree's elements connected as one. All of the tree's components are equally important, and if we take away one of them, the tree will lose its essence. If we cut the tree, the wood will be the only thing we have left…"

John was still puzzled, but curious now too. He was soothed. At the same time, he was intrigued to realise that his big bubble was present once again, and now made up a Whole, just as it had earlier. "But how can we apply all of this to our relationship?" he asked.

"We have to figure it out for ourselves!" Adele answered, smiling. "We can look at our relationship as a Whole. It is not just 'Adele and John'. It is something that *comes from* Adele and John, and it is only present when we are together. It never makes its presence known when we are separated. It is for us now to think about what keeps us together… Oh, John, look at the time! I'd like to get some details on the master's programmes here, before the administration office closes. Would you mind waiting for me for a little while?"

"No, not at all – take your time," John replied. "You'll find me right here."

Adele followed the sign for the academic administration department, and John walked up to the yew tree and leaned against it. He imagined his perfectly spherical bubble with all its arrows perpendicular to each other. The light coming from its centre shifted from bright white to golden, and then to every colour of the rainbow. He was still worn out and dizzy after the meeting with Professor Engelmann, but now he felt inspired and hypnotised by the image of the beautiful sphere that still floated in his mind. He was pleased by Adele's positive encounter with Engelmann, as well as the boost in her self-confidence that had resulted from it. The professor had clearly been impressed with her comprehension of such a complicated subject, and John began to realise that he was too. He felt very proud of his wife.

Today he had seen within her undiscovered depths that drew him ever closer to her. He was enjoying her company more and more.

32

New Vision

Left alone, John decided to put the time to good use and explore the campus and its buildings. He strolled in the central square, taking in the Gothic architecture as well as the more modern buildings. His mind was still focused on their recent conversation with Professor Engelmann, and Adele's interpretation of how that way of thinking could be applied to their relationship. Reflecting on this, John circled the square and found himself standing again in front of the yew tree that Adele had used as an example of the theory.

Well, all right, then!" he decided, sitting down on a bench to look at the yew tree just opposite him. *I can do my own* Gedankenexperiment *on my relationship with Adele.* He tried to bring to mind all the details and terminology that Engelmann had used in his dialogue with Adele, but it did not help him much. His knowledge of physics from secondary school, and the one occasion on which he had attended a general lecture on Einstein's theory of relativity, afforded him only a few vague ideas on the subject. *Damn!* he thought in frustration. *How can I get through this if I don't understand any of it?*

He stood up, walked around, and then sat down again. Suddenly, a novel idea came to his mind. *Hmm… so could it be that the real secret is abstract thinking applied directly to our everyday life?* he reasoned, as if he were lecturing to his students. *Let's think about us, John and Adele, as a Whole. The Whole shows itself through its functioning. It has its own inner structure, but it is also linked to the external world. All of these aspects of the Whole are connected by a mysterious and powerful ring at its point of origin.*

The bubble appeared again in John's mind. The three perpendicular arrows from Engelmann's graph stretched from its centre to its surface. John understood that they all had to be of the same length in order to form a perfect sphere. *Now, the same is true for our relationship. Everything must work in harmony to allow us to function well in the world. But how do we act in the outside world? What is the effect of our partnership on this world? What have Adele and I together given to the world?* He reflected for a few seconds. *Patrick! We have given Patrick to the world!*

John was satisfied with his conclusion. But then he acknowledged, with chagrin, that he could not think of anything else that he and Adele had created together. Patrick was an adult. He no longer needed their constant support. He would soon be independent both financially and in his decision-making. *Adele and I are accomplishing quite a bit separately: me in my academic and teaching activities, and Adele in managing the household and her voluntary work as a community companion for elderly people. But I can't think of anything that we are engaged in together.* He began to see that their partnership was not very creative or productive. In his imagination, the vertical arrow shortened, and that deformed his bubble.

John took a notebook from his backpack and drew the same

system of coordinates that he had just seen on Engelmann's blackboard. He then identified each axis with a letter in the same way. He titled the drawing *A Couple as a Whole*. "Functioning!" he said out loud, writing the word next to the y-axis. *That is not very impressive in our case. So, it's clear that we need to lengthen this arrow – that is, to make an effort to do more together.* He put in an arrow going up, and added a question mark. *But how will we do that? We'll set that aside for the moment.*

Then he moved on to the x-axis, writing 'structure' next to it. *The principal question here is how our life together is organised,* he reflected. *On what structural basis does it rest? Hmm... it was established by our legal union when we married; then we acquired our apartment and started to accumulate property together. That includes our furniture, our household contents, our car...* He continued to enumerate in his mind the different objects they had built, purchased or collected during their marriage that could be thought of as part of the material aspect of their life. But he was soon frustrated. *This is nonsense! What does this list of material things have to do with our relationship? They are not especially important to us... but on the other hand, how can a couple have a life together if they have nothing?* An image came to him of Adele and himself suspended together in mid-air, with nothing on which they could sit, nothing from which they could eat their meals, and nothing on which they could sleep. *Well, that's not very practical, or indeed very inspiring. I can see now that this x-axis – structure – definitely makes sense... but I'm asking myself how these ever-increasing possessions contribute to our life together. I have to say that the structural basis of our partnership has stretched the x-axis so far out of proportion that our perfect sphere has become more like a rugby ball. It's really out of shape.*

He continued his reflections and drew a further conclusion. *The good thing is that we can change the way our life is organised by changing its structure.* He smiled, recalling their experience with Christos at The Wellspring of Life. *As an example, we could look at the way our bedroom is arranged and make changes to it.* He pictured their bedroom transformed into a more special place: relaxing and comfortable, with soft furniture, scented candles, and luxurious cushions placed on a large bed. A basket of aromatherapy oils sat on a shelf. Decisively, he wrote 'e.g. our bedroom' next to the x-axis. *In making improvements to our bedroom, practising sensual massage, learning how to listen, and communicating with each other, we would gain new insight into what brings well-being to our partnership. We could then share that experience with others, or perhaps write some books together. So, if we go about changing the way in which our relationship is organised, that will have an impact on the way in which it works.*

Suddenly, the y-axis in John's mind stretched upwards, making the rugby-ball bubble more spherical. Next to it he wrote 'projects done together'. *Very good!* he thought, spurred on by the progress of his analysis. *So, now, what about this 'link'? Of course, our partnership has to be linked to the world... but how?*

John wrote 'link to the world'. The minutes passed. Slowly, he moved his pencil along the z-axis and traced the point of its arrow again and again. He still could not come up with an answer. *How are we linked to the external world as a couple? Through our actions? But that is already accounted for by the 'functioning' on the y-axis.* He looked up at the yew tree, and suddenly an idea struck him. He crossed out the tip of the arrow on the z-axis and drew another arrow below it, pointing inwards. *This new arrow representing the link* must *point inwards on the z-axis. Taking the example of this yew, the tree uses its roots to absorb water and minerals into its structure in order to gain strength and grow. Therefore, there must be a connection between the link, the structure and the functioning. What is it, then, that flows into a couple through the link?* He knew straight away, exclaiming out loud, "Information! Of course!" *The information that we take in from the external world, use to organise our life together, and afterwards take action based upon it.*

John wrote 'information' on the inward-pointing z-axis and underlined it twice. He bent closer to his graph. There was something important reflected within it that he still very much needed to comprehend. He concentrated even harder, focusing all of his attention on his drawing. *What has happened in our relationship recently? Why has there been such a transformation in the way in which we have been interacting during the past week? How and why have we become closer? We haven't changed the structure of our partnership yet; our bedroom is as boring as ever; nor have we created anything: we are not cooking our meals or writing a book together. All of that will need more time.*

Suddenly, he smiled. He felt encircled by illumination that seemed to shine over him like warming rays of light. Carefully, he wrote 'Darius, Marija, Mary Catherine (The Road)' next to the z-axis. *I see now that it is the experiences and the new perspectives that we have learned and internalised during this week that are changing us!* he thought in triumph. *It's up to each couple to choose what information they gather, what guidance they accept, and what they need to learn to allow them to take action in dealing with their problems. It is only this learning process, approached with love, that will permit them to change their lives for the better.*

John felt an indescribable lightness. The framework he had sought had now taken shape in his mind. He saw clearly what needed to be done to allow Adele and himself in their relationship to form a sphere with its own source of light, as in the vision he had experienced while leaning against the yew tree. *Fine, that's clear. But hold on a minute... what is this empty ring at the centre – that is, at the point of origin? What does that represent? It's marked 'coordination'. Hmm... perhaps it is what holds a couple together... So, what keeps Adele and me together?* he asked himself. He did not have to wait long before the answer came to him. *The golden thread! That is what keeps us together.*

The golden thread was formed in the instant we knew that we wanted a future together. We can't ever risk breaking it!

A Couple as a Whole

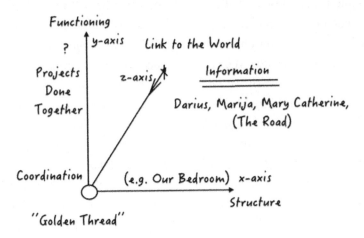

Immersed in his thoughts, John did not notice Adele approaching him. Holding some papers, she came up behind the bench and looked over his shoulder.

"I can see that you haven't been wasting any time," she said softly, sitting down next to him. "Tell me about your drawing. You've done quite a lot of work on it."

"Adele!" exclaimed John. "This abstract way of thinking about the world is amazing, and the most incredible thing is that it works! We can look at our relationship through the prism of my drawing. We can analyse different aspects of it and identify what we need in any given moment of our life together."

"The visual way in which you have set out our partnership and what you see within it is fascinating," remarked Adele. "It means a lot to me that you thought about it so seriously. I think that this may be the toolbox that Darius spoke about."

"Well, it still needs to be developed in order to become a tool," John said, moved by her praise. Then he carefully put away his drawing in his backpack and turned to her. "Now, show me your papers. How was your visit to the university administration?"

"It went very well! I found an interesting master's programme on environmental management, and it starts in two months. I need to make up my mind quickly. What do you think? I thought perhaps..." She stopped in mid-sentence and looked at John, waiting for his reaction.

"Absolutely, you should do it!" John looked directly into her eyes. "I'm sure you'll write an excellent thesis."

"Then I'll need your help, Professor!" Adele sang out happily. She took a breath. "Listen, John: this programme is incredible. When I saw it in the list I knew straight away that it would build on my previous studies and give me a practical way in which to apply what I learn. I also thought that if you could provide me with some practical academic support, I could progress even further."

"Me?" exclaimed John. "I'm no expert in the environmental field!"

"But you *are* an expert in economics, and you can help me with my calculations. I think that no matter what thesis topic I choose, the first thing I need to do is to prove convincingly that we as a society incur tremendous losses in continuing to act so irresponsibly against nature," explained Adele. "When, for example, I see mature, healthy trees cut down to make space for a car park, I know that we are losing an irreplaceable resource, and that we are not managing our environment correctly. That makes me angry as well as sad. Cars can be parked between trees, or some other solutions can be sought. Nobody can convince me that ignoring our environmental well-being is economically beneficial. We have to find a new way of planning our urban spaces. There must be another way to deal with humanity's endless expansion, and it's essential to encourage people to respect as well as enjoy nature."

John listened attentively to Adele's every word, her ideas

sparking fresh images in his mind. He had no doubt that he could and would like to contribute to her project. Still, his drawing remained at the top of his mind. *This could be a new opportunity to bring some creativity into our relationship*, he thought. *We'll make an excellent team, and we'll work well together.*

33

The Final Mission

Talking all the way, John and Adele returned to their car. As John opened the doors he noticed an envelope lying on his seat. He had left the driver's window a tiny bit open, and clearly someone had dropped the envelope through the gap. On opening it, he saw that it contained a single sheet of paper. He read the contents out loud to Adele:

> **FINAL ASSIGNMENT**
> *NOW GO TO A PLACE THAT HAS A SPECIAL MEANING FOR YOU BOTH. THIS PLACE SHOULD BE SOMEWHERE THAT YOU WANT TO VISIT TOGETHER. ONCE YOU HAVE COMPLETED THIS ASSIGNMENT, RETURN HOME.*

"Hold on… what a mission to set. I have no idea what kind of place this assignment requires," mused John. He put the paper back into the envelope and dropped it on the back seat. "Do you have anywhere in mind, Adele?"

"Um… I don't have any idea, either!" exclaimed Adele. "This task has really caught me by surprise. I'm not thinking straight because I'm still so excited about everything that has happened today."

"I understand. Well, what about our original holiday plan? The one we had on starting out? We could still try to call the spa and arrange to stay for a couple of days," suggested John.

Adele put her chin in the palm of her hand, reflecting on this. "Oh, but, John, I don't think that spa is somewhere that *you* really want to go. I don't believe it has any special meaning for you… or for me either, now," she answered thoughtfully. "Neither of us has ever been there. Perhaps the destination that the three counsellors have in mind is a place that is familiar to us both?"

They tried to recall the various locations they had visited in their many years together, but after their unusual week on The Road, none of them seemed relevant or interesting. They remained sitting in their car for nearly half an hour, trying to work out how to carry out their mission, but they made no progress. Adele began to sigh.

"I think I've had enough of this now," John said. "This task is harder than it seemed at the beginning. We can't stay here any longer; it's getting late. Let's see if we can find a hotel."

"Good idea, John!" Adele agreed. "If we're not sure how to move forward with this task, then it would be better to take our time to choose well, rather than settling for something meaningless. I don't mind staying in this lovely university town and having the chance to explore it a bit."

John drove off the campus and towards the town centre. He was surprised by the number of people in the streets. Posters announced a summer festival with music, dance and theatre. The central square of the town was set up with colourful marquees and food stalls, as well as long benches and tables for visitors. The inviting aromas of grilled meat, fresh buckwheat crêpes filled with Emmental cheese, and buttered popcorn wafted through the air. Slowly, John made several turns around the square and was disappointed to see that the first two hotels he spotted displayed 'No Vacancies' signs. They left the square, and in a side street came upon a third hotel. Nothing indicated that it was full.

"Let's try this one. What do you think?" John turned to Adele.

"Look, John! It's named for me," she said, laughing.

John parked the car in front of The Scholars' Guest House. Constructed over the preceding two centuries, it was of dark grey stone, fairly modest in size, neat, and well maintained. They entered a small foyer with a polished floor, also of grey stone, and narrow windows looking out onto a lawn. There was an old library just beside the guest house, after which it appeared to have been named. The staff, probably local university students, were well trained, polite and helpful. John and Adele spoke to a young woman with long auburn hair, with whom they registered and then obtained their keys. Their room was on the upper floor and had an arched ceiling. It was sufficiently spacious to contain a plywood wardrobe, several bookshelves, a large old-fashioned writing table with a lamp, and two single beds. The wooden furniture was of simple construction, but robust enough to have withstood constant rearrangement and hard use by many student guests. John and Adele left their suitcases in the room, and as they went out, they noticed that a 'No Vacancies' sign had appeared at the entrance.

"We arrived in exactly the right place at exactly the right time," remarked John, delighted with their change of fortune. "Let's keep our luck going and we'll eventually find what we're looking for. A little fun may serve as inspiration and help us think of somewhere to go."

The evening was warm and the air was calm. The town square was already crowded. Families sat on benches in the

227

open air, while their children revolved on a small merry-go-round. Young and old chatted together, queueing for food sold from the marquees. From a raised platform at one corner of the square came the strains of medieval music, played by musicians on a lute, a dulcimer, and several recorders, accompanied by two or three tabors and cymbals. The lively music was so appealing that it made people want to dance in the street. Performers dressed in costumes from the Middle Ages led the crowd in a circle dance. Adele took John's hand and they joined the circle. At first the music was light and soft, but gradually the beat of the tabors grew louder and stronger. Then the rhythm became progressively faster – much faster. As more and more people joined the dance, they began to form new circles, whirling and spinning around each other in a dizzying flurry of joy. Adele and John were overwhelmed by the power of the music and their happy mood. They danced hand in hand, and smiled at other people and at each other. The next dance was even faster. People began to laugh and stumble over one another's feet, forgetting their steps. Adele was out of breath, and John was gasping.

"Let's take a break," he panted.

They sat down at a nearby table.

"What incredibly fast dancing!" exclaimed Adele. "Let's eat or drink something, and then dance again."

John went to a food stall and returned with a tray laden with two pints of red ale and two portions of breaded haddock accompanied by chips sprinkled with cider vinegar and coleslaw.

As they were finishing their meal, the music stopped and a gong announced the beginning of a new performance. Two comedians appeared on the stage. One played the role of a student sitting his oral anthropology exam, and the other was his professor.

The student was clearly ill-prepared for the exam, so he told the professor, "My parents are sure that I'll fail this exam.

There's really a lot of pressure on me. If you could pass me with an excellent mark, I would be very grateful."

"Highly irregular... well then, I will start by asking you something rather straightforward," said the professor. After some reflection, he put his question to the young man. "The most puzzling mystery in the development of man is why the Neanderthals, our cohabitants for a certain period, disappeared from the face of the earth. What are your thoughts on this?"

"*Did* they disappear?"

"They certainly did. Do you have any doubts about this?"

"Hmm... ah... I was sure I had seen some late at night, at parties, with their hair messed up after dancing for hours."

The professor cleared his throat. "Be that as it may, why, then, did this species disappear?"

"Um... perhaps they were so unappealing that they couldn't find anybody to marry them?"

The professor stared incredulously at the student. People watching the little comedy began to laugh.

"I'm lost for words."

"Or perhaps they were afraid of dinosaurs?"

"Do you really think, young man, that the dinosaurs were still on earth when the Neanderthals lived?

"I think it's quite possible. It's such a pity that the Neanderthals are gone and so we can't ask them who they wanted to marry or if they lived with dinosaurs."

"I seriously doubt that your answers merit an excellent mark," said the professor firmly.

The comedian playing the student clasped his hands together and pleaded with the professor. "Please, sir, give me one more chance. I have rather bad luck where dinosaurs and marriage are concerned..."

"All right... now, a change of subject. Archaeology. What historical dating methods do you know?"

"What have you in mind, Professor?"

"Dating methods! Radiocarbon, for example."

"Ah, *dating*!" exclaimed the student with relief. "I have a lot of expertise in this subject. I could even advise you, Professor. The most essential thing is eye contact. Look into my eyes. Yes, that's excellent! I have already established a good rapport with you. What are you doing tonight?"

The audience burst into laughter.

John chortled, "What is he going on about? Incorrigible! If I were his professor, I'd show him the door at once."

The professor sighed. "I'm afraid that tonight someone will not pass his ancient history exam…"

"Hold on, Professor, don't lose hope so quickly. Try another question!"

"I'm losing the will to live. It's probably useless to ask, but is there any chance that you can tell me of any tools used by ancient man? I suppose that this question is too difficult for you."

"Definitely not! That is something on which I have reflected very profoundly."

The professor looked at the audience and smiled. "I hope," he said to them, "that this time this student can answer my question and obtain his excellent mark."

"I have read that ancient men hunted woolly mammoths for their dinner."

"Well, that's correct. Go on…"

"So they certainly would have needed toothpicks… and I have found myself that they make an excellent tool at the dinner table!"

The people in the square erupted into laughter once again.

The professor put his head in his hands in despair. "I honestly do not know what to do. This is hopeless! He is finishing me off; I just can't go on…"

The young man started to speak in a soothing tone. "Professor, don't be so upset. I have sympathy for you. Exams are a question of luck. You'll get through it next time. Let me know when you are ready, when you have some good questions, and we can meet again. See you soon!"

The actors bowed and the audience applauded loudly as the sketch ended. John and Adele, slightly tipsy from the beer and feeling as though they were part of the crowd, were very much enjoying themselves. Through the evening they had steadily let go of the constant introspective focus on their relationship to which they had become accustomed on The Road. They no longer felt any pressure to put anything into practice.

"I will remember that little strategy for turning the tables on a professor!" Adele leaned playfully against her husband. "It could come in very handy for my studies."

John assumed a serious professorial air, but his eyes were smiling.

With the comedy sketch over, their festive mood lingered and they looked forward to the other performances to come. A local band mounted the stage and started to play some soft rock music.

"Oh, Adele! I really like this kind of music. Especially live!" said John. "Will we have another pint?"

He got up and headed towards the beer marquee. On his way there, a new song began. Its soft, gentle rhythm appealed to him instantly, and as he advanced, he swayed to the beat. Suddenly, he stood stock-still, taking in the lyrics attentively:

Stay on the road, my friend,
Until the last mile!
For whatever will happen
Will be yours all the while...

He then understood the hidden meaning: the lyrics were referring to their final task. He rushed back to the table, and Adele was surprised to see that he was not carrying any beer.

"Don't tell me that they've emptied the last keg!" she joked.

"Adele," John said seriously, "I think we should move to a quieter place. It's getting dark, the evening is advancing, and there is still much we need to talk over. If we stay here, we will hardly be able to hear each other."

His unexpectedly sober words perplexed her, but nevertheless, she stood up, gathered her things, and followed him. They were moving slowly through the crowd towards a narrow, seemingly quiet street, when John suddenly noticed that Adele had dropped back and then disappeared altogether. He looked around and spied her in front of a stall selling religious icons, cards, candles, and jars of honey. *I can't believe it. Her bad habits are so ingrained*, he thought with disappointment, watching her rummaging through the merchandise. Adele sensed rather than saw John looking at her. She turned to him and signalled that she was coming. But instead of moving towards him, she continued to browse the stall. John shifted impatiently, waiting for her shopping to end, and when she finally came back to him, holding a small paper packet, he could not hide his frustration. But he said nothing. He firmly took hold of her hand and drew her towards the quieter street, not letting her go for a single moment. In that street they saw a tea room, which seemed less crowded and less noisy than the bars and pubs where people had gathered to have fun. They entered it, found a table easily, and ordered a pot of tea and some tempting home-made pear cake with almonds.

"John, I'm sorry that I kept you waiting," Adele said contritely. "I understand your irritation. I've probably bought another meaningless thing, but I couldn't pass that stall without speaking to the kind religious sister who was selling handmade goods from her convent. I wanted to do something nice for her."

"Don't take my reaction to heart," John soothed her. "At the height of all of this festivity, I just started to worry about our final task. We haven't yet decided where to go, and I really don't want to get up tomorrow morning with a hangover and no fixed plan. Can we make another effort to reflect on this?"

"Yes – it's a good thing that you've remembered. I was having such a good time that the fact that we still have no destination for tomorrow slipped my mind."

So they concentrated on their task again, but without much success. The pot of tea was soon empty and the cake gone from their plates, but they remained at the table, contemplating possible destinations and proposing clearly unworkable ideas. Unable to break through the impasse, they sighed in boredom.

Then, looking down at her empty cup, Adele opened her paper packet and took out a small hand-painted ceramic plate which she put over her teacup. "Look, John, it fits perfectly! I'm always in need of a lid to cover my tea to keep it hot."

John glanced at the object. It was a simple pale yellow saucer, but it was the painting on it that really attracted his attention. He took it in his hands and examined it closely. At the front of the image were bright purple roses. In the background there was an old stone wall covered with gracefully winding ivy. The branches of two large trees could be seen behind the wall. The image reminded him of something; something familiar to him. "Adele…" He articulated his words slowly and carefully. "You haven't bought something meaningless. Perhaps this saucer is bringing us a message about where our final destination should be."

Adele looked at him, amazed.

"Do you recall that, a long time ago, I promised to take you to see my mother's garden?" continued John earnestly.

"Of course I do, John. I remember well that, when we were first going out together, we told each other of our childhoods and our upbringing, and you spoke quite a lot about the marvellous garden in which you spent time with your mother."

In truth, Adele had been charmed by John's recounting of his memories of being a little boy and spending time with his mother in a magical garden in a demesne near their home. She had always wanted to see this intriguing place, and he had

233

promised to take her there. But the visit had never taken place. They had made several plans to go there during the course of their life together, but each and every time unexpected circumstances had arisen to prevent them from doing so. For example, on one occasion they had made a firm plan to visit the garden once Adele had been accepted for her master's degree. But when she had failed to gain acceptance and then fell ill, the excursion had been postponed. They had also proposed setting out to see the garden as a family one last time, shortly after Patrick's fifth birthday. But just before leaving home, they had had a very serious argument. John had been unaccountably anxious the entire morning; irritable and unable to relax for even five minutes, moving restlessly and without purpose from room to room, like a fly seeking an open window for escape. Adele had been doing the ironing when the milk warming for Patrick's hot chocolate had started to hiss and boil over onto the cooker. Rushing into the kitchen, she had forgotten the iron on top of John's shirt, and it had burned through the fabric. John had caught the odour of burning cloth and, on seeing his favourite shirt reduced to a browned rag, had flown into a temper. He had accused Adele of being incapable of doing anything properly, and she had responded that if he had wanted something done perfectly, he should have done it himself. In the end, they had remained at home. Deeply hurt, Adele had reflected many times on John's behaviour and the reasons for that quarrel. She could only contemplate forgiving him when she realised that he was unconsciously avoiding going to the garden. Eventually, she had stopped asking him to take her there. In addition, the garden had become associated in her mind with her own failures in life.

"When I saw this scene," John turned the front of the little saucer towards Adele, "my childhood memories came flooding into my mind. I saw my mother's garden. Then I realised that *now* is the time for us to go there. *Now* is our chance to see it;

now is the time for me to go back there as a man and deal with my childhood emotions."

"Are you not afraid?" Adele said gently, putting the question directly.

"No. I am ready to go back," John answered in a determined tone. "And I want to go with you, Adele!"

Adele thought for a moment. John's suggestion to have the garden as their final destination had been sprung on her unexpectedly. It brought again to the front of her mind her own failures as a partner and as a person. She reflected on all the other times they had attempted to visit the garden, and how the fact that they had always failed to do so still cast a shadow over her life. She had just taken the decision to apply for the exciting master's programme, and she was afraid of feeling like a failure again. But it was clear to her that what she wanted most in this moment was to prevent the dark clouds of her past with John – their misunderstandings, their arguments and their long silences – from obscuring her bright future. She needed to face her fears, and like him, she was ready and determined to do so.

"Do you still feel that that place means something important to you too?" asked John.

"Yes," said Adele, looking into his eyes. "My wish to see your secret garden has never left me."

The couple did not linger over the details of their travel plans. They would be left for the next day. They hurried back to their guest house, light-hearted and anticipating their adventure. Propelled by their excitement, they flew up to the top floor and entered their room. John went to the window and opened it, breathing in the night air. The darkness was almost all-encompassing, except for the blurry light from a few lamp posts. One or two distant voices were barely audible in the now-quiet square. The town's boisterous festivities had come to an end. An atmosphere of tranquillity was descending slowly over the blue of the night, and this spread languidly through their bedroom and soothed their minds.

Adele had already made herself comfortable in her bed, and was yawning. John closed the window, undressed, and sat down on his own bed. "Adele, these two beds look so lonely apart. Don't you think so?" Having said this, John then stood up and moved his bed next to Adele's.

34

Together

Early in the morning, as soon as John and Adele woke, they started to prepare for their journey. There was an old-fashioned radio beside the window, and Adele switched it on. A loudspeaker transmitted the voice of a young man with a strong regional accent giving the weather forecast.

Adele looked out. "No worries; it's only a light drizzle," she remarked.

Meanwhile John was absorbed in examining the map. He noted that Kilbride, the village in which he had lived as a child, was not very far from where they were now. "We should reach Kilbride in a couple of hours," he announced with satisfaction. "So, we can have our breakfast without the need to rush."

"Keep in mind that in a place like this, meant for students, they often skip the morning meal," Adele said, doubting that a decent breakfast would have been set out for them downstairs.

But when Adele and John went down to the ground floor and entered the breakfast room, they were pleasantly surprised.

Considering how modest the guest house was, the breakfast was truly copious. Just-baked rye bread, ham, smoked salmon, eggs, muesli, and fruit were placed on large ledges against the wall. Freshly squeezed orange juice stood in glass pitchers on a chest of drawers beside the pots of coffee and tea. The couple chose their breakfast and entered the dining area. In the middle of the room were two big wooden tables covered with linen tablecloths and decorated with vases filled with cornflowers and poppies. A group of six people, four men and two women, were having breakfast at one of the tables. John and Adele said a polite hello to them and then turned towards the empty second table.

"Would you like to join us?" suggested one of the men. "We're a small group for such a big table, and we'd be glad to have your company."

The man – slightly built, balding, and with a tied-up ponytail – appeared to be the eldest of the group. He was perhaps a mentor for the others. They were all friendly and welcoming, and John and Adele did not hesitate in accepting their invitation.

"We're folk and ballad singers. We sang at the festival yesterday." The man introduced his group, and each member shook hands with the couple.

"The audience was very responsive to our music. I must say, we gave an excellent performance!" said one of the singers with enthusiasm. He looked across at the older man. "Thanks to Alain, the guiding light of our team."

Everybody raised their teacups. "Cheers, Alain!"

"Thanks to all of you... you were all so brilliant!" replied Alain, proud but also embarrassed. Then he turned to Adele and John. "I'm really lucky to be the lead singer in this band."

"Yes," said another man, with a beard and a knitted black cap on his head, "but we have no idea how that happened."

Everyone laughed, and then a young woman with long chestnut hair in plaits addressed John and Adele. "What about you? I assume that you also came here for the music festival?"

"Well…" answered John, drawing out his words, "not really."

"On business?"

"Not that, either." John was trying to find a suitable way to explain the purpose of their stay in the town. "We're on holiday, but I must admit that this holiday is very… unusual… and we have been doing some work with regard to—"

"We are here quite by accident." Adele intervened. "Since the beginning of our holiday, we haven't known exactly where we would find ourselves the following day. We are just travellers on the road, so to speak."

"That sounds great!" exclaimed Alain. He looked at his group. "We know that feeling, since we're often on the road as well, with our music. The road makes us think of possibilities, and doing things we have never before considered. It can be very motivating to bring something you haven't yet experienced into your life. It calls for great imagination and courage. The only thing that you'll miss on the road is boredom." He laughed, and then paused. "In fact, you're like us: you're both creative artists. You are the principal actors in your own lives."

"Believe me, Alain, the two of us are far from being actors," responded John. "Adele and I are dealing with reality, and we are not on stage."

"Are you sure of that? It depends on your perspective. We all have many roles to play in the different situations we encounter in life. In fact, it *is* the same as being on stage," continued Alain. "When we put all our energy and creativity into our performance, our life can become a wonderful drama. The ultimate goal for all of us is not to perform to someone else's script, but to be the playwright for our own life."

Alain's words launched a lively discussion about well-known people whom the group thought of as remarkable, and their paths in life. Everyone agreed that the distinctive qualities that these people had in common were the capacity to understand and accept themselves, the ability to question society's views on popular life choices, and the courage to live their lives in accordance with their own values and beliefs. The day was advancing, and everybody had finished their breakfast. John and Adele said goodbye, feeling as if they were leaving behind good friends.

Once on the road again, still invigorated by their pleasant and unexpected encounter with the musicians, Adele and John continued their discussion in the car.

"John, I am really struck by the fact that it's possible to have such a thought-provoking conversation with someone you have never met before and will most probably never see again," mused Adele. "It's true that we can occasionally meet people in ordinary situations who offer us advice that we might need just at that very moment."

"I was also very impressed by Alain and his idea of writing the script for your own life," said John. "You know, in looking back over everything we have gone through this week, I have come to realise that we were the actors in the stories crafted by Darius, Marija and Mary Catherine. We did exactly what we were asked to do and we played our parts as best we could, but with this final task we have begun to tell a new story about our relationship. Listen to me, Adele. When I reflect on it, I have to admit that the life we were living before going on The Road was staid and monotonous. We felt trapped in our past; our future was already mapped out. Wasn't that so? Now I can sense the infinite number of choices in front of us. But I also have to say that this doesn't make it easier."

"That's true," said Adele. "It's certainly not easy. Life is always complicated. The greater the choice, the greater the difficulties in making it. We have to take responsibility for our choices. We cannot blame anyone else for the decisions we make freely as a couple. But at the very least, we know we can rely on each other."

They fell into a contemplative mood, watching the countryside roll out in front of them. Summer was coming to an end, but the hills were still covered in wild flowers. Mossy woods alternated with uncultivated green fields. The mountains through which they drove seemed to regard them as intruders into their private world. John and Adele gazed out almost respectfully as they moved across the landscape. The surface of a light azure lake flashed brightly in the distance.

"Here we are – this is Lake Ellyn, near Kilbride, my home village," John said. "But I'm not sure that I'll manage to find the way to the garden. It was so long ago; the last time I visited the garden was when I was nine years old… I was there, of course, with my mother." He swallowed hard. "You know, when… God took her… my father and I were all alone here, and then a year later we moved to the coast." He paused briefly to look at Darius's map while still keeping an eye on the road. "When I was a child, speaking to my classmates, I called it 'my mother's garden'. But in fact, it was an old monastery garden at quite a distance from our village."

"Did you go there often?" asked Adele.

"Not very. The excursions to the garden with my mother were rare enough and took place mostly during the summer. They remain so memorable because of her full presence on those occasions. Her undivided attention was so precious to me. You know that she was the local pharmacist, and was often on duty even after working hours. She also had to care for my grandmother, who had fallen ill and come to live with us. But once she was in the garden, my mother no longer felt burdened by the stress of her constant responsibilities, and we could really enjoy each other's company. We would usually collect many different herbs, lay out a cloth on the grass, take the things from our basket, and have a picnic. My mother would tell me stories – that was the part of our time together that I truly loved. The magic of her stories was always inspired by what we saw around us. Our garden had a very distinct character. Despite the fact that the monastery had been abandoned, the place retained an ambience of prayerful tranquillity. I felt a sense of freedom and security. Sadly, when I lost my mother, I lost the garden too. My world became less secure." John was thoughtful for a few moments.

"What else do you remember?" Adele asked him gently.

"I remember an elderly man tending the garden. He was probably the last surviving monk connected to the monastery. He was very different from the other elderly men I saw in the village, who sat gossiping in front of their houses. He seemed as old as time to me, and equally wise. I was fascinated by him, since I had no living grandfather. One day, he was weeding a row of carrots, while my mother and I were picking raspberries a short distance away. He was struggling to kneel down on the ground to reach them, and then he held his back as he slowly rose again. I watched him repeat these movements each time he advanced along the row, and so I went to him and offered to help. He agreed to let me pull the weeds for him, and after showing me how to do it he went over to water the radishes in another section of the garden. I started my work with good intentions, but I quickly lost patience – there were too many weeds and my progress was too slow. So, I came up with an idea to make it go faster. I would simply tear off all of the weeds' leaves and throw them between the rows. I proceeded to do this throughout all the rows of carrots. When I had finished, I ran to him, extremely proud of what I had accomplished. We went back to the carrot bed and the elderly man looked at my work. He could see that I had left the roots of the weeds embedded in the soil.

"He told me, 'Look carefully, John. These troublesome weeds are like our problems in life: you need to find them and root them out. Otherwise, the problem remains there, deep down.' Then he knelt again to pull out the roots in order to correct my negligence.

"I felt my face burning with shame and I tried to repair what I had done. But in tearing out the leaves I had made it harder to see the roots. They were too deep or too strong, and I felt that it was beyond my power to pull them out. I began to despair. I remember putting my fists over my eyes and sitting down on the ground.

"Then I felt his hand on my shoulder. He spoke to me in a quiet voice that I found soothing. 'Sometimes, John, we need to ask for help if we find that we cannot solve a problem on our own. And always remember, there is no shame in that.'

"My mother arrived soon after and asked him what we had been doing.

"He answered, 'He's a good lad; he was a great help to me.'

"'Yes, he's very kind-hearted,' my mother said. 'I knew you would find that in him.'

"The gardener said nothing of my little catastrophe, and my mother was full of praise for me."

"But, John, you've never told me about that elderly man before," said Adele in surprise.

"I know, it's strange that I'm remembering him just now. As we're approaching this place, everything that has been buried deep within my memory for so many years is coming back to me."

John pulled the car over to allow him to open out the map and search for a route to the monastery garden. They were just outside Kilbride and he was certain that there had never been a direct route from Kilbride to the garden, and perhaps that there would not be one now. He recalled the roundabout way he had taken with his mother, following her through the long grass of a meadow, climbing up hills covered with masses of bramble, and jumping through overgrown hedges to reach the little pathways that eventually led to the garden. Nonetheless, he was determined to find a route by which he and Adele could get there by car. John concentrated on trying to bring to mind any relevant information that might still be concealed within his childish recollections. "I do remember that, when we returned home from the garden in the evenings, I often saw our village church lit up by the setting sun. Its stained-glass windows reflected the light and showed us our way home." John smiled as he recalled the church tower bathed in the rose-gold rays of the sunset. "So that means that the garden is located to the west of the village. Then we will need to take this road." He pointed to a thin dotted line on the map. "I hope we can access it by car."

"I'm sure we'll be able to do that," Adele said supportively.

John turned back to the main road, and some minutes later he took another narrow, dusty road to the west of Kilbride. "You know, Adele, even though that elderly man probably only spoke to me that one time, I trusted him so much." He began to reminisce again. After a minute of deep reflection, he continued, "His eyes… there was something special in his gaze: something calm, strong and encouraging… And now I realise that when I met Darius for the first time, his face was somehow familiar to me. I'm certain that I saw the very same wise and encouraging look in his eyes, and that's why, deep in my heart, I felt the same trust in him, though I didn't recognise it at the time."

"Yes, John, I understand exactly what you mean," said Adele thoughtfully. "I had the same feeling of trust, and also of affection when I was with Marija. I felt as though she were my closest friend."

"Apart from me." John winked and smiled.

They drove slowly through the landscape in silent contentment, happy in each other's company. The road was becoming narrow and difficult to navigate. It had not been maintained for a long time and was used only occasionally by farmers and foresters, whose heavy vehicles had left deep tracks. The rain had washed away the gravel, and large stones protruded from between the ruts. John was obliged to drive very carefully to avoid getting caught on one of them, or even sliding off the road. Finally, they had to stop, because the road became even more treacherous, sometimes disappearing from view, since it had become overgrown with bushes and stunted trees. Nature was obliterating it and taking the space back to its original state.

"Why don't we get out and walk a bit, just to see what we find?" suggested Adele.

John nodded, stopped the car, and turned off the engine. Then he took their coats from the boot, placed Adele's raincoat over her shoulders and, glancing up, remarked, "The sky is beginning to darken. Those clouds above us may hold some rain, so let's be on our way!"

They had been walking for only a couple of minutes when it became clear that the road had ended and was leading onto a path that was rarely used. This trail appeared to be quite isolated, with nothing on one side but untilled fields, while the other bordered a large forest. There was no sign of any houses, buildings or people. As they followed this rough path, littered with broken branches, pebbles, and fallen tree trunks, and suffocating with dense grass and weeds, it became more and more difficult to walk. Neither John nor Adele had shoes suitable for outdoor walking, since it was a new activity to them.

"It's all too easy to lose your footing here and fall. Take my arm, Adele!" But just as he offered her his arm, John lost his balance. Adele caught him.

They continued to move forward, helping each other to find their footing, until they came upon an old iron gate. It was hanging partly open, its handmade metal hinges rusted, tipping forward, leading nowhere. The gate opened onto nothing but another field. Beyond the gate were piles of dark grey stone; clearly the ruins of an ancient structure. Deer of all ages and sizes, from fawns to adults, ran about the ruins, tripping over them lightly while continuing to destroy whatever shape the stones had originally formed. Their keen hearing soon sensed the approach of humans, and their hooves made a soft pattering sound as the timid, gentle animals retreated into the wood. Adele and John were touched by how hard the fawns tried to keep up with the others. Three of the smallest glanced back curiously at the couple, just before they disappeared into the forest.

Just beyond the stone piles there was a wall. A clear opening within it, topped by a brick arch, had been the original entrance to the monastery garden.

"Let's go inside," said John, like an intrepid explorer discovering an unknown land. "This has to be my mother's garden. Let's see what's still left within these walls."

Adele looked at him and then back at the archway in consternation. John had never been attracted to adventure. It had always been comfort and security that had appealed to him. Now the tables had turned and it was she who was a little hesitant. "Are you sure it's safe?" she asked quietly. "After all, so much time has passed and we have no idea what we'll find in there…"

"Have faith in our choice; have faith in the journey!" responded John with enthusiasm. "I believe that whatever we find there will be important for our life together. Remember, this is our final task!"

He held out his hand and she took it, breathing in his confidence. She had been pleasantly surprised by the changes in him over the last few days, and this one was the most promising of all.

As they approached the entrance to the enclosure, they noticed that it was getting warmer. The old stone wall had been built to raise the temperature within it to help the growth of the fruit, vegetables and herbs. They had come upon a huge, abandoned garden. Old apple trees along the back wall had shed their fruit, which lay rotting on the grass. Adele took in the pleasant scents of a multiplicity of flowers. There was also a large variety of trees and bushes, both well-known and very rare. In looking closely at nearby raspberry bushes choked by overgrowth, she suddenly spied an antique pear tree, heavily laden with unpicked fruit.

"Look at the colour of these pears, John! It's unbelievable that this tree can still produce fruit."

"It's marvellous! It feels as though we're in an open-air museum," John responded, absorbed in trying to pull away masses of ivy from a little stone angel.

The couple were like two children let out to play after a long stay indoors: as soon as they made one discovery within the old garden, they moved on to another. There was a stone rotunda in a far corner. Its six columns supported a beautifully shaped Eastern-style dome. Compared to the ruins of the monastery, the rotunda was exceptionally well preserved; perhaps because of the protection afforded by three ancient oak trees that surrounded it as if they were its guardians. Adele went inside the rotunda and found a small wooden bench. On it was a tiny china pot on a stand; full of dried-up old leaves reduced to almost nothing but dust.

"It looks as if they were burning plants under this pot – perhaps lavender – to keep the tea hot," she remarked to John. She bent over the leaves and sniffed lightly. "Yes, these are the remains of lavender buds."

A light, handmade willow basket for fruit or flowers looked as though it had been blown from the bench years before and now lay exactly where it had fallen. A vixen had been tending her cubs near the stone wall to the left of the rotunda. The cubs had been curled up around her to shelter from the breeze and stay warm, and their tiny bodies had flattened the grass where they had been lying. They were probably out with their mother now to search for food, but they would return to the garden at twilight to continue to frolic with their furry brothers and sisters. The grey stone walls made the garden a kind of wildlife sanctuary. It had blackbirds, song thrushes, and chiffchaffs. It was full of goldfinches, known for their bright red face as 'the spark in the woods'. Collared doves cooed soothingly in the high branches: *Ooboo-oo, ooboo-oo…* Adele and John could not even recognise the many other bird species in the garden as they sang out from their niches, hidden in the bushes and trees.

A small patch of sky just above the couple began to clear and shed direct light onto the latticework of the distant church tower, and on the purple clouds chasing each other over the higher ground. This view revived John's childhood memories once again. He had had multiple interpretations of this landscape in his head that he wanted to reproduce on canvas, and now his hand longed for a paintbrush. He wanted to represent the changing seasons within the colours of the trees on the distant hills, the play of the wind in their branches, and the shifting reflections of light on the garden's rotunda and stone walls.

Adele had her own perspective on the landscape. A warm and pleasant feeling was spreading in her chest. She had felt it before, in the lovely countryside near her grandparents' house. They had been farmers, and in their world practical considerations had always prevailed. Everything they had built on their land, including paths and benches, had had its purpose and yet fitted harmoniously into the countryside. Despite the fact that their house had not much followed the progressive improvements demanded by modern life, Adele had loved every inch of it. In that simple, natural environment, she had felt happy and carefree; able to be a little girl rather than an older sister in charge of her siblings. Unlike her mother, her grandparents had considered her to be the child she was. She ran and played and did as she wished, without caring about discipline, or timetables, or younger children. She smiled, remembering the narrow flame of the burning candle as her grandmother had recited her evening prayers. Her Aunt Helena had often been there too, and later, when the younger children and Adele's grandparents were in bed, she had remained with Adele in pleasant conversation at the small table, under the holy pictures illuminated by the soft light of that candle.

The sweet nostalgia of these recollections, in all their vibrant colour, affected Adele deeply. Her previous association of this 'secret garden' with a fear of failure vanished. So much joy emanated from each branch and flower that it made her curious to know what else she would find here. She felt a strong impulse to explore more of this beautiful place. She was drawn again to the ruins of the monastery garden, the outlines of which could still be discerned in the way the plants were growing. She started to see and appreciate the meticulous layout put in place by unknown gardeners, centuries before. The high chestnut trees which framed the inner structure of the garden had been planted very carefully to leave enough space for various fruit trees and berry bushes. At the same time, they sheltered delicate herbs and flowers from cold winds and hard rain. This loving human touch could also be seen in the traces of old paths which followed the natural landscape. Their purpose was to allow dainty plants and fragile flowers to be tended and admired. Incredibly, the centuries-old rose bushes were still blooming, and over time cross-pollination had allowed their colours to mix. At the furthest reaches of the garden were deep yellow roses and on the other side deep red, but those in the middle comprised every combination possible: light orange mixed with yellow on the petal fringes; vibrant peach with patches of red; dark apricot. The same had occurred by the side walls, with roses of a strong claret colour and those of pure white combining to give every shade of dark cherry, light cerise, and even a violet purple. Some varieties were unknown to Adele, and so old that they were probably no longer grown in modern gardens. Some of the shapes seemed to resemble Persian roses; others perhaps Chinese. *The elderly ladies I work with would love these flowers,* thought Adele. *How I wish I could bring them a bunch with their groceries!* The temptation she felt to study and know the variety of plants in that small space was endless. Her mind was fully engaged in discovering nature; yet it had not tired her. This place made her feel calm, but at the same time refreshed and revitalised. She wanted to understand the age-old principles that the gardeners here had put into practice in order to achieve their spiritual and alimentary goals. They had accomplished their objectives in a non-intrusive way, and in harmony with nature. Adele knew instinctively that those principles would be very useful in the arrangement of modern living spaces. She could apply them in a practical way to environmental planning for her master's thesis.

Meanwhile, John had arrived in a section of the garden that was protected by the remnants of two walls forming a corner. He knew, on careful examination of the plants lying underneath the top growth, that for centuries this space had served as a plot for growing medicinal plants. That had been his mother's purpose in visiting the garden. She had been less interested in beautiful flowers than in plants with healing properties, which she had wanted to use as natural medicines and to increase the atmosphere of well-being in her home. In uncovering a lavender bush, John realised that that was why she had rinsed the household bed linen in lavender water, and brewed sage tea for his coughs and colds. She had sprinkled fresh tarragon on the chicken she had served for his lunch, and had him cutting basil for her tomato salads. She had used the garden's blessings to express her love for her son. That was exactly what Mary Catherine had shown him, but he had been unaware of it at the time. Mary Catherine had known that he would be at ease in her garden. Slowly but surely, she had sparked all of his pleasant yet deeply buried childhood memories that were rooted in nature. John now knew that this knowledge was a gift that would remain with him for the rest of his life, and felt the desire to share that legacy with Adele and Patrick. He was glad to have finally come here with Adele, and certain that it had happened because they had met Darius, Marija and Mary Catherine.

35

Resourcing

Coming across a rosemary bush, John stopped stock-still in front of it. He recalled standing in this exact spot as a child, when his mother had showed him how to gather the herb from its thick stem. Now he pulled some of the spiky needles from those stems and rubbed them between his fingers. They released the powerful fragrance he had been expecting, surrounding and suffusing him with memories of his mother. Putting his hand on his chest, he let out a strong sigh.

Looking over at him in concern, Adele stood up from her crouched position where she had been trying to identify a pointed red flower, and moved towards her husband. He did not even hear her approach. She caught the strong scent enveloping him and whispered, "Rosemary: the scent of remembrance."

"Remembrance," John repeated slowly. "Remembrance and loyalty."

They stood in silence as his eyes filled with tears.

Adele put her arms around him. "She would be happy to

know that she meant so much to you," she said in a low, soft tone.

John said nothing for a moment and then added, a little too loudly for such a quiet garden, "Nine years of age is too young to lose the most important person in your life."

Adele looked at him with compassion, realising for the first time that this old wound had determined much of the behaviour of the man John had become: his desire to avoid expressions of strong emotion, whether of joy or sadness; his inability to deal with even the possibility of impending grief; and his obsessive worries over Patrick's future. This rare display of grief on his part also gave her an insight into his inability to manage his temper: throughout his life he had channelled his sadness into anger. Keeping her head on his shoulder, she looked at the open sky as the breeze picked up. Nearby birch trees swayed gently, and a giant linden spread its thick, dark branches over the garden. White patches of sky winked through its mass of leaves, beckoning to her. "John…" She gestured towards it. "The linden tree is calling to us. My grandfather often told stories of the lindens. I've never seen such an ancient one."

John shook himself out of his reverie and they moved towards the giant tree.

"It's in full bloom. That's quite strange. It usually only happens in July." She reached out and touched the trunk with the palms of her hands. "When I was a little girl my mother's father told me that beneath a linden tree you could do nothing but tell the truth – it stands for justice and what is right." She turned to John and embraced him again. "Lindens have always been meeting places for those in love. My grandfather said they have great power to bring about good in the world. So, tell me the truth: do you think we're going to succeed on our journey through life? Do you think we'll stay together? Is our marriage going to survive?"

John held her tightly. "In answer to your three questions, Adele: Yes, yes and yes."

These words pronounced firmly and without a single note of hesitation, moved Adele. She looked deep into her husband's eyes. "Under this linden tree, I promise you that I will do everything I can to honour our relationship. I won't run from my emotions, or from any difficulties between us. I'll try to be honest with myself and more open with you, so that from now on I will be completely truthful, just as you have been with me on The Road." She paused. "I trust you, John, and I hope that you trust me!"

They remained silent for several moments, and then John whispered into Adele's hair. "I have taken you for granted since the moment you came into my life: your patience, your optimism, your hard work for Patrick and for me. I never made the effort I should have made to keep us as close as we could have been. I'm so sorry, Ad. Please forgive me."

She made no answer, but continued to embrace him. John smoothed her hair, looking out at the garden, and caught sight again of the group of birch trees still waving in the breeze, their leaves rustling and shimmering in the now fading light.

"Adele, let's go over to the birch trees. I've got something to say to them."

She looked at him in surprise. Was he acknowledging the trees' awareness of their presence in the garden? That would be quite unusual for him.

They walked over to the four slender trees, their white bark still shining in the descending daylight. John encircled the narrowest trunk with one arm, and reverently touched one of its leaves. "The Lady of the Woods," he said quietly. "My mother told me of her. The birch holds ancient wisdom, but always appears to be a young tree. It offers protection and hope to humanity, and a source of light as the sun reflects off its pale bark." He turned to Adele and touched her cheek. "Did I tell you the story of Lughnasa?"

Adele shook her head.

"Lugh, the Celtic god of sun and light, received a warning from the birch tree one summer. It told him that the fairies intended to kidnap his wife and carry her away to their land, never to be seen again. The birch warned him in the rustling of its leaves. Thanks to this rustling sound, Lugh was able to save his wife and live in eternal happiness with her. The ancient Celtic priests, the Druids, called on the trees to act as their army in entering the battle for good against evil." John closed his eyes and recited some lines from memory:

The Druid's chants, a rhythmic hum,
The ancient words, the beating drum,
They called upon the trees in song,
In fierce alliance, kinship strong.

With leaves that shimmered a vivid green,
A beacon in the battle scene,
The Birch would weave a mystic spell,
And tales of courage, it would tell.

He sighed and took Adele's hand. He gently removed the raincoat from her shoulders, placed it on the grass and helped her into a sitting position, then sat down himself beneath the next tree. Both had their backs against the trunks of the slim birches.

"Before I even went to school," John said softly, "I had trouble controlling my temper. Since I had no brothers or sisters, I played with neighbouring children, but I always wanted to be in charge; I always wanted them to fall in with my demands, my needs, my wishes. I expected everyone to play by my rules, and I carried that into my adult life. I have done the same to you, Adele." He looked her full in the face. "When I was six years old and about to start school, my mother brought me to a birch tree in this garden. She showed me that if I sat quietly with my back against its trunk and thought about what was bothering me, the birch would guide my emotions into wiser ways when they were too intense, too destructive or too overwhelming. She told me that when I grew to be a man, it would be good to remember that the tree's power is strongest at the Spring Equinox, when day and night are of equal length, and that no matter where I was on this earth, I could use that knowledge to help to control my emotions." He took a deep breath. "I'm ashamed to say that I left my mother's words far behind me. I never really thought of them again."

"Don't be so hard on yourself, John. When thinking about the past, being kind to ourselves as well as to others is important."

"But I was a hard man. Do you remember how I lost control with Patrick when he was accused of taking another child's bike? Our son... he had nothing to do with it." John winced at the memory.

Adele was the one to sigh now. "It's best to focus on what you did that was helpful in his life, and there are many examples of that."

John fell silent, lost in thought, his back still pressed against the birch trunk. "My mother was like the birch tree: strong in spirit, but not long-lived."

"We both deserve more than we've had from each other in the past," Adele pronounced slowly. "In the past..." she repeated. "The past is gone, and now we face our future."

Suddenly, a bird with a brown back and a black-spotted yellow belly took up a place on one of the birch branches. He jumped up and down several times, obviously feeling at home and showing no signs of anxiety at the presence of two unusual visitors. *Fillip-fillip-fillip quitquiquit quitquiquit tereret tereret...* His melodious and lively song brought John and Adele back from their valley of remembrances.

The garden was getting a bit chilly now. John stood up and approached Adele, taking her hands in his and raising her up from the ground. "It's time to go, Adele. These trees have given us their wisdom, and this cheerful bird brings us a new message, encouraging us to move on."

Hand in hand, they walked slowly through the garden towards the gate. The sun softly caressed the trees, in casting its last light and in turn the trees began to throw their long shadows onto the grass and pathways. Despite the hour, the garden was still full of life. The flowers released their fragrances, the birds sang their perpetual songs, the bushes were filled with the restless rustling of small animals. A palpable sense of the old monastery's warmth and benevolence enveloped all within the garden.

John squeezed Adele's hand gently. "It's strange: in coming here, I was expecting to be overcome by nostalgia and by reminders of my painful loss in childhood... and I was afraid of those memories. I must admit that that *did* happen – I *was* overwhelmed by those feelings – but you stayed close to me and helped me to confront my fears of the past. Here in this garden, I seem to have unexpectedly found a new source of energy; a life force that has revived and inspired me for the future." He paused. "*Our* future."

He looked at Adele, and she could see both strength and tenderness in his eyes.

"When you look at me like this, I can imagine wonderful times ahead for us." Her own eyes smiled.

"Our future belongs to us, Adele! We can do anything we want to do. We can grow *our* garden..." John stopped in mid-sentence, astonished by what he had just said.

"How?" Adele was also astounded by her husband's idea. "We don't have any space for one."

John's momentary uncertainty turned to determination and optimism. "But we can buy a piece of land or rent an allotment and set up our own garden. We can even sell our apartment and buy a house outside the city with space for a garden."

"That's a bold stroke… I don't recognise you, John," exclaimed Adele in delight. Suddenly she realised that she had already begun to envision the two of them living in a house in the country. This proposed garden project had also piqued her interest in creating a life-affirming space in nature, in order to build her new life with John.

"If we had a garden, I could build a pergola, and paint there when the weather is good," continued John.

"Wonderful! And I'd like to have a kitchen corner there to make you tea," suggested Adele.

"Then, I'd make a swing for you!"

"John, that's so lovely. I've dreamt of having a garden swing since I was a child…"

They looked at each other, surprised by the new wave of energy created by these ideas. They both knew that this was why they had been brought to this garden. This place in nature, tended and loved by others before them, had inspired them to realise their goals, both independently and together. Here, their contentment in each other's company, blocked for so many years, had finally been released.

"I think we should go home, Adele," John said quietly. "We've been away long enough."

36

On the Way Home

The warm orange glow of the sun that was sliding down behind the hills enveloped the silver hatchback as it glided smoothly along the motorway. The approaching headlights in the opposite lane added further light to the surroundings. Adele looked out of the window. This same landscape that she had seen just one week ago looked different to her now. Her more tranquil state of mind had perhaps transformed her impressions of it, making it appear vivid, multicoloured and distinctive. Adele glanced at John. The lights of oncoming cars took the form of bright sparks and were reflected in his blue eyes. Despite a long and intense day, he wore no air of fatigue. Beaming, he looked back at her and began to laugh.

"I've just remembered how we ran out of petrol," he said. "I can only imagine how my face appeared to you, when in anger I threatened to kick and hit the car. It was so childish! I understand now why you were so furious with me."

"Yes, I *was* furious. I was incandescent with anger,"

confirmed Adele. "But on the other hand, if you hadn't been so stubborn, we would never have come upon the Couples' Counselling Office, so there was something positive to be found in that situation." She paused. "Perhaps sometimes we have to go right to the limit of our stubbornness to see the stupidity of it; to realise how ridiculous it is. Then we can move beyond that stupidity."

"Everything that happened to us on The Road was outside our previous experience and our normal world," John mused. "At the start, it was beyond our comprehension. All of it finally came together in the last task, culminating in our visit to the monastery garden. In fact, can we really say that we'll be returning to the same world we were living in just one week ago?"

There was a moment of silence.

"But, John, do you think we've completed all the tasks?"

"Yes, Adele, I believe we have." John tousled her hair gently. "We've done all the work we were given. I can sense the progress I've made in my understanding of myself, and I'm proud of it. The best thing of all is that I feel closer to you. I'm so glad we're together."

"Oh, I feel the same way. My heart is full of gladness, and of gratitude to our mysterious guides – and to you, John." Adele leaned towards him and touched his neck lightly with her fingertips. "Nonetheless, I am already longing to experience again that sense of adventure that we had on The Road. It was so exciting to receive a challenging task, complete it together, and await our next assignment."

As night fell, they passed a filling station. Instinctively, Adele glanced at the fuel gauge. There was still enough petrol in the tank. Suddenly the thought came to her that perhaps they could continue their adventure. "I can't honestly believe that that was our last task," she said, and she turned to reach for the envelope on the back seat. She opened it and took out the single sheet of paper that had informed them of their final task, then read it to herself, expecting to extract some more information. Turning the paper over, she saw an additional note written in much tinier letters. She took out a little torch from the glove compartment and read the note out loud.

Dear John and Adele,

There is no single formula for a happy relationship. Each couple is different, and your partnership is unique. You have followed The Road together, and in many complex situations you have acquired a deeper knowledge of each other, with an awareness that cannot always be expressed in words.

Perhaps some simple advice will remind you of what you have experienced on The Road and help you to move forward into the future. Here it is:

The moment when you were drawn to each other, and understood in your hearts that you wanted your destinies to be linked, is very important. That is the source and foundation of your relationship. When you are in trouble as a couple, return to that moment. Listen quietly to what it reveals to you. This may give you a new perspective on your problems.

Remember that you live in an ever-changing world. Nothing remains the same, and your partnership should also evolve. Don't be afraid of your ups and downs or your crises. They are natural in a growth process.

Once in a while, take a detached view of your partnership. Analyse how it is built, how it functions, what it gives to the world, and what it takes from it. What is its essence? What values, aspirations, feelings and interests lie at its core? Are you satisfied with what you have? Is everything balanced? Do you need something to change in order to make your relationship more harmonious? Stay open to the world and the messages it sends you. If new ideas, activities or opportunities inspire you both, then go ahead – these are the fuel that keeps a couple going!

You are both responsible for your relationship. Devote time and energy to each other, communicate, and be sincere and creative! Work to find a solution even when you see none.

Your bodies always need a loving touch. Be sensual and cherish your intimacy.

Finally, being in a relationship should never hinder your personal growth. We all have latent talents and abilities. Encourage and help each other to discover as well as to develop your uniqueness.

With love and trust in you!
Darius, Marija and Mary Catherine

37

Much Done, More to Do

As they left the motorway for the main route to the city centre, Adele noticed that the arrow on the fuel gauge was indicating that the tank was almost empty. She blew out her breath in annoyance. "John, can't you see that we're nearly out of petrol again? Why is this still happening?"

"What do you mean, 'Why is this still happening?'" retorted John. "The car is using up the petrol! *I'm* certainly not using it!"

"But I thought you'd finally realised that you have to keep an eye on the petrol gauge to avoid running out!"

"So, I'm the only one that has to watch everything?"

Suddenly, Adele's phone rang. She answered it. "Oh, hello, Patrick, dear. How are you getting on? Are you going to stay with us the whole weekend? Did you heat up some soup? Yes, yes, we're still on the road, but your Dad and I are almost home. Are we what? What? Fighting about the fuel? Well, erm…"

As the old silver hatchback passed along the road, a familiar voice carried by the breeze was saying, "Please stop sighing, Mary Catherine, my dear. We don't expect miracles."

"But honestly, Darius, after all this work – and it was *so* much work…"

"But we don't expect miracles, do we?"

"I do. I must admit, I do."

"Now, now… just be patient. They need time. They will always keep their memories of what they experienced this week."

Epilogue

"Adele, I'm so happy today, and so proud of you." John was at the wheel of their new car, looking with admiration at his wife. "You are really beautiful in that red dress."

"Thank you, John. I have to say that this master's diploma also belongs to you," answered Adele sincerely, putting her hand on her husband's knee. "You've encouraged and supported me so much over these twelve months, and you made a magnificent speech today. I'm so touched by all of this, and I could see that Patrick was delighted as well."

"Well, we have to celebrate and have a party!" John exclaimed enthusiastically. "What about next weekend?"

"But next Saturday is the opening of your first exhibition!"

"Of course, you're right. I pushed it to the back of my mind!" John rubbed the bridge of his nose. "Sometimes I get so worried about the public reactions to it that I try to persuade myself that the exhibition is not really going to go ahead. What if people don't like my paintings?"

"Johnny, don't even think like that! You are a true artist. People will see that. They'll respond to the emotion you put into your paintings," Adele reassured him.

"Yes, you're right again... I'll get through it," he replied, comforted by Adele's heart-warming answer. "But now, let's get back to *your* day. We have to honour it in some way. What do you think?"

"Well... maybe we can make a surprise visit to Darius and Marija?" Adele said, tentatively and after some reflection. "After all, they're very much involved in this incredible turn my life has taken."

"That's an excellent idea! And look – we're not even very far from where those changes began." John laughed. "I can still remember how I found you sitting among the cows in the moonlight."

"They were quite good company!" Adele giggled. "And I'm sure that they thought I looked lovely..."

John turned off the motorway. Unlike the old silver hatchback, their new SUV forged ahead smoothly and confidently on the steep and winding road. The familiar surroundings ran colourfully into one another, evoking memories of their magical journey one year ago. Eventually they reached the area just at the side of the road where they had run out of petrol. It was surrounded by the same tall trees. They parked their car and took the narrow path up the hill. This time, the path was illuminated by the soft afternoon sun. They reached the gate of the house, but the Couples' Counselling Office sign was missing. In its place there was an ordinary letterbox on the gate with the name 'Peter Devereux' written on it. Surprised, John and Adele looked at each other.

Just at that moment, a small white dog approached, wagging his tail in friendship. A second later, an elderly man appeared in the yard. "Mickey, don't bother our guests with your curious nose!" he admonished the little creature before turning his attention to Adele and John. "Hello – can I help you? Are you looking for someone?"

"Oh... uh... Good afternoon. Sorry to disturb you," began

John. "It's just that we were expecting to find our friends who had their business here."

"Ah, yes, that nice couple, the previous occupants who were here, Darius and Marija," replied the man. "I knew them. They moved away just a few months ago. It's a wonderful house, and I'm happy to be living in it." Here he stopped, having noticed his visitors' obvious disappointment. "Would you like to come inside for a cup of tea?"

"Thank you very much for your kind invitation. We'd love to, but we still have a long journey ahead of us," John said apologetically. "But we're glad to meet you, Mr Devereux, and to know that you're happy here."

"I'm sorry; we didn't introduce ourselves. I'm Adele Ross, and this is my husband John," said Adele.

"Adele and John?" Peter Devereux raised his eyebrows curiously. "In that case, I have something for you, left by Marija and Darius. They were so considerate; really not of this world. Would you care to follow me?"

Bewildered, they followed the man, who led them to the inner yard behind the house and stopped in front of two plant pots containing young trees. Labels hung from their trunks: 'Birch' and 'Linden'.

"Here you are! These are yours," he said, smiling and pointing at the pots. "They must have been gardeners, that couple."

Amazed by such an unexpected gift, John and Adele thanked the kind-hearted man and carried the saplings back down the path to their car. They fitted nicely into the boot of the SUV. Then John started the engine and moved out onto the road.

"How could they know?" asked Adele, after a long silence.

"Don't try to understand it, Adele," John replied thoughtfully. "When I started to paint, I realised that it isn't always possible to have an explanation for everything. Some things just appear. What is most important is that these two trees mean something

special to us… and that we now have somewhere to plant th
They will be an essential part of our new garden."

"Perhaps you're right. Marija and Darius were alwa
somewhat mysterious," agreed Adele. "But today is particularl
important for me. I wanted to share my happiness and express
my gratitude for everything we learned on The Road…" All at
once, an idea came into her mind. "What if we go to Columbine
Cottage? Maybe we could find Mary Catherine there. Then we
could at least thank *her*."

John turned to his wife and smiled enigmatically. "Believe
me, Adele, she's not there either. Marija, Darius and Mary
Catherine have finished their work. Now it's up to us to go on."

Authors' Word to the Reader

Dear Reader,

You have now accompanied John and Adele for an entire week on their turbulent, romantic and mysterious journey. You have witnessed how these two people changed their dull, distant and tired coexistence into a vital, vibrant and intimate relationship.

If this story inspires you, set yourself a similar challenge and take it on. Perhaps this little volume will give you a bit of encouragement.

Good luck!

The Authors

Couples' Counselling Office

.

Made in the USA
Columbia, SC
04 August 2024

39971993R00153